Damaged Goods

DAMAGED GOODS

a novel

Paul Scheufele

WOLF HOUSE PUBLISHING, LLC
BOSTON, MASSACHUSETTS

ISBN 979-8-9928397-0-8 (paperback)
ISBN 979-8-9928397-1-5 (ebook)

Library of Congress Control Number: 2025913752

Wolf House Publishing, LLC
Boston, Massachusetts

Damaged Goods is a work of fiction. The names, characters, businesses, places, events, locales, and incidents are either products of the author's imagination or used in a fictitious manner. Any resemblance to actual persons, living or dead, or actual events is coincidental.

Book design by C'est Beau Designs.
Author photograph by Anna Chernobaeva Photography.

For
my wife, Susan;
our children, Darren, Michael, and Jack;
their spouses, Sarah and Elizabeth;
and our grandchildren, Emma and Caleb.

In loving memory of Bobby and Karen.

PART ONE

Brendan

December 2007

Brendan stared blankly at the snowflakes skipping off the limestone office tower and settling on the musket of a bronze Civil War soldier in Madison Square Park as he waited for the street vendor to hand him his coffee. "Try to stay warm out here, Joe," Brendan said with a faint smile, giving him a five-dollar bill for a two-dollar cup, "and keep the change."

"Have a nice day, Mr. O'Shay," the street vendor said.

If only I could, Brendan thought as he passed through the turnstile into his office building. He reached in his pocket for his vibrating cell phone and glanced at the number. Oh no. His Irish twin sister, Cassie, born ten months before him, was calling. What dramatic ending of one thing or hopeful beginning of another would she share this time? His mind was flooded with premonitions of disaster, yet it also held distant, unrealistic hope for her.

"Bren, how've you been? Long time no talk," she chirped.

Her biting cheerfulness always unnerved him.

3

"I know this is last minute, but can I see you for Christmas?"

"Sorry, Cassie. We plan to be at the chalet," he said while walking to the elevator.

"I really want to see you guys," she said, her cheerfulness eroding into pleading.

"The holiday is right around the corner," he said. "We've already ordered our food for Christmas dinner and asked a few of our skiing friends to stop by."

"Please, Bren," she groaned. "What about stopping by my place for an early meal, say one o'clock, then going back to your place in Vermont to meet your friends at night? You can make sandwiches with the leftovers like we did when we were kids."

"That's complicated," he said, trying to come up with a reason it would be complicated before she asked why.

"It's not complicated, Bren," she said. "You come to my place in New Hampshire then scoot across to Vermont in the late afternoon."

"I don't know, Cassie."

"Bren, it's been three years," she said. "I really want to see you and Laura and Shannon. Shannon must be shaving by now."

"He's bigger than me," Bren said.

"He was a skinny runt last time I saw him," she said.

"I don't know, Cassie," he repeated.

"Christmas is a time for family," Cassie pleaded. "You're all I've got left."

He could rattle off a thousand good reasons to say no again, yet something inside told him to give in. He even had some magical thinking and considered inviting her to spend the day with his family in Vermont. But the truth was she'd drink too much, cause a commotion, and end up passing out on the couch and spending the night.

"We can't change our plans now."

"Please, Bren, it's important to me," she said.

He thought he heard her whimper. Maybe she was begging for a lifeline. He hated himself for fearing the worst, but how often had he read about people ignoring desperate calls for help only to find a loved one doing something drastic? How could he live with himself if he stood in the way of her chance at a better life? Being there for her might be enough to turn her life around. Damn, he thought, I'm engrossed in magical thinking again, but before he could stop himself, the words slipped out of his mouth.

"Sure, Cassie. I'll ask Laura if we can change our plans. Assume we'll be there unless I call you to say otherwise."

He tucked his phone back into his pocket, trudged to his trading desk, and plopped in his chair. He removed the lid from his paper coffee cup and let the hot steam bathe his face, soothing him as he contemplated how he would tell Laura about their change of plans. A tap on his shoulder interrupted his thoughts.

"Sarah wants to see you," his boss's assistant murmured.

"Can I finish my coffee?"

"I wouldn't do that if I were you," she said.

He snapped the lid on and hustled across the floor, passing a hundred other traders slouched like beasts behind walls of Bloomberg terminals, slowing to a strut as he approached Sarah Whetstone's glass office door. Gus Marchetti bull-rushed past him, knocking the coffee from Brendan's hand onto Sarah's new white Berber rug.

"Whetstone, you gotta hear this," Gus said in his staccato voice, skipping an apology. "Was in Boston yesterday. Trey Williamson is building a gold mine up there. Has original Hopper and de Kooning paintings hanging in the lobby. Those painters hated women. Had dinner at a fabulous French restaurant . . . for Boston, I mean. Finished the night at a boutique strip club in a refurbished brownstone in the South End. Secret doorways. Passwords. Completely discreet. Dancers smelled like ambrosia. Could talk about anything— books, movies, art, Kama Sutra. Anything. Almost the kind of girls you'd take home to Mother."

Sarah winced.

Gus ground his thumb into the gap between his pectorals. "Williamson knows how good *I* am, Whetstone. They want *me* as a deal partner."

"How good *we* are. Want *us*," Sarah said.

"But the deal comes down to our lending rate. If O'Shay can muster a competitive rate, I'm in." He tapped his forehead with his Stanford University Phi Beta Kappa Society ring. "It's a fucking no-brainer, Whetstone, even for him." He pointed his thick index finger at Brendan.

As Brendan formulated a response, he contemplated the subject of Gus's pitch—Trey Williamson. Trey was a superstar financier who'd grown frustrated with his multi-million-dollar annual bonuses, so he hijacked a group of partners from Goldman Sachs and established Williamson Trust Financial. WTF was a hedge fund that trafficked in teaser-rate mortgages, packaged them into mortgage-backed securities, hoodwinked the credit rating agencies into assigning the MBS an investment-grade rating, and sold the securities to pension fund managers at a substantial profit. The WTF partners were earning a decent living—five to ten million bucks a year each—by investing their capital. But they aimed to make a killing and needed leverage—lots of borrowed cash—from investment banks like J.P. Morgan and Brendan's employer, Global Investment Bank. He reflected on the old Wall Street adage: "Pigs get fed. Hogs get slaughtered." Brendan felt a noose around his neck as Gus guided him to the slaughterhouse.

Gus spat out the terms of the deal, and Sarah tapped on her calculator, nodding as if she had just scratched off the winning numbers from the lottery ticket she played religiously every week. "We'll earn a buck twenty—a hundred and twenty million—in two years on this deal!" she crowed, her eyebrows raising into rainbows. Her eyes sparkled like shiny pieces of gold.

"The mortgage market is unstable. The deal's imprudent," Brendan said, wiping the optimism from Sarah's face.

"Imprudent? Who the fuck on Wall Street uses the word 'imprudent'?" Gus said, forming a loose circle with his hand and jerking the air. "Grow a pair, why don't ya?!"

"I know my market," Brendan retorted.

"Not according to WTF. I don't want to throw you under the bus in front of Whetstone, but the word on the street is you're a . . ." Gus formed an inverted triangle in front of his crotch with his hands.

"That's bullshit, Gus."

"Don't fear success, O'Shay."

"If WTF defaults, we'll be offloading these shitty mortgages into a cesspool market," Brendan protested.

"These 'shitty' mortgages give hardworking hairdressers, nurses, and auto mechanics a pathway to the American Dream," Gus said, swatting his hand in Brendan's direction. He turned to Sarah. "Whetstone, you just bought shares in a private jet. D'ya seriously want to let this deal slip away?"

Sarah sharpened her eyebrows.

"I'll take a closer look at it," Brendan murmured.

"Way to man up, O'Shay. There's still hope for you," Gus said, charging out.

Sarah came around to the front of her desk. Her black leather pencil skirt accentuated the nautical-rope thighs she'd honed as an all-American field hockey player at Princeton. "Don't underestimate Gus," she said. "Our business is part engineering problem and part wrestling match. He's the best at both."

Brendan didn't need reminding that Gus was the smartest person in the room and an NCAA champion wrestler.

She caressed the white plastic Gulfstream G550 model on the front corner of her desk. "We're going through with this deal. I trust you'll make it happen." Then she gestured toward her rug. "Have my assistant arrange for maintenance to clean up your mess."

As Brendan strutted back to his trading desk, trying to hide his humiliation from the other traders on the floor, he thought about Cassie. She wouldn't have taken Gus's and Sarah's shit, even if it meant getting fired.

●

On the train home that night, Brendan squeezed into the middle seat between a guy watching porn on his laptop and another guy snoring with drool dripping down his chin. Just as the doors were about to close, a young woman with brown hair pushed a baby stroller into the vestibule. The nearby passengers glanced at her, then raised their newspapers to shield their faces.

"Excuse me," Brendan said to the person watching porn, "but could you turn that shit off?"

The guy shook his head at Brendan without looking up from his computer screen.

Brendan slammed the screen shut as he pushed past the guy into the aisle. He walked over to the young woman leaning against her baby carriage.

"Please, ma'am, you and your baby can take my seat. I'll watch the carriage. I get off at Westport station."

"You're a nice man," she said, picking up her baby and walking down the aisle to sit in the seat he had just left.

He smiled and considered Cassie. He was sure that she would disagree.

Cassie

December 2007

Cassie rolled in bed, her knees tucked to her chest, searching for a position that wouldn't hurt her stomach. No luck. She got up and hobbled into the bathroom. The light bulb was dead. She reached for the sink, leaned forward, and coughed hard, dislodging a bloody mucus blob that splattered off the porcelain onto her hand. She wiped it on the thigh of her sweatpants and stumbled back to her room, where she lay awake until the morning light slanted through the window and burned her tired eyes. She got up, filled the tub, tossed in a handful of Epsom salts, and eased into the soothing water, massaging herself with a bar of soap, begging for the pain to dissolve. But it only got worse. She slid her head under the soapy surface until her breath expired. Then she burst from the water, gasping for air. If only she had the courage to stay under until the end. She climbed out, knotted a towel around the top of her swollen breasts, and gazed into the mirror, searching for traces of the thirty-year-old woman who had come to New Hampshire from Greater Boston two decades earlier in pursuit of a better life.

Cassie had a rule to avoid hospitals at all costs. They drained her money without easing her pain. But this time felt different, so she slipped into clean socks, underwear, jeans, a plaid flannel shirt, and snow boots, struggled into her rusty red Toyota pickup truck, and drove across town to New Ash Hospital. She could barely see through the dirt streaks on her cracked windshield as she squeezed a Styrofoam coffee cup between her swollen thighs.

She slipped and fell hard as she stepped out into the icy hospital parking lot. "Shit," she shouted, lying there, half hoping someone would either help her up or run her over, unsure which one she preferred. She felt so weak as she grabbed the side-view mirror and pulled herself up. It was a minor miracle that she had had the strength to shoot a buck the week before. Its antlers were beside her Winchester rifle and an ice chest full of venison steaks in the back of her truck.

As soon as she entered the ER, the intake nurse handed her a clipboard and pointed toward the waiting area. Filling out forms annoyed her.

NAME: "Cassidy O'Shay." She crossed it out. "Cassidy Whitman." She crossed it out again, then scribbled "Cassidy (O'Shay) Whitman."

MARITAL STATUS: "Divorced."

INSURANCE CARRIER: "None." It had always been none, even during her steady jobs at the animal clinic in Nehoiden, the dog kennel in Canada, the staircase manufacturer, and various seasonal jobs in New Ash.

She passed the clipboard to the nurse.

"PCP?" he inquired.

She shook her head and sat down, flipping through a stack of outdated magazines until a gray-haired nurse escorted her to a clean, well-lit examination room. The nurse cradled Cassie's forearm against her body, took her vitals, and rubbed her back like a mother comforting her child—something Cassie's mother had only done once for her.

"Please take everything off down to your underwear and wear this gown, Ms. Whitman."

"You can call me Cassie," she said. "Everyone calls me Cassie."

"Keep the back of the gown open, Cassie," the nurse instructed.

As the warmth of the nurse's hand lingered on her back, she thought about the venison, antlers, and Winchester rifle in her truck bed. Anyone could steal them while she was stuck there. Soon, the sound of heels clicking on the linoleum floor echoed in the hallway, and a young Indian woman in a white lab coat entered the examination room, reminding her of the Indian oncologist who had cared for her dad at the VA Hospital in Boston years ago.

"I am Dr. Prana," the woman said, frowning as she reviewed Cassie's chart. "What brings you in today, Ms. Whitman?"

"Cassie. Just call me Cassie. I've been hacking up dark, coffee-ground-colored loogies . . . I mean phlegm . . . for the past few weeks."

"Are there any other symptoms?"

Cassie described the sharp pains and bloating in her belly.

"How many cigarettes do you smoke?"

"A pack a day."

"Alcohol consumption?"

"Not more or less than anyone else I know."

Dr. Prana pursed her slender salmon-hued lips.

"Five or six a day," Cassie admitted.

The doctor cast a sideways glance at Cassie.

"Maybe ten or twelve. It depends."

"On what?"

"The day of the week, who's around, lots of things. I like to party with my friends."

Dr. Prana wrote in her notepad. "Have you had any surgeries or chronic conditions?"

"No surgeries."

"Pregnancies?"

"No," Cassie replied weakly. "I have DES syndrome. I can't have kids. I wouldn't want to bring a child into this messed-up world anyway." It felt strange to share her condition with a stranger, even if the stranger was a doctor. She had kept it private for so many years.

"Are there any other conditions?" Dr. Prana asked, writing down more notes.

Fear, loneliness, despair, she thought, then said, "No other conditions, Doc."

Dr. Prana examined Cassie's face, eyes, arms, stomach, and legs. "The nurse will collect blood and urine samples. After that, you are free to go. I will call you with the test results."

It was past sunset at 4:15 p.m. when she drove home along the dark country roads, hitting potholes that rattled her teeth. Upon arriving home, she removed the rifle, antlers, and cooler from her truck bed, placed the venison in the fridge, opened a beer, and leaned the gun against the corner of the kitchen. She carried the antlers into the living room and noticed the deflated football on the mantel. It was inscribed with the words NEHOIDEN 20 WASHBURN 0 and bore the faded signatures of fifty players from Brendan's high school team. She tossed the football into a kindling box and replaced it with the antlers. "Try to live in the present," her old friend Emily had advised her recently. "Live in the present. Live in the present." As she repeated the mantra, she fell asleep on the couch, not waking until her phone rang the next morning.

"Hello, Cassie," Dr. Prana said in her distinctive voice. "The lab was slow last night, so I was able to expedite your test results. They are concerning. You have elevated BAL bilirubin, low albumin, and low total serum protein."

"Come again, in English this time?"

Dr. Prana cleared her throat.

"Sorry, Doc. It's not your accent; I don't understand the medical jargon."

"Your liver seems to be failing due to your alcohol abuse."

"Abuse? I can handle my liquor." She sipped from the beer glass on the end table beside her. It was warm and flat.

"The bruises on your arms, the spidery capillaries around your eyes, and the swelling in your abdomen and ankles are all indicators of a serious condition known as cirrhosis of the liver. The test results suggest this, but I want to confirm it with an ultrasound and CT scan. Can you come tomorrow?"

"I'm not sure, Doc," she said.

"Cassie, you need to come in. There's a risk of variceal bleeding."

"More mumbo jumbo," Cassie said.

"Increased pressure in the portal vein connecting the liver and intestines leads to enlarged, swollen veins in the esophagus and stomach. If untreated, these veins can rupture, causing severe bleeding. A coffee grounds color in your phlegm is a symptom."

Cassie felt as if she were sucking on a rope. She took another swig of beer.

"If the scans confirm my initial diagnosis, the results can speed up your admission to an alcohol treatment center. It is late but not too late. So please, come to the hospital tomorrow."

"Even if I do, I can't afford the treatment."

"There are charities available, Cassie. You might qualify for Medicaid. The hospital social workers can assist you with the paperwork."

"I'm not a charity case," Cassie said, recalling her dad's words from long ago. "Thanks for the call, Doc. I'll think it over and get back to you. Have a Merry Christmas."

Cassie pushed off the couch and walked to the kitchen window, staring blankly into the dark woods as she thought about the oncologist at the Veterans Administration Hospital in Boston who had treated her dad's stomach cancer only for him to suffer a slow, miserable death. She thought about her mother, Rose, who had suffered a massive heart attack not long ago, and her ex-husband, Warren. The only family member left was Brendan. Before she could talk herself out of it, she dialed his number. "Bren, it's me, Cassie."

Brendan

Christmas Day 2007

"You owe me, Bren," Laura whispered as she settled into the black leather passenger seat of her white Range Rover. Her long legs were dressed in black tights and shearling-lined calfskin boots. She gazed intently through purple-framed eyeglasses that matched her lipstick, threading yellow yarn through the needlepoint canvas depicting a golden retriever nursing her pups. Shannon, their seventeen-year-old son, sprawled in the back seat with a beanie pulled down to cover his eyes and his headphones over his ears.

Brendan wondered why he owed Laura anything. Didn't he support and create the secure life she desired? He was a good husband, unlike half the guys he worked with who drank too much, stayed out too late, and cheated on their wives. Sure, he worked long hours and sometimes struggled to leave his job stress at the door, but that was all part of the deal. The obsessive behavior came with the paycheck. He was tempted to say what he was thinking, but today, he needed her on his side.

After driving for three hours on the dull, snow-covered highway in near silence, he turned onto Cassie's dirt road, passing houses with paint chipped from their shingles, old pickup trucks resting on cinder blocks, and overgrown patches of bare bushes poking through piles of snow. The Range Rover hit a pothole, jolting Laura's hand so violently that she stabbed her finger, smearing a drop of blood onto the needlepoint puppies.

"Look what you made me do! How am I going to fix this?" She rolled up the canvas and stuffed it into her bag. "I can't believe I let you bring me here after what Cassie did to your mom. God rest her soul."

Three years earlier, on Christmas Day, Cassie had jumped up from her dinner chair and slapped their mother, Rose, on the head, muttering something about overcooked vegetables. The stunned expressions on Shannon's and Laura's faces made him realize Cassie's outbursts were abnormal. He regretted that his mother had passed away before he'd had a chance to talk to her about what had happened. He wished he had a second chance to make things right.

"That was ages ago," Brendan said weakly. "She sounded much more mellow on the phone."

"'Mellow'? There are plenty of words I could use to describe Cassie, but 'mellow' isn't one of them," Laura huffed.

"I'm nervous too, Laura. But she's taken the initiative to reach out to us. Let's make the most of it."

"All right. Maybe she has changed. We all deserve a chance to change. Still, I'm skeptical."

"Stop arguing and give Cassie a chance," Shannon said drowsily, sitting up as they pulled into her driveway. "I like Cassie. She's a free spirit."

Shannon has no idea how wild Cassie can be, Brendan thought. As he made his way to the side door, he noticed the coat hanger suspending the bumper of her truck and heard the torn tar paper on her roof snapping in the wind. The skeleton of a wood-burning stove leaned against the cracked concrete steps.

Laura turned to Shannon. "Remember, Cassie's . . ."

"I know, Mom, Cassie's sick," Shannon said.

Cassie flung open the door and flicked a lit cigarette at Brendan's feet, bouncing it off his boot. "Welcome to my humble abode!" she exclaimed, flashing her false front teeth as they stepped inside. Her graying blond hair was clean and shiny, pulled back from her face, exposing a jagged purple scar on her forehead. Brendan was responsible for the broken teeth and scar, but he had kept that secret for thirty-four years. The only other person who knew was his old girlfriend, Emily Winter, whom he hadn't seen since high school. Suddenly Cassie's dog, her second Alaskan Malamute, named Nomad like the one she'd lost, dashed in from the living room and sniffed at their crotches.

"Trying to see if she recognizes you," Cassie said.

Laura crossed her legs like she needed to pee and pushed the dog aside. Shannon knelt to pet him.

"Careful, he'll lick your face off," Cassie said, pulling Nomad by the collar and guiding him back into the living room. As Cassie rushed past him, Brendan caught that familiar scent of stale beer and fresh nicotine. The smell brought back memories of their dad. So did the clutter on the kitchen countertop, which was littered with empty beer cans and extinguished cigarette butts. Amid the chaos, he spotted the red gun-shaped bottle opener he'd given her for her thirtieth birthday. If he'd only known how prophetic that keychain would be, he'd have picked something different, like a lifetime membership to Alcoholics Anonymous.

"Come in here," Cassie said. "The fire's burning good."

They followed her into the cozy room, bathed in a soft orange glow. Shannon gestured toward the antlers on the mantel. "Cool rack, Cassie," he remarked.

"Shot the buck myself," Cassie said. "We're having him for Christmas dinner."

"You're a throwback, Cassie, a frontierswoman from the past living in modern times. Someone ought to write a book about you," said Shannon.

Laura wrinkled her nose. "We're having venison for Christmas?"

Brendan ignored Laura's comment and pointed to his belt buckle and the bathroom door. "I drank too much coffee on the way here," he said.

"You're addicted," Cassie said.

"Yeah, that's *my* addiction," he said, instantly regretting it.

Cassie winced. "Ouch."

The bathroom appeared cleaner than Brendan remembered from his last visit three years ago, but no amount of scrubbing could eliminate the thin layer of black mold that stained the caulking along the edge of the sink. A toothbrush stood upright against the porcelain wall, its handle resting in a murky puddle of water. He lifted the seat with his foot, urinated, and then flushed the toilet with his foot. The soap dish was empty, so he rinsed his hands under hot water, rubbed them against his thighs, and went to the kitchen for a bar of soap.

Cassie glanced at him as if expecting a sarcastic comment, but he refrained. He was proud of himself for holding back.

"May I hold the antlers?" Shannon asked.

Cassie took them off the mantel and handed them to Shannon. He twisted and turned them, examining every angle, then held them up to his forehead with one hand.

"That's a damned heavy rack, Shannon," Cassie said. "I can't believe how strong you are. Just like your old man—when he was in half-decent shape."

Brendan reached for the roll of belly fat concealed beneath his loose cashmere sweater, humoring her, trying to make up for his comment about her addiction, which had clearly stung her.

"I have a gift for you, Shannon," Cassie said as she glided across the wide-plank oak floors in her woolen socks. She grabbed a sturdy hickory walking stick leaning against the knotty pine wall and handed it to Shannon after he'd placed the antlers back on the mantel. "I carved it myself. A branch fell during the last nor'easter," she added, pointing to the trees behind her house. "I tapered it with a hunting knife and drilled an eyehole so you can insert a rawhide lace and hang it on a hook. D'you still like to hike, Shannon? Remember when we climbed Mount Krystal when you were no taller than my waist?"

"Vaguely," Shannon replied. "Still, the walking stick is incredible! Thank you." He handed it to his mother.

"Heavy," Laura said, lifting it with both hands before handing it back to Shannon. "It will outlast us all. You must have put a lot of effort into this, Cassie."

"I did," Cassie said, smiling uneasily at Laura.

Brendan thought he detected a subtle compliment in Laura's words. Perhaps it marked a small breakthrough. He strolled into the sunroom and watched a family of beavers building their den outside.

Cassie sneaked up behind him. "Sometimes I watch them working on that den all day," Cassie remarked. "I admire their work, but it dams up the brook. I'm thinking of shooting them."

"Shooting them?!" Brendan was stunned.

"The water is flooding my basement," she said.

Uncertain about what to say, he changed the subject. "Your pigpen is empty. Where have the pigs gone?"

"I butchered them in the fall. We're having pork sausages with the venison today."

"You mean you had them butchered," Brendan said.

"Why do you always try to fix me, Bren? *I* butchered them."

"Just like Dad, for better or worse," Brendan quipped. Strike two.

He locked eyes with her, unable to recall the last time he had done so. Her gaze unsettled him. Her once emerald-green irises had transformed into the color of absinthe, and the whites appeared bloodshot and yellowed. He began to sweat. "Now I see why you call it a sunroom," he joked, wiping his forehead.

Cassie glanced over her shoulder and then turned back to Brendan. "I'm glad we have some time alone," she said. "I need something from you, Bren. That's why I asked you to come here today."

Brendan let out a sigh. Over the years, he had lent her money to waterproof the basement (not that it had done much good) and to pay back taxes. Her roof and siding needed repairs, and her car was on its last legs. But he was tired of supporting her. "We'd better get started on the meal," Brendan said. "A storm's on the way." Cassie followed him out of the sunroom before she could ask her question.

"There you are, Cassie," Shannon said, intercepting her in the living room. "We have a gift for you. I chose it myself." He handed her a box, and she ripped off the wrapping paper, crumpled it, and tossed it into the fireplace. The paper hissed as it turned to ash and floated up the chimney.

"A fruit basket," Cassie said. "A person can always use another piece of fruit." She sneered at Brendan before smiling at Shannon. "Thank you, Shannon."

Cassie stood with the fruit basket while the others watched like statues in a diorama until Cassie moved into the kitchen, cleared the counter, and set the fruit basket down. She removed the venison stew and pork sausages from the oven, along with a bowl of green salad from the refrigerator, and arranged them on the edge of the table. She also pulled four placemats from a cabinet and laid them out.

"Aren't those the placemats you gave Mom for Christmas when we were in elementary school?" Brendan asked.

"Good memory," she said. "I picked them up at the church bazaar for twenty-five cents each. I inherited them when she passed away."

Lastly, she set a pine cone and holly centerpiece on the table. "Made it myself," she declared, just as a pine cone broke loose and rolled across the table. She quickly reached for it, accidentally knocking over her beer bottle and spilling it onto Laura's lap.

"Look at the mess you made, Cassie," Brendan exclaimed, handing Laura a stack of paper napkins. "You should cut back on your drinking. You look terrible. We're worried about you." Strikes three, four, and five.

Cassie jutted her chin and flashed her yellow teeth like a wolf ready to pounce. "*Should?* Are you telling me what I *should* do? I invited you here for a meal that I hunted, prepared, and cooked myself, extended my hospitality, and you lay that bullshit on me?"

Laura glared at Brendan before turning to Cassie. "I'm fine, Cassie. These are just an old pair of leggings," Laura said. "As for Bren, he could have been more sensitive, but Cassie, we *are* worried about you. Is there anything we can do to help?"

"I'm doing just fine, Laura. I haven't heard from you in years, but I appreciate your offer. Bren is too important to be burdened with me. I brought him here to ask something significant, but forget it now."

"I'm sorry, Cassie," Brendan said. "I'll give you more money, but you need to go to rehab. That's the deal. I'll even cover the rehab costs."

Cassie fumbled her matches onto the floor while trying to light a cigarette. She bent down to pick them up, and tears streamed down her blotchy cheeks as she stood. "I don't want your money!" she exclaimed. "It's not about money. Keep your fucking money!"

Laura grabbed Brendan's arm, nearly yanking it from its socket. "Stop talking, Bren," she said. "You're making matters worse."

"Okay, okay," Brendan said. "I'll stop. But Cassie would feel better if she went to rehab."

"Stop!" Laura shouted.

Cassie sat silently, staring at her smoldering cigarette until a long ash fell onto her dinner plate. "You're a cruel bastard, Bren," she remarked. "You should leave."

"But. . ." Brendan began.

"Go away," Cassie yelled.

Brendan, Laura, and Shannon stood up, and Laura put her hand on Cassie's shoulder. "I'm sorry it ended this way," Laura said.

"It always ends this way," Cassie whimpered. "I'm such a fool for thinking it could be different."

Shannon walked around the table and hugged Cassie. "I'm sorry too," he said. "I have my driver's license now. Once the weather improves, I'll come to see you. It'll be better next time, Cassie," Shannon assured her.

"Thanks, Shannon," Cassie said. "You're a great kid. My brother was a great kid once, but he's changed. Try to hold on to your goodness and pass some of it up to your old man."

As Brendan backed out of the driveway, he glanced at Cassie standing in the kitchen window, gazing past him into the woods beyond, smoking a cigarette and sipping her beer. He wondered why he had spoiled the day. As he drove down the dirt road leading to the highway home, his eyes fell upon a stand of birch trees swaying in the wind like restless ghosts adorned with beards of fresh snow. A solitary scraggly fox with a field mouse dangling from its mouth scrambled in front of the car. Brendan braked hard as it darted from beneath the wheel well and vanished down a snowy embankment.

"Be careful!" Laura shouted, tears rolling down her face and smudging her black mascara. "You nearly sent me flying through the windshield."

"Yeah, Dad," Shannon said from the back seat. "You're out of control, driving like a maniac and lecturing Cassie about rehab. It's Christmas Day. Have a heart."

For the entire ride to Vermont, Brendan suppressed his urge to rehash his childhood, growing up with an alcoholic father and a hysterical mother. Cassie frustrated him. If he could escape their past, why couldn't she? He hated that she didn't seem to have the strength. But perhaps he was being too harsh. Should he go back and apologize? Maybe, but the snow was falling so heavily that his windshield wipers struggled to keep it at bay.

When they reached their ski chalet just after dark, Brendan watched Shannon using his new walking stick for balance as he maneuvered through the knee-high snow and headed straight to his room, flicking on his bedroom light once inside. Laura followed in Shannon's footsteps, stomping the snow off her boots in the mudroom. Brendan remained alone in the dark car until the cold outside over-took the warmth inside. Then he made three trips carrying their duffel bags down the path, slipping and falling onto his side. Snow filled his collar, sending shivers down his neck. After placing the last bag in the mudroom, he removed his wet boots and jacket and entered the great room, where Laura sat on the leather couch with her legs folded underneath her, sipping tea in front of the fireplace.

"Wyatt was supposed to shovel the path," Brendan said, expressing his disappointment in the caretaker. "But at least he delivered the tree, and his new girlfriend decorated it beautifully." Brendan pointed at the fifteen-foot-tall tree twinkling with white lights and gold ribbons. He poured himself a cup of tea and took a small box from his pocket.

"This is such poor timing, Laura, but with all the chaos today, I couldn't find the right moment to give you my gift." He tried to hand her the box, but she waved him away.

"Bren, I don't understand what happened today. You changed our Christmas plans to be with Cassie and were so cruel to her when we arrived. What's going on?"

"It's the same old pattern," he said. "I have good intentions, but then she triggers me. I don't know how to control it."

"You stay down here and think it over. I'm going to bed."

Brendan heard the bedroom door close and thought about following her upstairs. Instead, he sprawled on the couch, staring at the three-story stone fireplace, the oak-paneled walls, and the timber beams. Laura had designed the 10,000-square-foot chalet with an architect from the Stein Eriksen Lodge in Deer Valley, Utah. Brendan tried to remember whether Cassie had ever visited here. As he started to doze off, his cell phone vibrated in his pocket. Maybe Cassie was calling to apologize for kicking them out.

"Brendan, I'm sorry to bother you on Christmas, but I thought you'd want to know," said Bill, his attorney at Global Investment Bank. "WTF missed its margin call last night. I just found out myself; otherwise, I would have called you sooner."

"No way," Brendan groaned. "Did you tell Sarah?"

"I assumed you'd prefer to call her yourself."

"Thanks for calling, Bill," Brendan said, "and Merry Christmas."

"Same to you, Brendan," Bill sighed.

As Brendan dialed Sarah, he wanted to remind her that he'd warned against lending money to Williamson Trust Financial. Yet, if he did, she would cut off his balls at the first opportunity.

"Merry Christmas, Sarah," he said.

"Well, this is quite a surprise," Sarah said. "What reason could you possibly have for calling me tonight?"

"WTF missed the margin call," he said.

"Go to the office tomorrow morning and fix it," she said.

"I'm skiing in Vermont with my family," Brendan said.

"Shit flows downhill," Sarah said. "Call me when it's done."

He wondered why Sarah was such a jerk. Not even a "Merry Christmas" greeting when she'd answered the phone. Her greed, along with Gus's, was why he found himself in this situation in the first place. Couldn't she at least acknowledge it? But who was he kidding? Nobody on Wall Street took the blame; they only took the credit. Brendan went upstairs to tell Laura the bad news. The bedroom door was locked.

"I have an emergency at work," he shouted from the hallway. "Gotta go back to Connecticut. Tonight."

"Tonight?" Laura's voice was muffled by the door. "You've already had a long day, and it's still snowing. Go in the morning."

"I don't have a choice," he said. "Make sure Shannon finishes his application to Painter before I get back here in a few days, but don't let him submit it until I've reviewed it."

Laura opened the door, wearing a red cashmere robe over black satin pajamas. "Shannon doesn't want to go to Painter," she said. "The place doesn't offer what he's looking for."

"We've donated over half a million bucks to pave his way," Brendan said.

"You're not listening, Bren. He doesn't want Painter."

"Shannon's not listening. He doesn't know what's best for him."

Laura frowned. "Come downstairs. I'll make you a thermos of coffee and a peanut butter sandwich for the road."

"After I put you through such a terrible day, you would do that for me?"

"I'm furious with you, Bren. But I lost my father in an accident, and I don't want to lose my husband the same way. Drive safely."

Cassie

Christmas Night 2007

Cassie rolled back and forth in bed, her arms wrapped around her gut, wondering why Brendan constantly degraded her for drinking or needing extra cash. She hadn't invited him there for money. She wished she hadn't exploded. The pain in her gut worsened. She tried to stand up, but her head spun, and she flopped back down on the bed, coughing. Something thick like a doughnut climbed up her throat. She gagged and spit a glob of dark, bloody bile onto the sheets. A warm, coppery aftertaste coated her cheeks and tongue. Then another glob climbed up her throat into her mouth. Then another.

"Holy mother of Jesus." She gasped and stumbled into the kitchen to grab her gun-shaped key chain. But she was in no condition to drive on dark, slippery roads. She called Emily, reaching her answering machine. "Help," she uttered, then lost her grip on the phone. She spit another bloody glob onto the linoleum floor as she bent over to pick up the phone. She called Brendan. No answer. She pressed

DAMAGED GOODS

9, but before she could dial 9-1-1, she fell against the wall and landed beside her loaded rifle. She dragged it into the bedroom and laid it beside her on the bed. As she reached for the trigger, she noticed the bottle of painkillers and a jar of whiskey on her night table. She dumped a palmful of painkiller pills into her hand and washed them down with the whiskey. Then she pointed the rifle at her head.

Brendan

December 26, 2007

Brendan hurried out of Grand Central Terminal and down Park Avenue South. The empty pre-dawn streets the day after Christmas reminded him of September 12, 2001, the day after the Twin Towers fell, when Manhattan's streets were filled with smoke and dust all the way uptown. Although six years had passed, the memory remained vivid. He had worked twelve-hour days for three straight months, collaborating with funding managers from other banks under the supervision of the Federal Reserve Bank of New York to save the financial system and then attending countless funerals at night. But unlike the tragic events of 9/11, the deteriorating mortgage market was a self-inflicted wound that threatened the solvency of greedy hedge funds and banks every day. The struggle for financial survival reminded him of Jack London's *Call of the Wild*, a novel he had read in high school. The Wall Street dogs were turning on each other. Brendan's mandate was to kill the hedge funds before they killed him.

Outside his office building, the coffee vendor was off for the day. Without coffee and a good night's sleep, Brendan would have to rely on adrenaline. He headed directly to the war room, where his attorney, Bill, handed him the marked-up lending agreement that governed the loan between his bank and WTF.

"I know these contracts inside and out," Brendan said, setting it aside. "Have you talked to anyone at WTF about why they missed the forty-million-dollar margin call?"

"Tom Gallagher, their outside attorney, states that WTF has the funds, but he's blaming an operational glitch at their prime broker," Bill explained. "He and Trey Williamson will be calling any moment now."

"The CEO and outside counsel are calling about an operational glitch the day after Christmas. That's a bad sign," Brendan said, wiping the sweat from his brow with his sleeve.

The speakerphone rang, and a disembodied, boisterous voice echoed in the war room. "Hi, Brendan. Hi, Bill. It's Trey. I want to thank you for your business . . . and your patience. We at WTF love doing business with everyone at Global Investment Bank. I hope our prime broker's operational snafu didn't ruin your Christmas. Ha-ha. It ruined mine," Trey said. "On another note, I finished a tennis match with Sarah about half an hour ago. Who says women aren't as athletic as men? She has a great forehand. Gets her power from those field hockey thighs. After resolving this situation, I told her we plan to move even more business to your bank."

Brendan frowned. Why hadn't Sarah told him she had already spoken to Trey?

"We're currently on the phone with our prime broker. Rest assured, we'll pay you before the close of business tomorrow," Trey said.

"You need to pay us today," said Brendan, "or else . . ."

A deep, raspy, no-nonsense voice boomed from the speakerphone, interrupting Brendan. "Tom here. My client will resolve this operational error that was entirely outside of its control and was completely the fault of the prime broker. But it will be resolved by the end of tomorrow, not today."

They couldn't see him, but Brendan puffed out his chest and clenched his fist. He despised arrogance, and they were serving him a double dose of it. "The world's on fire, Tom. We're worried about this loan and have the right to liquidate the collateral if you don't meet the margin call today."

"You're wrong, Brendan," Gallagher said. "Flat wrong. Your mortgage attorney gave WTF an extra business day to meet margin calls."

Brendan's heart sank. He muted the speakerphone and turned to Bill. "Is he correct?"

"Gus made a last-minute concession to seal the deal," Bill said. "Sarah gave her approval."

"You knew this and didn't mention it to me?" Brendan asked.

"I tried, but you said you knew the contract inside and out."

"Fucking Gus," Brendan said, slamming the table. "And fuck Sarah with her private jet and field-hockey thighs." His chest deflated as he unmuted the phone. "Okay, Tom, I stand corrected. What's your plan?"

Tom explained a complex series of collateral movements that would complicate the deal but ultimately resolve the issue.

"Tomorrow by the end of the day," Brendan said weakly before hanging up.

"Gallagher outsmarted us," Bill said. "He's not the type of guy I'd want married to my sister, but he's one hell of a lawyer."

"Maybe we should hire him," Brendan joked, not fully understanding the marriage analogy.

He called Sarah to explain what had happened.

"Just a minute, Brendan. I'm on the first hole, 150 yards out. Let me hit this six iron, and then I'll call you from the cart." Eight minutes later, she called him back. "Sorry it took so long," she said. "I landed six inches from the cup and wanted to sink my birdie putt. What's up?"

Son of a bitch, Brendan thought. Here I am in this empty office while she plays tennis and golf in Florida. He could kick himself for being too afraid to say those words to her. Instead, he said, "Trey Williamson mentioned that you and Gus gave WTF an extra day to meet margin calls, so we'll find out if they're solvent tomorrow."

"Did I not mention that to you? My bad, Brendan. Unfortunately, it seems there's nothing you can do until tomorrow. Take the rest of the day off. I have to go now. We're on the tee box, and I have the honors."

Brendan wanted to pull Sarah through the phone and strangle her with the cord, but what could he possibly do? Why does she treat me like shit? he wondered while glancing around at the hundreds of empty seats on the trading floor, sparsely filled with junior traders babysitting the senior traders' positions. It wasn't even eight o'clock yet. He checked in with the junior traders in his department.

"Why are you here, boss?" asked Simon, a recent graduate of Painter College whom Brendan had hired as a favor to the college's head of career placement. Painter was small, and he knew that anything he could do for one department would reach the head of admissions, which might be enough to tip Shannon's application into the "accept" pile.

"I had to take care of a few things," Brendan said. "But I'm leaving now. Call me if you need anything." Brendan patted Simon on the shoulder and left for Grand Central to take the train home. As the near-empty train moved slowly along snow-covered tracks through Greenwich and Stamford on its way to Westport, his phone vibrated in his pocket.

"What a coincidence, Cassie. I was just about to call you. I was such an ass yesterday. I'm sorry for what I said. I don't know what comes over me. I promise to do better. I hope you can forgive me?" he said. It felt good to take the high road.

"Bren, it's Emily Winter. I know it must be bizarre to hear my voice. I hope you're sitting down."

"Emily Winter? I'm confused," he said.

"Cassie called me in distress last night and left a message. When I returned her call this morning, she didn't answer, so I went to her house. Nomad was barking nonstop when I arrived."

"What's happening?"

"Cassie's . . . Cassie's . . . Oh, God, Cassie's dead, Bren. She's gone. Just gone."

"She can't be dead," he said, catching his breath between words. "I was with her yesterday. How could she be dead today?"

"It seems like she OD'd, Bren. On painkillers. A whole bottle of them. The coroner's taking her away now."

"Where?" he whimpered.

"I'm not sure. It's really confusing here. They said you should contact the coroner, Mary Bassett, as soon as possible."

"Oh my God, Emily! I'm on the train home. Please give me your phone number. I'll call you when I'm on my way there. Oh my God!"

He hung up and then dialed his boss, Sarah, to explain the situation.

"I'm so sorry to hear such terrible news, Brendan. I didn't know you had a sister. Losing a family member is so difficult. But listen, I'm one under par on the ninth hole. It's the best round of my life. Give my assistant the funeral home address so she can send flowers. Try to return to the office as soon as you can after your sister's funeral. I've got to go."

Her words sent him beyond his breaking point. He hung up on her and pounded the wall of the train with his fist. A woman ran and came back with the conductor.

"My sister is dead," Brendan said. "Please, leave me alone."

The conductor stepped back, and Brendan called Laura.

"Dead? Good God. We were just with her," Laura said. "Poor Cassie. I'm so, so sorry, Bren. Where are you? How are you holding up? Do you want Shannon and me to come home?"

"I'm in shock, honey. Cassie overdosed. I don't know if it was intentional or accidental. Given how I treated her yesterday, I can't shake the feeling that I'm to blame."

"You shouldn't blame yourself," Laura said. "A person doesn't accidentally overdose because of one bad incident."

"I know, you're right," he said, unconvinced. "But still . . ." His voice caught in his throat. "I need to hang up and call the coroner. Then I'll pack a suitcase and head to New Hampshire."

"Where are you planning to stay tonight?"

"I suppose at Cassie's house."

"You're not thinking clearly," Laura said. "Stay at a hotel."

"I'll come up with something."

On his drive north to New Ash, Brendan talked to himself aloud. "Why is everything collapsing around me?" he said. "I've tried to do everything right in my life. I've tried to be a good brother. But Cassie's dead, and I'll never get to reconcile with her. I'll never be able to show her how much I care. Sure, I was hard on her. Too hard, I suppose. But that was because I wanted more for her. I wanted her to live the life she deserved. I wanted her to thrive, not be trapped in her shabby existence, drowning in booze. Whatever I did that made her hate me, I did out of love. And look where it got me. Look where it got her!" He began to cry. He hated himself whenever he cried. Thank God he was alone. "I've tried to be a good father to Shannon and a good husband to Laura. I've worked my ass off at a job I hate so I can earn enough to give them good lives. I don't always give them the time they deserve, but it's only to provide them with what they deserve—a nice house, nice cars, a good private school, better opportunities to get into a good college—all the things Cassie and I didn't have."

The snowbanks along the roadside grew thicker and taller the farther north he drove. By the time he reached the New Hampshire border, daylight had faded and the sun painted the sky in shades of orange and purple. For a moment, he grasped why Cassie had chosen to live in New Hampshire. It could be a beautiful place in the right sunlight and location. His phone rang, but he didn't recognize the number.

"You haven't called me," Emily said.

"Sorry, I'm a mess. But the good news is that I'm only an hour away. It's funny—the closer I get, the more I want to distance myself. I'm dreading what lies ahead."

Emily spoke, but he could only concentrate on the soothing sound of her voice. He was unnerved by his desire to wrap himself in it, to stay sheltered from his complicated world.

"Where are you staying?" she asked.

"I'm going to search for a hotel room, but I don't expect much availability in ski country during the holidays. If I can't find one, I'll stay at Cassie's, but I don't want to."

"I have a spare bedroom. Come stay with me."

Her offer knocked him off-balance. The idea of staying in the home of another woman, especially Emily, didn't feel right. He had once been in love with her—it was youthful love but love nonetheless. Her voice dredged up their painful ending, and he didn't have the emotional capacity to deal with Cassie's death and Emily's reappearance at the same time.

"That's a lot of trouble for you," Brendan said. "I'll find a place to stay."

"Don't be absurd," Emily said. "You shouldn't spend the night alone."

"Okay. Thank you," he said. "You were always kind."

"Don't think twice about it," she said and told him her address. "See you soon."

As he hung up and entered Emily's address into his car's navigation system, he wondered why he hadn't tracked

her down at her New Hampshire boarding school and pro-
fessed his love their senior year in high school. He had been
hurt and overwhelmed back then, but sports distracted him,
and slowly, the pain faded. After graduating high school,
he went to Painter, fell in love with Laura, and completely
forgot about Emily. Now, thinking about Emily felt like a
betrayal to Laura. It was a ridiculous notion, but he felt it
nonetheless.

He called Laura. "I found a good place," he said.

"I rented a car and will meet you there the morning
of the funeral," Laura said. "I'm sorry you're going through
this. I'm worried about you."

"Everything's gonna be all right, Laura," he said and
hung up.

He exited the main highway and followed a pothole-
riddled road that encircled a vast, ice-covered lake deep in
the forest before turning down a spur road, half expecting
to find a witch's lair. Instead, he arrived at a paved driveway
that led to a redbrick mansion on the estate of a farmer who
cultivated medicinal herbs. Emily lived in an apartment
above a three-car garage. She was waiting for him inside.

"I'm happy you're here, Bren." Emily hugged him
tightly before gently releasing her hold.

He could still see the seventeen-year-old girl in her
eyes and her smile.

"Would you like a drink?" she asked.

"I stopped drinking a long time ago," he said. "But
please, pour one for yourself."

43

"I'll brew a pot of chamomile tea," she said. "It'll help you relax."

"Better make a gallon," he joked.

They settled onto a soft couch packed with pillows and sat beside each other, their knees brushing. She rested her hand on his forearm. He remembered that in high school she always touched people when she talked to them, but it wasn't like they were still seventeen, chatting at a house party surrounded by a hundred people. Was she coming on to him? He felt the urge to push himself away, yet her touch was comforting.

"Cassie and I hadn't spoken in decades," Emily said. "Then she called me out of the blue a few years ago. She had heard I lived in New Hampshire and wanted to see me. I was nervous about reconnecting with her because of what you and I had done to her."

Brendan frowned. "We were young, drunk, stupid, and afraid."

"I know," she said, "but those excuses don't diminish the guilt. I haven't forgiven myself."

Brendan nodded. "It was my fault, not yours."

"When we finally met, I had to hold back my tears. She looked so depleted. My first thought went to your father's drinking, and then I thought of you, hoping you had avoided their fate."

Brendan shook his head.

"But deep down, I knew you had. You were so incredibly determined," she said. "I asked Cassie about you. She mentioned that she admired you but couldn't be near you.

Ultimately, though, I believe she wished she was more like you."

Brendan cringed. Why had it taken Cassie's death for him to realize how awful he had been to her?

"She knew her days were numbered," Emily said.

It was all too much for him. He shifted the conversation. "Tell me more about yourself, Emily. What do you do for work? Have you ever been married? Do you have kids?"

"Ahhh, you're looking for lighter conversation. I get it." She smiled. "I'm a doula—a birthing coach. I practice in an office just across the way." She pointed toward a small outbuilding on the farm. "No, I've never been married, but yes, I have one child, a daughter who lives in Massachusetts."

"In Nehoiden?" he asked.

"Nehoiden isn't as affordable as it was when we were kids."

He kept to himself that Nehoiden was well below his means. "We had good times growing up there," he said.

"I don't remember those days as carefree for you, Bren. You were on a mission."

"Why'd you leave high school, Emily? Cassie said you went to a Catholic boarding school for girls, and your dad wanted you to be a nun. You were about as far from a nun as anyone could imagine."

Emily smiled and sipped her tea. "Another shift in the conversation, huh, Bren? We had fun, didn't we, exploring our, how should I say it . . . our physical attraction for each other."

"We had too much sex, if that's even possible," Brendan said with a laugh.

"Dad knew we were at it all the time, and he didn't want me involved with a boy from the wrong side of town, even if he was a football star like you."

"I hated your father," Brendan said.

"He had no idea who you truly were, Bren. He simply assumed that you would amount to nothing based on the size of your family's house, your father's job as a butcher, and his views about wild Cassie. And he knew I would do anything for you. So he sent me away. I loathed every moment at that place, but my time there led me to my passion—becoming a doula."

"I wish Cassie had discovered her passion," Brendan lamented.

"Oh, she did, Bren. Many times! She was incredible. I admired her spunk and sense of adventure. She told me how she hunted deer, raised pigs and vegetables for food, and built staircases worth tens of thousands of dollars, installing them in McMansions outside of Boston. She was so talented, and the way she handled dogs was truly remarkable. She was a genuine dog whisperer. But . . ."

"I know," Brendan sighed.

". . . most of us outgrew the partying and risk-taking. If only she could've tamed the beast inside her. A few weeks ago, she mentioned she would tell you about her diagnosis at Christmas dinner, but I gather she never did."

Brendan wondered why he hadn't seen how gravely ill she was and showed some compassion instead of jabbing her with insults and snide remarks.

"Her overdose hastened the inevitable," Emily said, withdrawing her hands from his forearm before leaning in to hug him.

Warm tears streamed down his face into her hair. Sure, he had cried alone in the car on the way there, but he hadn't cried in front of anyone else, not even Laura, since his parents had passed away. But those deaths didn't come with this overwhelming sense of guilt. He lifted his head from Emily's shoulder. She touched his face with her fingertips, gently wiping away his tears. They locked eyes and moved their lips imperceptibly closer. As Emily closed her eyes, he suddenly pulled away. "I can't," he said.

"Still the disciplined Bren I once loved," she said, smiling gently. "You should probably get some rest. Tomorrow is going to be a tough day. I'll show you to the guest room."

An hour later, Brendan was still lying on his back, staring up at the dark ceiling. He got out of bed and opened the window shade, letting in the moonlight and casting his shadow on the adjacent wall—the apparition of another self. He wondered where life would have taken him if Emily had stuck around. Thank God he hadn't kissed her. The last thing he needed was another complication in his life. Yet he couldn't stop pondering the road not taken.

Brendan

December 28, 2007

Brendan sat with Laura and Shannon beside Cassie's pine casket in the front pew of the small Catholic chapel, bowing his head. The priest completed a prayer and nodded to Brendan, who stepped up to the pulpit, looking out at men and women clad in heavy winter work clothes, seated shoulder to shoulder, filling every pew and spilling into the aisles. He was ashamed for thinking that no one would show up. He fumbled over his words, mumbling and mixing them up as he tried to express the sibling love between Cassie and himself, sucking in air between his teeth to keep from fainting. When he finished the eulogy, the room emptied quickly. They probably have to get to work, he thought; or perhaps Cassie had told them he was a son of a bitch.

As they were leaving, Emily approached them in the chapel vestibule.

"Emily's a childhood friend of Cassie's," Brendan said, introducing her to Laura and Shannon. As the women shook hands, Brendan's face turned red. He hadn't cheated

48

on Laura; he had simply chosen not to mention that he'd been staying at Emily's house. He had nowhere else to go. He would tell Laura when the time was right. There was no need to complicate an already confusing situation. Yet, how could telling Laura about Emily be a complication if there was nothing to feel guilty about? He pushed the conundrum out of his mind.

"Shall we head to the cemetery?" Laura asked, gesturing toward the car outside.

"Before you leave, Bren, I have something for you," Emily said, reaching into her satchel and handing him a large sealed manila envelope. "Cassie asked me to give this to you when she passed."

Brendan's lips trembled.

"What's this about?"

"It was sealed when she gave it to me," Emily said, squeezing Brendan's hand. "God bless Cassie's soul. There won't be another like her. You saw only a small fraction of Cassie's friends here today. They're all working-class people. Getting time off from work is tough, especially during the ski season. Her friends could have filled three chapels if they didn't have to work."

"We should get going," Laura said, giving Brendan's arm a gentle tug. "It was nice to meet you, Emily."

Laura climbed into the Range Rover as Brendan and Shannon brushed off the snow that had piled up during the funeral mass. He opened the driver's door and whispered to Laura, "Give me a minute. I need to tell Emily something."

Before Laura could reply, Brendan quickly headed back into the church. Out of Laura's view, he hugged Emily and, without thinking, kissed her lightly on the lips. "Thank you," he said. "I'm glad you reconnected with Cassie."

"I'm thrilled we reconnected," she said, her brown eyes glistening.

He squeezed her hand. "I need to sell Cassie's house," he said. "Are you interested?"

"Doulas don't earn enough to afford a house," Emily said.

"I don't have time to sell the place," he said. "Make me an offer. Whatever you can afford—if you want it, it's yours."

Emily threw her arms around him. "You're a good man, Brendan."

"Cassie would disagree," he quipped. "But I'm sure she would've wanted you to have it." He hugged her once more and inhaled the amber scent of her perfume. "I've got to go."

Brendan returned to the car and tossed the manila envelope into the back seat with Shannon. Then he activated the emergency flashers and pulled in behind the hearse waiting for him. They formed a two-car procession to Cassie's grave site at a small cemetery a few miles outside town, near Mount Krystal's foothills. When they arrived, the snow was ankle-deep and falling heavier.

"You can stay in the car," Brendan said to Laura and Shannon. "You've been through enough today."

He followed the pallbearers from the funeral home along a snow-cleared path to Cassie's grave site. A snowshoe hare huddled against a gravestone. He helped lower the casket into the ground, then took a handful of dirt from the slouching mound beside the open grave and tossed it in. He recalled what Emily had said about Cassie: "Adventurous." "Talented." That was only the beginning. She was fun-loving and fiercely independent, not to mention infuriating and incorrigible. She was an enigma. How could someone with so much potential end up in a pine box at the bottom of a six-foot hole at fifty years old? What a fucking waste.

He grabbed the shovel and plunged it into the mound, dumping the dirt into the hole. A hidden rock struck the pine, echoing like a gunshot. The snowshoe hare stood up, its forelegs raised in prayer, wiggled its ears, and then bounded away. Brendan wanted to bound away too. A million miles wouldn't have felt far enough. Breathless and machinelike, he shoveled dirt until the mound, hole, and Cassie were no more.

●

When they arrived home that night, Brendan took their suitcases and duffel bags from the trunk, went inside, and turned on the lights. Laura immediately went to the wine rack while Shannon handed Brendan the manila envelope before going to his room.

"I've been wondering about something the whole way home, but I didn't want Shannon to hear." She uncorked the wine bottle and poured herself a glass. "Was there anything between you and Emily beyond her friendship with Cassie?"

"I'm not sure what you mean," Brendan dissembled.

"Well, as far as I know, there are two people in the world—well, one now, I suppose—who call you Bren: me and Cassie."

"My mother called me Bren sometimes," he said weakly.

"Now, this beautiful woman shows up out of nowhere, calling you Bren. What's going on?"

"Nothing's going on," he said, a bit more adamantly than he intended. "She calls me Bren because Cassie called me Bren. And besides, you're much prettier."

Laura frowned.

"Okay," he said. "It's absolutely nothing, which is why I've avoided mentioning it. We dated during our junior year of high school, but she went away at the start of our senior year, and we never saw each other again—until now."

"She's still in love with you," Laura said.

"Love? We were never in love," he replied. He had been about to mention that he had spent a couple of nights at Emily's, but how could he say that now? He changed the subject. "I want to open Cassie's envelope. That's more important than Emily."

He tore open the envelope and pulled out two pristine tan moleskin notebooks with the words *My Memoir* written neatly on the covers. Then he tipped over the manila envelope, and a white business envelope slipped out onto the table. He picked it up and examined it. "My God," Brendan exclaimed, "you won't believe what this is!"

"If it involves Cassie, I'll believe anything."

"Do you remember when Cassie lived in Canada?"

"Vaguely," Laura said. "Didn't she train sled dogs at a kennel there in the eighties?"

Brendan waved the document in the air as if it were on fire. "This is an agreement with a fertility clinic in Winnipeg."

"That poor woman," Laura said. "What other secrets did she hide?"

"According to this contract, I'm the legal custodian of Cassie's frozen eggs."

"Custodian? Are you saying we're responsible for her frozen eggs?" Laura gulped her wine and topped off her glass.

Brendan dropped the contract on the table. "Cassie said she'd never bring a child into 'this fucked-up world.' Those were her exact words. What possible reason could she have for freezing her eggs?"

"It doesn't matter why," Laura said. "We don't have time for this. Call the fertility clinic tomorrow. Tell them no, you're not going to be the custodian of your deceased sister's eggs. My God, did I actually say those words?"

"Stop with the imperatives, Laura," Brendan said, rubbing his forehead. "It's been a horrible few days. Give me a little time to think about this. Let me sleep on it."

"What's there to think about? The answer is no," Laura insisted.

"I can't just abandon these eggs. We're talking about the potential for human life—Cassie's biological child. These eggs could give Cassie a second chance. I need to think this through."

"It's about time you think about Shannon and me. He's having a tough time. So am I."

"Shannon? What's wrong with him? Stellar grades, well-liked by both students and teachers, outstanding athlete, involved in community service, National Honor Society scholar, and he dates a smart, beautiful girl," Brendan said. "Next year, he'll be at Painter College . . . hopefully. I'd give my left arm to be in Shannon's position."

Laura shook her head. "You're only reciting his CV and overlooking how he feels. He doesn't want Painter."

"And what about you, Laura? What grievance could you possibly have against me?"

"Bren, don't you think it's a red flag that we haven't made love in six months? When was the last time we had dinner together? When was the last time you showed any interest in me? And now you want to spend what little free time you have on Cassie's eggs? She's gone, Bren. No matter how guilty or sad you feel about her death, her eggs won't bring her back."

"Maybe they will, Laura. Maybe these eggs can bring a part of her back. Maybe the good part."

"You've lost it," Laura said. "This day has to end. Good night, Bren."

Brendan sat alone at the kitchen table, the moleskin notebooks before him. He had countless questions about his sister, her eggs, and why she had given them to him. What would the memoir reveal about her? What would it say about him? What long-forgotten memories would it revive? Reluctantly, he opened the first notebook and saw a note written in perfect cursive penmanship taped to the inside cover. It was addressed to him.

PART TWO

Memoir and Remembrance

Cassie

Dear Brendan,

It's been a few years since we last talked. With Dad, and Mom, and now Warren gone, and with both of us too stubborn to be the first to try to end our estrangement, the truth is I'm alone and hurting. I got bad news from my doctor last week, and I want to try to make peace with you. You're all that I've got left.

I wrote this memoir when things started falling apart. It's my feeble attempt to try to sort out my life and to leave something of myself behind when the time comes. Hopefully, that moment will be far in the future, but we don't know what fate has in store for us. I want you to have this memoir as a keepsake and record of who I am—who I truly am. I know that I've disappointed you over the years, but you've disappointed me, too. It's sad that our adult relationship hasn't been as good as our time as kids. We had some crazy times together. Fun times. Not so fun times.

Along with this memoir, I have something else to share with you, but I'll share it face-to-face next time I see you, which hopefully will be on Christmas Day. I know that in our family, the word "love" has never been spoken. But I want to end this note by saying that I love you and hope we can make things better before it's too late.

Love,
Cassie
December 2007

Cassie

Fall of Junior Year 1974

Bren hated that I liked Larry. Said he was trouble. But to me, he was the coolest kid in high school. So when Larry invited me to a party with him in Devil's Den on Halloween Friday night, I almost peed my pants. On the night of the party, I wore a red tube top, hip-hugger jeans, black dingo boots, and a black belt with a peace-sign buckle, sneaking out the back door so Mom and Dad wouldn't see what I was wearing. Bren had a football game the next day, so he wasn't gonna party with me and Emily. She met me at the entrance to the town forest, and we followed a narrow, moonlit path covered with pine needles through the pitch-dark woods. As we entered the clearing known as Devil's Den, I fixed my tube top so it pushed up my boobs and tugged down my hip-huggers to expose my belly. Emily didn't need to make any last-minute adjustments. She could look sexy in a burlap sack. She pulled out an empty peanut butter jar filled with sloe gin from her shoulder bag, and we pinched our noses and chugged it. The taste of cherry cough syrup coated my mouth and lips.

The first person I noticed in the Den was Larry. He stood atop Satan's Throne—a fifteen-foot-tall rock in the center of Devil's Den—with his legs straddled, daring the other boys to knock him off. No one even tried. When he spotted me, he climbed down from the rock, pushed his sweaty long black hair back from his face and kissed me. My stomach churned. Then he pulled two beers from his leather motorcycle jacket and handed one to me.

"I'll leave you two alone," Emily said, fading into the crowd.

Larry stood quietly, one fist on his hip, the other holding the beer, legs apart, gazing at me with a smile. "Drink up," he said.

The beer was warm and tasted awful. But I didn't want to disappoint him, so I forced it down.

"Did you hear that noise?" Larry asked, his eyes glossy. "It's a coyote. Let's track it down."

"No freakin' way," I said.

"Come on. I'll keep you safe," he said, grabbing my hand and pulling me down a path deep into the darkness. I didn't want to go, but I did anyway. We stumbled forward, stepping over rocks and fallen trees until we reached a narrow clearing and sat on a damp log. The moisture soaked through my blue jeans and made my backside clammy. The night air felt cold against my exposed belly and shoulders.

"Let's go back," I said, attempting to stand up, but he tightened his grip on my wrist and pulled me back down.

"Don't be such a baby," he said. "I thought you were cool."

We sat quietly on the log for a few minutes, listening to squirrels rustling in the leaves. I convinced myself the coyotes were creeping closer. I said I was cold. Larry removed his leather jacket, draped it over my shoulders, and tightened his grip on me.

"Let's go back," I whined.

With that, he grabbed my hair and pulled my mouth to his, prying my lips open with his tongue before shoving it in.

"That was gross," I said. It was nothing like the soft, warm kiss he had given me when we first arrived. "I want to go back."

Then he did it again, shoving his tongue so far down my throat that I thought he was going to lick my tonsils. Before I knew it, he had pinned my wrists behind my back with one hand and yanked down my tube top with the other. I struggled to free myself, but he was too strong. I cursed myself for letting him lead me so deep into the woods. It was entirely my fault. But he was acting insane. He must have been so drunk that he didn't know what he was doing. I was scared, but I tried to stay calm.

"That's enough, Larry. Let's go back."

He stopped kissing my lips and began kissing my boobs.

"Stop struggling," he said in a low, angry voice that I'd never heard before.

"Please, Larry. This isn't why I came here with you. I want to go back."

"Shut up," he shouted.

I was so scared I didn't know what to do. I wanted him to stop but didn't want to anger him further. What would he do next? I didn't want to find out. I wondered where Emily was. Did she see us go into the woods? How long had we been gone? Wouldn't she know enough to come after me? I prayed she'd rescue me. Suddenly, he stopped. Thank God.

That's what I believed, at least.

"Let's go," I tried to say sternly, but it came out like a whisper.

Instead of letting me get up, he grabbed my belt and unbuckled it. I tried to say no, but the words caught in my throat once more, and before I realized it, I was lying on my back with my jeans tossed onto the leaves beside me. I clung to the waistband of my underwear as if my life depended on it.

"Take them off," Larry insisted.

"No, Larry, please, not that."

Suddenly, he was on me, his thick thighs pushing against mine, his hard penis grinding against my pubic bone. I reached down and felt strangely grateful that my underwear was still on.

"Stop, Larry. Please stop," I said, unsure whether I had spoken or thought the words. My head spun, and I lost all sense of time. After what felt like an eternity, he finally stopped. I gasped for breath, struggling beneath his weight, until he rolled off me, buttoned his pants, and yanked me up from the ground, nearly pulling my arm out of its socket. I quickly adjusted my tube top, found my pants, and pulled them on, brushing the damp, decaying leaves off my legs and back. As I zipped up my pants, I felt a thick, slimy wetness on my belly. I thought I was going to be sick. I wiped it with a handful of dead leaves, then finished buckling my belt.

Larry was just a few feet away, peeing on the ground. I sprinted away as fast as I could, my boots slipping on the rocks and leaves, unsure of where I was going, following the path, listening for sounds from the party and moving toward them. I climbed a steep trail and realized I was close. I could hear him panting behind me. Just when I thought I couldn't take another step, I burst into the clearing and dropped to my knees, my lungs burning and too exhausted to cry.

Emily approached me with a crooked smile. "What happened to you?"

I wanted to scream at her for not saving me. Instead, I grabbed her jar of sloe gin and chugged what was left. A moment later, I puked cherry-red liquid all over my boots. Emily reached into her bag and handed me a breath mint. We both sobered up instantly.

"Let's get out of here," she said, wrapping her arm around my waist and guiding me out of the woods. We went to her house and up to her bedroom, where I shared the entire terrible story, or at least what I could recall. I was still shaken.

"Promise me you won't tell Bren," I kept repeating.

"You can count on me," she said.

I got home past midnight, took off my boots, and tiptoed past my parents' bedroom, where Dad was snoring so loudly that I worried he might wake up Mom, forcing me to come up with some excuse for coming home so late. I ducked into the bathroom, washed the vomit off my boots, and tossed my clothes into the hamper. I scrubbed the crusty residue off my belly and threw the washcloth in the wastebasket. I stared at my body in the mirror; my pubic area was bruised and sore, and my boobs were marked with hickeys.

I kept revisiting why I'd gone to the party. I'd wanted to make out with Larry but not that way. The longer I stared into the mirror, the more I convinced myself it had all been a big mistake, that Larry was drunk and didn't mean what he'd done. I was sure Larry would call me in the morning to apologize. But he didn't.

On Monday morning before school, I was smoking a cig with Emily in our usual spot, holding my thick science textbook. Despite Emily warning me to stay a hundred miles away from Larry, I waited for him to come over and apologize. But he stood across the parking lot, smoking with his friends, talking and gesturing with his arms and hips, rolling his eyes, and laughing. I knew what he was telling them. Then the school bell rang. He dropped his cigarette and walked past me, purposely looking away. I stepped into his path, holding my textbook like a shield in front of my chest. "What were you telling those guys?" I asked.

"None of your business," he said.

"I thought you'd call me over the weekend," I said.

"Come on, Cassie," he scoffed. "See that girl, and that girl, and that girl." He pointed to three other girls smoking in the corner. "Join the crowd."

I heard Larry's friends laughing and calling me a slut. Without a second thought, I slammed the sharp edge of my textbook against the side of his temple. He collapsed and hit the back of his head on the asphalt. For a few seconds, he lay there, rubbing the back of his head and checking for blood.

"You cunt!" he shouted at the top of his lungs.

"Fuck off," I said, flicking my cigarette at him as he staggered to his feet.

That marked the end for Larry and me.

●

Brendan's hands trembled as he finished the passage. He had no recollection of the party and could barely remember Larry, one of those guys who came and went in his life without leaving a ripple behind. Yet for Cassie, Larry felt like a heavy boulder plummeting from above and shattering her. Everyone carried the memory of their first kiss throughout their lives, and while Brendan cherished a beautiful memory with Emily, Cassie carried this . . . was "rape" too strong a word?

Brendan

Summer before Junior Year 1974

"D'you wanna come to the beach with me, Lisa, and Emily?" Cassie shouted through Brendan's closed bedroom door. "Emily's picking us up in her Camaro in twenty minutes."

"You're inviting me to hang out with you guys?"

"We're planning to have a few beers, so we'll need a driver," she said.

Brendan jumped out of bed, showered, slipped into his lucky blue gym shorts and a white sleeveless Nehoiden Football T-shirt, poured a cup of coffee, and wolfed down a stale doughnut while gazing out the window, thinking about Lisa in a bikini on the beach. When Emily pulled up in the white Camaro her daddy had given her, the ragtop down, he strolled to the car, trying not to seem too anxious about going with them. He spotted Lisa in the back seat wearing an oversized red Coca-Cola T-shirt that hung off her slender shoulders, revealing the straps of her black bikini top. Her silky blond hair was styled in a French braid. Brendan started to climb into the back seat.

"Sit up here. You're our chauffeur, Bren," Emily said, smiling widely, leaning forward and revealing her large, beautiful breasts spilling from her tiny pink bikini as she hopped over the stick shift and landed in the passenger seat. Cassie climbed into the back.

"First stop, the packie," Cassie said. When they arrived at Lucky's Liquors, Lisa went inside and came out with two six-packs of Schlitz, a few cans of Coke, a bag of corn chips, and a sleeve of ice. She wasn't eighteen yet, but the old guy behind the counter didn't seem to care. The girls drained a six-pack as Brendan sped along the highway on the hour-long trip to Duxbury Beach. Once they arrived, Brendan carried the cooler and his towel while the girls raced ahead to claim an open patch of sand on the crowded beach. As Lisa laid out her towel, Brendan tried to spread his towel next to hers, but Cassie got there first.

Emily spread out her towel, which was big enough for two people, and patted the space beside her and said, "We'll share yours to dry off, Bren." Brendan glanced at Cassie and Lisa, who rolled their eyes and nodded for him to comply.

Settling beside Emily, he closed his eyes and inhaled the fresh scent of salt and sand. Soon, the smell of Emily's amber-scented perfume and warming skin overwhelmed the scent of the shore. When he opened his eyes and glanced her way, she smiled and leaned on her elbows like the Sphinx, pushing her breasts together with her slender biceps and licking her lips. Sweat dripped in her cleavage like condensation on a cold glass of water.

"Tell me about your football team," Emily said, taking off her sunglasses and revealing brown eyes like tea saucers.

"I didn't realize you were interested," Brendan said.

"I'm suddenly curious," she said.

Brendan told Emily about the upcoming season.

"That's sooo fascinating," she said, crossing her arms beneath her ribs and pushing up her breasts as she leaned closer to him.

"Come to a game," he said.

"I want to come," she said, sliding her hand onto his biceps, "as long as you don't hurt anyone with those guns."

He felt a bulge in his lucky gym shorts.

She handed him a tube of suntan lotion, tied her long brown hair up in a band, and rolled onto her stomach. "Let's lather each other up. You go first."

He dropped the tube on the sand to create a diversion and rolled away from her until he regained his composure. Then he knelt beside her and rubbed slow circles on her back, hamstrings, calves, and around the pukka bead anklet on her right ankle. She rolled onto her back.

"Don't forget my toes, Brendan. Rub your fingers between the gaps of my toes."

Her wish was his command. He worked the lubricant between her toes and, for a moment, thought he was going to explode. But somehow he managed to calm himself as he worked the lotion up her shins, stopping at her knees.

"Keep going," she urged. "You wouldn't want my thighs and belly to burn, would you?"

He compliantly reloaded his hands with lotion, rubbing it into her thighs, belly, along the snow-white sides of her breasts, and across her décolletage. It was the closest he'd ever come to second base.

"Okay, okay," she said with a smile. "We're in public. Try to keep it PG." She took the lotion from him. "Now take off your T-shirt and roll down the tops of your shorts. I don't want to miss a spot."

He sensed the bulge once more.

"Don't worry," Emily said, glancing at his gym shorts. "These things happen. Just relax." After she finished rubbing in the lotion, she lay beside him, pressing her arm and leg against his side. "That feels nice," she said. "I'm glad you came today."

Gradually, Brendan relaxed and started to doze off until Emily suggested they go for a walk.

They strolled along the shoreline, weaving between toddlers digging in the sand as the small waves lapped over their feet. By the time they returned to their towels, Cassie and Lisa had polished off the second six-pack and were passed out, turning red under the relentless sun. Brendan nudged them to wake up.

"Let's go home before you do any more damage to yourselves," he said, packing the towels as Emily guided them to the car. Cassie and Lisa flopped in the back seat while Emily settled in front, resting her head on Brendan's shoulder. Soon he felt her drool on his biceps and glanced at her, accidentally catching a glimpse of brown nipple that had slipped out of her pink bikini top. He thought she was asleep until he felt her hand sliding up his leg, creeping into his lucky blue gym shorts. He jolted the gas pedal and nearly crashed into the black Gran Torino ahead. The Gran Torino's driver honked the horn and flashed his middle finger out the window. Despite Brendan's erratic driving, Emily remained undeterred for the rest of the ride home. When they reached his driveway, Emily pulled her hand away, kissed him on the cheek, then slid into the driver's seat and drove off.

The following afternoon, Emily called his house.

"Are you looking for Cassie?" Brendan asked, pretending that the day at the beach had been a wonderful dream.

"I'm looking for you, Bren. What are you up to tonight?"

"The football team is lifting weights at the high school gym, but I'll be finished by eight."

"I'll pick you up outside the gym," Emily said.

They drove around town in her Camaro with the ragtop down, reveling in the cool breeze on the hot August night, stopping for ice cream, and finished around midnight in the parking lot at Raven Bay. They climbed into the back seat and gazed in awe at the gazillion stars painting the sky milky white. He was still wearing his sleeveless T-shirt and blue gym shorts from the workout, and as she rested her head on his lap, he worried about his sweaty smell. But she didn't seem to mind. She pulled her shirt over her head, unclasped her bra, and tossed them aside. "Much better," she said, smiling blissfully, her eyes rolling back. "Take off these shorts, Bren," she whispered. But before he could react, she tugged them down to his ankles and did things to him that made his head spin. The wonderous dream is real, he thought, the dream is real.

Cassie

Junior Year 1974

I was balled into the fetal position on my bedroom floor, feeling like I'd been gutted with a hunting knife. Larry had broken something inside me. The next thing I knew, an ambulance was taking me to Nehoiden Hospital, where a white-haired doctor asked me questions and said that an exam was necessary. I closed my eyes, took deep breaths, and tried to relax as he probed inside me. Little did I know how long the hurt would last.

A nurse led me to the doctor's office, where he sat behind his desk and handed Mom a piece of prescription paper with a name and phone number scribbled on it. "I've arranged for Dr. Horowitz at the Boston Hospital for Women's Dysplasia Clinic to examine Cassie on Tuesday. He's the top cervical specialist in Boston." Then he turned away and gazed out the window at the large elm tree in the center of the hospital's expansive front lawn as if watching the leaves change color.

"Mrs. O'Shay, is there any chance you were given diethylstilbestrol—DES—the anti-miscarriage drug, during your pregnancy with Cassie?" he asked as he turned back to face us.

Mom's eyes darted nervously between the doctor and me. Her face went pale.

"Could we have some privacy?" she asked the doctor. He pressed a button, and his nurse entered the office and guided me out to a chair in the hallway. The nurse left the door slightly ajar, and I could hear Mom. "I had several miscarriages," Mom said, weeping. "My ob-gyn prescribed DES, and it worked. I had a healthy baby girl, and I was prescribed the drug again when I was pregnant with my son, Brendan, who was born ten months later. Then, last year, I read in *The Boston Globe* that daughters of women who took DES were developing cervical cancer."

Cancer! The word freaked me out. I realized that my condition had nothing to do with Larry.

"The stories terrified me," Mom said. "But the newspaper articles claimed the odds of having an affected daughter were minuscule, so I pushed the whole mess out of my mind. Cassie had a better chance of getting hit by a car than of getting cervical cancer." Mom sobbed louder. "If the drug was so dangerous, why did that damned doctor give it to me?!"

I felt sorry for Mom.

"We can't change the past," the doctor said, "but we can address the consequences. Bring Cassie to Dr. Horowitz's office on Tuesday."

"What about my son?" Mom asked.

"There's no evidence that DES harmed boys," he said.

"Thank God!" Mom cried out. She sounded so relieved.

I got up and quietly peeked into the office. The doctor handed Mom a pamphlet. "This should answer most of your questions," he said. She stuffed the pamphlet in her pocketbook.

Mom hung her pocketbook on the back of a kitchen chair when we arrived home and went to the basement to do laundry. I read the pamphlet.

> Diethylstilbestrol (DES) was regarded as a safe drug in the 1950s. However, since 1967, several girls aged fourteen to eighteen have been diagnosed with clear cell adenocarcinoma, and some have undergone removal of their bladder, ovaries, uterus, and, in rare instances, vagina. One in four thousand daughters of women who took DES may develop cervical cancer.

One in four thousand. I couldn't be that unlucky. Could I?

The night before my appointment with Dr. Horowitz in Boston, I was in the living room reading *The Bell Jar* for English class when I overheard Mom and Dad talking in the kitchen. Dad had been drinking. He was shouting and complaining that he couldn't afford to take another day off work to drive me to the hospital.

"Our health insurance coverage doesn't start until I've been on the job for three months," he stammered. "I need to work!"

"I told you not to quit your old job," she said. "A little extra salary isn't worth losing medical coverage when a family depends on you. You were shortsighted to take this new job, Rick."

It was hard to hear Mom's complaint because Dad was so happy when he got the new job. I stopped reading and went to bed but didn't sleep a wink. I worried about Dad . . . and myself. I prayed we would be okay.

The next morning, Bren was heading out the door for school when he saw the three of us getting into Dad's car. "Where are you guys going?" he asked. But Dad said it wasn't Bren's concern. For the first time in as long as I could remember, I would have given anything to be on my way to school that morning.

On the road to Boston, Mom kept looking back at me, asking how I felt. I think she was praying that I would say the pain had stopped, but it hadn't. I believe she was hoping this was just a bad dream. I know I was.

Dad dropped us off at the hospital, a massive redbrick structure that resembled an insane asylum from a Hitchcock movie. Dr. Horowitz, a short, chubby man with slicked-back dark hair and thick horn-rimmed glasses, explained in a no-nonsense voice that the nurse would apply an iodine solution to my vaginal area, and if the tissue were completely stained, I'd be out of the woods. If it weren't, there would be additional steps.

Dr. Horowitz was so intimidating with his Harvard diplomas displayed behind him. I didn't dare ask stupid questions about the additional steps. Mom didn't ask, either. Then he brought me to an examination room and poked and prodded me so much that I thought I might faint. When it was over, he met Mom, Dad, and me in his office. As we sat, he removed his glasses and explained the results.

"I examined Cassidy for cervical erosion, vaginal hood, pseudopolyp, rim, collar, and cockscomb cervix." I felt like crawling out of the room as I listened to the doctor explain to my parents what was happening down there. Dad fumbled with a cigarette until the doctor pointed to the NO SMOKING sign on his desk. Mom looked scared. "The good news is that Cassidy doesn't have precancerous vaginal adenosis. However, cancer can appear at any time, so we'll actively monitor her every three months."

"For how long?" Mom said.

"For the rest of her life," the doctor stated.

"If that's the good news, what's the bad?" Dad said, lighting a cigarette and flicking the ashes into his hand.

"Cassidy has a T-shaped uterus," the doctor said, "which means she can conceive but cannot carry a child to term."

"She'll miscarry?" Mom said.

"Worse. The fetus could develop outside of her uterus in her fallopian tubes, which would be a life-threatening condition if it occurred. And it most likely would occur."

Dad suddenly jumped up and kicked his steel-toed work boot through the front of Dr. Horowitz's mahogany desk, yelling that he was going to strangle the son of a bitch who gave my mom DES.

Dr. Horowitz backed up his chair hard against the wall, scared shitless that Dad was coming after him, knocking the diploma to the floor and shattering the glass.

I felt outside myself, looking in, trying to process the crazy scene and terrible news. I didn't have cancer, but I might at any time. I could conceive, but I couldn't carry a child. None of it made sense.

Dad finally calmed down, and Mom apologized to the doctor. The doctor was so rattled that he didn't even try to clean up the broken glass. As we left the building,

Dad hugged me so tightly around the shoulders that I thought he would dislocate them.

That night, Bren sat on the couch in the living room while I finished reading *The Bell Jar* for English class. The main character, Esther, is a talented writer who struggles with emotional issues. We all faced our share of problems, except for Bren, who always seemed confident and composed.

"Why'd you miss school today, Cassie? Is everything okay?" he asked.

"I'm fine."

"Cool," he replied. "Emily wants to hang out with you tomorrow."

"I can't believe you and Emily are hot and heavy," I said. "I figured you wouldn't last a week."

"I like her," he said. "But enough about that. I haven't even opened the worksheet for my math quiz tomorrow."

Bren left the door between the living room and the kitchen open when he left. I heard Dad and Mom talking too loudly.

"I wouldn't have let you take DES if I had known this would happen," he said, slurring his words.

"At least we have our children," Mom said. "Without the DES, I might have miscarried again."

"Yeah, but now my only daughter is damaged goods."

"Don't call her that," Mom said. "It's not her fault."

I closed my book and pondered what Dad had called me. Damaged goods.

●

Brendan finished reading this chapter and wondered why his family hadn't told him about Cassie's medical condition. It finally made sense why she hadn't wanted children. Why then did she freeze her eggs?

Cassie

August before Senior Year 1975

The day started so well. I got a letter from the high school notifying me that I'd been recommended for a brand-new experiential learning program because of the gap between my high standardized test scores and low grades. It sounded cool, and for the first time since elementary school, I genuinely looked forward to the start of school. I called Emily to share the news, but she blew me off. All she wanted to talk about was the party at Raven Bay and how she'd pick up Bren and me at eight.

I couldn't believe Bren was still dating her. She was a total wild child, even wilder than me, and Bren was the most uptight guy I knew. Maybe they liked each other because they were so different. Who knows? Bren wasn't exactly the type to talk about his feelings, at least not with me.

When Emily arrived, Bren jumped into the driver's seat, and I settled into the back. He loved Emily's Camaro, probably because our dad's car was a five-year-old blue

Chevy Impala with dents in the rear side panels that Dad couldn't afford to fix. A few minutes later, we pulled into the Raven Bay parking lot, where massive oak trees and dense tangles of honeysuckle underbrush shielded us from the main road—perfect for partying and screwing. Knowing Emily, I was sure she and Bren had been doing plenty of screwing all summer.

As soon as Bren parked the car, I got out, and they jumped into the back. I lit a joint and passed it to them. Emily took a long hit, but Bren passed. I knew he would. Then I left them alone to do their thing while I wandered around the party, saying hi to kids perched on the hoods of cars, smoking weed, and drinking beer. The air buzzed with the sound of a hundred teenage voices mixed with the music of the Grateful Dead, the Allman Brothers Band, and Elton John blasting from car radios. I moved from one group of kids to the next, hitting on joints and taking shots of whatever hard liquor had been swiped from their parents' cabinets. I was flying high when I came to a pickup truck playing Elton John's "Rocket Man." Without hesitating, I swung my legs over the side of the truck, hoisted myself into the truck bed, then climbed onto the roof, crossed my legs like a guru, listened to the lyrics, and watched the scene unfolding before me under the light of a full moon.

In the corner of the parking lot, I spotted Emily straddling Brendan with a beach blanket draped loosely over them, trying to conceal the obvious. They could've been a little more discreet. Whatever. I took another hit from a joint I had picked up on my travels. The world suddenly felt like a better place.

That's when I noticed the blue lights flashing and heard the sirens wailing. I was scared to death. The last thing I wanted was to get arrested. Strangely enough, even though Mom and Dad would kill me, I was more afraid of being expelled from the experiential learning program I had just been accepted into. I jumped off the truck and ran toward Bren and Emily, hoping to hightail it out of there with them. But with a wall of headlights from all the cars trying to exit the parking lot before the cops could arrest the kids inside, I was running blindly. Then, my world went dark.

●

A week later, after I was released from the intensive care unit, Bren visited me in my hospital room and explained what had happened next.

"It was a madhouse after the cops showed up," he said. "I saw you running into the light. A car hit you, and you went down hard. Two cops jumped out of their cruiser. One grabbed his bullhorn and ordered everyone to clear out, while the other bent over you and shined a flashlight on your face to get a better look. You were in rough shape. I gave the cop your name. He kept whispering your name in your ear, but you were out cold.

"Honestly, I thought you were dead. He kept saying your name, and finally you squeezed his hand. The cop started crying. I didn't know cops could cry. I cried, too. You were alive, and I felt so relieved. When the ambulance arrived, the cop asked me to ride with you, but I thought it would be better to go home and tell Mom and Dad. When I got home, Dad was passed out in his chair. I took Mom to the hospital in Dad's car. Mom stayed with you day and night until you regained consciousness."

Bren's story sounded strangely rehearsed. I couldn't believe he would share that he'd cried over me! While he was telling his story, my head throbbed incessantly from a cracked skull and broken front teeth. Would I ever be able to think clearly or smile again? I closed my eyes and drifted off. When I opened them an hour later, Bren was still right there. Even though I doubted his story, I felt grateful that he chose to stay with me.

"You left something out of your story, Bren," I mumbled.

He blushed.

"Who hit me?" I asked.

"Nobody knows. Nobody came forward. There was so much mayhem and commotion. I bet the guy thought he bumped into another car; he probably didn't even realize he hit you."

"It was a guy?" I asked.

"He? She? Who knows? Nobody came forward," Bren said.

I slumped into the bed. What kind of piece of shit person wouldn't own up to mangling me, to almost killing me?

Brendan

August before Senior Year 1975

The Raven Bay party was rocking, but Brendan and Emily were having their own private party in the back seat of Emily's Camaro. Emily reached behind her ear to pull out a tightly rolled joint. She lit it while Brendan cracked open a beer. They passed the joint and beer back and forth, gazing up at the star-filled sky with the ragtop down.

"You know not to tell people I smoke weed, don't you?" Brendan said.

"I wouldn't want to damage your reputation, Bren," Emily said. "All of your secrets are safe with me."

She took another toke, snuffed out the joint, and draped a beach blanket over them. Brendan pulled off his gym shorts while Emily tugged down the top and jacked up the hem of her strapless babydoll dress, wearing it around her waist like a red sash falling loosely over her curvy hips. She pushed Brendan onto his back and straddled him, rubbing back and forth, the full moon casting light on her face and breasts.

"You're not wearing underwear," he said.

"Of course not," she moaned. "Get your condom."

"Damn. I ran out of them," Brendan said. "I didn't have a chance to buy more."

"Rookie mistake, Bren," she groaned. "Just be sure you pull out in time."

As he lay beneath her, cradling her breasts and watching her brown eyes roll back in their sockets, he was sure he was in love.

"Don't come," she pleaded. "Not yet. Just a few more seconds . . . a few more seconds . . ."

Suddenly sirens blared and blue lights flashed all around them. He tried to get up, but she held him down.

"Not yet," she said. "Just a little longer . . . That's it . . . That's it . . . Okay . . . Okay." She collapsed forward, pressing her chest against his.

"Get up! What's happening out there?" he asked. He sat up and nudged her aside. "It's the cops," he said, pulling his shorts up from around his ankles. "If I get arrested, my football season is done. Let's go!"

Emily fixed her dress and reached between her legs. "Did you come, Bren?" she asked anxiously. "I don't feel anything on me. I hope you didn't come inside me. You said you wouldn't."

Brendan hopped into the driver's seat. "Get in the passenger seat, Emily. We gotta go!"

"Did you pull out in time?" she said. "Did you?"

"Stop asking me! We gotta go. Now!" He slammed the car into reverse and floored the gas pedal, but the bright headlights from the other cars in the lot blinded him when he glanced back. Before he could hit the brakes, he felt a thud.

"Damn, Bren. You hit a car. I hope you didn't dent my car. My daddy will crucify me."

He threw the car into drive, but there was nowhere to go. "Damn it! Coach John will kick me off the team. I'll be stuck in Nehoiden forever." He opened the car door. "I'm making a run for it, Em. Don't tell the cops my name."

As he started for the woods, he heard the cop shouting, "Who knows this girl on the ground?"

The thud, the fear in the cop's voice, a girl on the ground, sent a shiver through him. He turned back and ran up to the cop shining a light in the girl's face.

"Fuck!!" Brendan yelled. "Cassie! Oh, fuck!"

"Who is she?" the cop asked.

"Fuck! It's my sister. Cassie O'Shay."

"Are you Brendan O'Shay, the football player?" the cop said.

"Yes, sir," he responded. "I shouldn't be here."

"That doesn't matter," the cop said. "I'm not gonna rat you out. We have to help your sister."

Another cop must have called in the accident because an ambulance raced into the parking lot and the medics loaded Cassie into the back before speeding away. Brendan sprinted back to the Camaro, where Emily had moved into the driver's seat.

"I was scared to look at her, Bren. How is she?" Emily asked.

"Bad. Really bad," Brendan said, motioning for Emily to scoot over and let him take the wheel.

"You're too emotional to drive, Bren, and you've already caused enough damage. I'll drive."

"Move, Em," he said. "I can't mess around right now. I need to get home to tell my parents what happened."

Brendan slammed on the gas, screeching out of the parking lot and along the winding road toward his house. "Slow down!" Emily yelled. "You're going to kill us!"

But her voice sounded like it was a thousand miles away. His mind raced from one thought to the next. Would Cassie survive? Would his football career be over? How would his parents react? He pressed harder on the gas pedal, and the moonlit trees lining the roadside became a blur in the night.

Emily started to cry. "Bren, you were going to leave me to get arrested by myself."

"I had to run, Emily. It wouldn't matter if you got caught. You're wealthy. Your dad will take care of you. If I got caught, I'd lose my future."

Emily pounded her fist on her thigh. "I thought you loved me!"

A few minutes ago, he had loved her. But he had never said the words. She couldn't hang him with his words.

"It's not about whether I love you, Em. Don't you get it? If I miss my shot at a football scholarship, my future is toast. Do you wanna be in love with a total loser? Without football, that's what I'll become. A total loser."

"I love you, Bren," she yelled, "but you're frightening me."

"What's important right now is Cassie. Please, stop distracting me!"

Emily buried her face in her hands, her sobs growing louder. As they pulled into his driveway, she clutched his forearm. "I'm scared to ask, Bren, but are we the ones who hit Cassie?"

"No!" Brendan said. "She was too far away from our car for me to hit her."

Emily nodded and bit her lip. "Good," she replied. "I couldn't live with myself if we did."

Brendan leaned the car hard into the next corner. "Neither could I."

Cassie

Fall of Senior Year 1975

Brendan was my savior. Every day while I was in the hospital, he'd ride his bike to. visit me after football practice. He'd sit at the foot of my bed and talk to me for hours about what was happening at Nehoiden High—who picked up whom, who was in trouble, and how his football season was going. Hearing voices other than the doctors and nurses was good for me. I asked him why he was talking about everyone except Emily.

"She went to a Catholic boarding school for girls in some boondocks town in northern New Hampshire. Can you believe it? Never even said goodbye to me."

"A Catholic girls' boarding school?" I muttered. "What could Emily possibly do there, sleep with the priests?" I felt totally crushed. She had been my best friend since junior high. We shared each other's secrets. How could she leave without visiting me even once in the hospital, or just letting me know she was going away? I sank a little deeper into my pillow and closed my eyes.

"She was a distraction anyway," Bren said. "I was going to break up with her regardless. I have to put a college football scholarship first. I need a career where I can make some money, not end up as a lowly laborer like Dad, Grandpa, and every other O'Shay man since we got off the boat from Ireland." He paused. "And seeing you here has made me realize that life is too short to screw around. Me and Emily were just screwing around. But she was getting serious. She even said she loved me and wanted me to say I loved her back. Can you believe that?"

"Do you?" I mumbled.

"How am I supposed to know?" he asked. "I don't know what love feels like!"

I opened my eyes and saw him gazing at the wall. He was in love, I thought, but he was on a mission, and nothing would stand between him and his goal. Nothing.

●

On the morning of my release in mid-September, Nurse Nancy gently unwrapped the gauze from my head and removed my eye patch. No matter how much she warned me about what I would see when I looked in the mirror for the first time since the accident, and no matter how many times she assured me I would eventually heal, I wasn't prepared for who and what stared back at me. Remnants of cinder ash from the parking lot had settled into my forehead. My cheekbone was lopsided and bruised. My once-perfect little nose was crooked along the bridge. My front teeth were broken, and the hair on the right side of my head had been shaved off. I looked like a ghoul from a horror movie. No boy would ever want to be with me. I wanted to crawl back into the hospital bed and stay there forever or maybe run away to wherever Emily was. Why did she leave me?

But my physical appearance was far from the worst part. My pounding headache wouldn't let up. I didn't have much confidence in my ability to manage the pain at home. Mom was super helpful for the first few weeks, assisting me to the front stoop, settling me in a lawn chair to watch the cars drive past our house on the main street through Nehoiden, and bringing me food and drinks when I asked for them. I also had a steady stream of friends visiting me after school, bringing small gifts like chokers and bracelets made of feathers, stone, and wood—things I wouldn't be caught dead wearing, but they were thoughtful gestures. Bren was great too, always chatting with me after football practice, but he stayed silent about Emily. He asked me to attend a football game, but I wasn't ready to leave the house.

On the last Saturday in September, the temperature dropped to the low forties, and the leaves were starting to turn. I sat on the front stoop with a blanket across my lap, waiting for Bren to ride his bike home from his football game so he could tell me how they did. It's funny; I never cared much about his football team, but I looked forward to hearing his game stories. Around five in the afternoon, a yellow school bus stopped in front of our house. Fifty huge guys dressed in muddy football uniforms filed out and formed a massive semicircle in the front yard. Coach John was the last one off the bus. The line of players parted, and Coach John handed me an enormous bouquet of roses and baby's breath, a get-well card, and the game ball signed by every player on the team.

"This game ball is for you, Cassie," Coach John said. "We just ended the twenty-game winning streak of the number-one team in the state. Brendan ran for two touchdowns and earned the game ball, but he asked us to give it to you instead. We hope you feel better and return to school very soon."

I was too stunned to cry, but when I looked around, half the players had tears streaming down their mud-splattered faces, including Bren.

●

When I finally returned to school in early October, six weeks after the accident, it wasn't a moment too soon. Mom was tired of waiting on me, and the stream of visits from friends had dried up. I met with the head of the experiential learning program, Teacher Dave, on a brisk Monday morning. I liked him, which was unusual for me when it came to teachers. He was a cool guy, not one of those loser teachers who tried too hard to befriend students. And he was quite a hunk—big blue eyes, a full head of shaggy brown hair with bangs swept off his furrowed forehead, and a neat brown beard. He reminded me of Kris Kristofferson in *Alice Doesn't Live Here Anymore*. I guessed he was in his late twenties, maybe ten years older than me, but the wrinkles made him seem older and wiser. He said he'd help me catch up on my schoolwork and arrange a work-study job at the Nehoiden Animal Clinic based on a personal essay I'd written for English class the year before about my love for animals. He said it moved him.

Funny, I scribbled that essay in one draft the night before it was due. It was a soapy story about when Bren and I were nine. With our combined life savings of thirteen dollars, we bought a black-and-white guinea pig named Ginny. We carried her home in a shoebox and kept her under my bed for five years before she passed away. I loved Ginny.

Teacher Dave drove me to my first day at Nehoiden Animal Clinic, where Dr. Johnson, the owner, greeted me by having me clean the cages and wash the floors. Eventually he let me watch him examine the animals. I loved the job, except when owners who had lost interest in their healthy pets chose to euthanize them. Dr. Johnson said it was best for the pet in the big picture, but I didn't believe that.

By the end of the term, I researched and wrote a paper arguing that Massachusetts should pass a law to prevent pet euthanasia for reasons other than terminal illness. Dave gave me an "Outstanding" grade on my paper (we didn't get a letter or number grade in the experiential learning program), wrote me an encouraging note, and asked to see me in his office. When I arrived, he sat close to me on his couch. For a brief moment, I thought he might try to kiss me.

"Where do you want to attend college next year?" he inquired.

"That's not in the cards," I replied.

"You've been dealt a new hand," he said. "My college roommate is the dean of the animal science program at UMass Amherst."

"We can't afford college tuition," I said. "My dad works as a butcher at a grocery store."

"Scholarship money is available," he said.

The following week, Dave drove me home from school in his blue Ford Pinto and came inside to meet my parents. Mom crossed her arms over her belly while Dad shoved his hands into his pockets, leaning against the wall as Dave took off the long white scarf braided around his neck, unbuttoned his navy-blue peacoat, tucked his black leather gloves into his coat pocket, and placed his palms on his long, thin thighs.

"You a Navy man?" Dad asked.

"Ah, the peacoat," Dave said. "It's in style."

"I served four years on an aircraft carrier in the Pacific," Dad said. "Korean War."

"I received a college deferment from the Vietnam draft," Dave said.

Dad gave a nod.

"Cassie's an up-and-coming student," Dave said.

"We get her report cards," Mom said. "We know where she stands."

"Indeed, she didn't perform well in the regular curriculum," Dave said, "but she's flourishing in the experiential learning program. She has enormous potential. College potential."

Dad pulled a pack of Camels from his shirt pocket and tapped it against the back of his hand. Then he leaned over, cupping his hands around the end to light it as if shielding the flame from the wind sweeping across an aircraft carrier's deck. Dad took a hard drag, exhaling a smoke cloud that drifted up to the ceiling.

"Cassie's always had potential," Mom said.

I'd never heard her say that before.

"I'm encouraging her to apply to the animal science program at UMass," said Dave.

"We don't have that kind of money," Mom replied.

Dad glared at her as if she'd just said he wasn't a man.

"There are scholarships available," Dave said. "I've also talked to Dr. Johnson, the animal clinic owner, about Cassie's situation, and he's agreed to cover any financial shortfall."

"'Cassie's situation'? I don't appreciate your words, sir. We're not a charity case," Dad said, flicking his ashes into his hand and rubbing them into the thigh of his pants.

"It's not charity, Mr. O'Shay," Dave said. "Cassie will have to work at the clinic for two years after graduation. That's the arrangement the veterinarian is offering."

Dad inhaled the smoke deeply into his lungs and held it. Finally, he exhaled, speaking like a fire-breathing dragon. "We'll think it over," he said.

I walked Dave to his car, apologizing for what my parents had put him through. "I've had dozens of conversations like this one when I taught in Boston. Parents want the best for their kids. Eventually, they come around."

"Mine won't," I said, "but thanks again for trying."

Mom and Dad were waiting for me when I came back inside the house.

"I think he's a little light in the loafers," Dad said. Mom nodded.

"Dad, please, he's just trying to help me. Not many teachers have tried to help me."

"You haven't given them much reason to," Mom said. "Forget this ridiculous college idea. You're meant to work."

"Mom's right, Cassie," Dad said. "What's college gonna do for you?"

"What about Brendan?" I asked, struggling to hold back the tears welling in my eyes. "He wants to go to college too."

"Only if he gets a football scholarship," Dad said. "Otherwise, he'll be a working stiff like the rest of us."

I dashed to my room, where I could cry in private, and tore the UMass application into a thousand tiny pieces.

Brendan

Winter of Senior Year 1975–76

Brendan received a flurry of recruiting form letters from college coaches, but they were meaningless scraps of paper unless the coach called to follow up. Coaches were not calling, and he felt hopeless, until one December night, in his bedroom, he heard the phone ringing and ringing on the kitchen wall. His mom finally answered it.

"Hello. Sorry for letting the phone ring so long, but I'm washing the dishes. Who am I speaking to?" Mom said. "Hold on, I'll get him.

"Brendan," Mom hollered down the hallway. "A coach from Pinto College is on the phone."

Brendan hurried to the kitchen and took the phone from her.

"Hi, Brendan. This is Coach Smith from Painter College. Let your mom know to remember the name, because that's where she'll be watching you play football for the next four years."

"Yes, sir." Brendan nodded as though the coach could see him.

The coach spoke for five minutes about how Brendan would be an ideal addition to their football program.

"This all sounds great, sir, and I'm happy you called me, but where's Painter?"

"Nestled at the foot of the Green Mountains, in God's country, a place where the life of the mind flourishes."

Brendan didn't know where the Green Mountains were or what it meant to have a life of the mind, but he knew enough not to ask.

"I invite you to spend a Saturday night here, tour our academic and athletic facilities, and meet some of our players."

This time he had to ask. "Excuse me, sir, but where are the Green Mountains?"

"Haha. I appreciate a kid with a sense of humor. In Vermont, naturally."

"I'd love to visit, sir, but Vermont is pretty far from Boston. I hoped to stay closer to home, maybe at Tufts or Amherst."

"Are those schools recruiting you?" Coach Smith asked. Brendan sensed urgency in the coach's voice. "You'll have a better experience at Painter; I can guarantee that. Come here with your parents this weekend; I'll show you around and answer your questions. I'll give you the name of a good hotel."

"Dad works on weekends and needs his car," Brendan said. "But I can thumb up there, sir, if you're truly interested in me."

"Hitchhike?" Coach Smith said. "We don't want you doing that, especially in the snow. They say it's going to snow up here this weekend."

"I hitchhike all the time," Brendan said, "but I usually don't go that far away."

"I tell you what. I've watched enough of your game films to know you'll be a star at Painter. Your high school coach says you're the hardest hitter he's ever coached, and we could use that kind of toughness on our team. He also mentioned that you're a good kid and a solid student. So here's the deal: I'll send you an admission application, and you can return it directly to me. I'll walk it over to the director of admissions—a good friend of mine—to let him know you're one of my top recruits, boosting your chances of acceptance. But you must promise me you'll come to Painter College if you get in—and I truly believe you will. Deal?"

Brendan covered the phone's mouthpiece and ensured his dad was out of earshot. "Thank you, sir," he whispered. "But my family doesn't have the money to send me to college, so I'm not sure I can make the deal."

"We take pride in making college affordable for everyone, no matter their economic situation. We provide financial grants and offer work-study programs for students in need. If we can make it financially feasible for your family, do we have a deal, Brendan?"

"Deal, sir," Brendan said. "Thanks."

Brendan hung up and let the call sink in. Everything had happened so quickly. Had he just committed to a school he'd never heard of? And had he given the coach the wrong impression that Tufts and Amherst were recruiting him? They were merely examples of schools closer to home.

"What did that coach say?" his mom asked, wiping her hands on a dish towel.

"He's recruiting me to play football," Brendan said.

"Will he pay your way?" she said.

"Said he would," Brendan said.

"Good," she said, "'cause that's the only way you can go."

"Don't you think I know that, Mom?"

"Just making sure," she said.

Cassie

Winter 1975–76

I didn't understand how Emily could allow her father to send her away. She had been looking forward to partying during our senior year, and she was definitely in love with Bren. I was so surprised when I received her Christmas card. It was one of those "12 Days of Christmas" cards where you open a tiny door, revealing two turtle doves or three French hens. Behind the door for five golden rings, I found a neatly folded piece of writing paper tucked inside. I pulled it out and read it.

> *Dear Cassie:*
> *I have to keep this brief. I miss you so much. I hope you've recovered from your accident. I hate Dad and Mom for sending me to this horrid place. It's worse than you can imagine. I'll share more someday if I survive.*
> *PLEASE, DON'T TELL BREN I wrote to you.*

I don't want to interfere with his journey.
Love you.
Emily

The letter blew me away. Why did she have to be so cautious? It sounded like she was in jail. I should've told Bren, but I couldn't betray my best friend. And I wanted to protect Bren from himself. He'd probably hitchhike to see her and help her escape. He could be righteous that way. That's why I never mentioned that horrible night with Larry or my DES. Even though Larry could have beaten Bren up, Bren would have fought him regardless. There was no point in bringing up the DES; he couldn't do anything to solve that problem. I think we're better off keeping our secrets. It's easier for everyone.

Brendan

Painter College Early Fall 1976

On the first morning of preseason football camp, Coach Smith shook Brendan's hand. "Brandon O'Shaw, right?"

"It's Brendan O'Shay, sir. It's nice to meet you face-to-face, sir," Brendan said.

The coach pointed down the hallway. "Follow the guys. Practice begins in twenty minutes."

As Brendan walked down the dark hallway to the locker room, he felt irritated that the coach had forgotten his name. Was he the same guy who seemed so upbeat during the recruiting process? Maybe he treated all the players this way as some strange psychological attempt to motivate them to compete harder. It didn't make sense.

But he brushed off the coach's coldness as he stepped into the locker room. It was twice the size of his house, with cherrywood lockers towering above his reach. Gleaming shoulder pads and helmets rested neatly on the top shelf. Clean, pressed practice uniforms hung on hooks, and shiny, polished black cleats were stored in the footlocker below.

Each locker had a three-legged wooden stool for players to dress comfortably. Player names and numbers were stenciled on them. He scanned the room for his name but found nothing.

"Freshmen are in the Cage," said a shirtless guy with pectoral muscles the size of supper plates, pointing farther down the hallway and giving Brendan a *you-dumb-shit* look. The Cage was a mildew-smelling cement box of a room with twenty-nine lockers made from flimsy, unfinished plywood, covered with chicken coop wire across the front. The problem was that Brendan was the thirtieth player to arrive. The other freshmen had already claimed their lockers and were rummaging through a pile of shoulder pads, hip pads, helmets, pants, and jerseys on the bare cement floor. First come, first served.

"Thirty high school all-stars, and this is how they treat us," one player reflected. "I guess they don't want us to get too cocky."

"I don't even have a locker," Brendan complained.

"You can share mine. I'm Andy," another player said. "Problem solved."

What a nice gesture, Brendan thought. Things might be okay.

An assistant coach poked his head through the doorway. "Practice in five minutes. Get your tails out there!"

The freshmen dressed quickly and joined fifty upperclassmen on the practice field, forming a matrix of large boys standing five yards apart in every direction, doing calisthenics and stretching as the late-August sun rose in the east, burning off the morning dew and drying the freshly mowed grass. In the distance, mist rose from the Green Mountains, reminding Brendan of the Christ's Ascension fresco behind the altar of his church in Nehoiden. He would need divine intervention to win one of the four spots in the starting defensive backfield. Still, he wasn't there to warm the bench.

After two hours in the sweltering heat, the coach lined up the players and blew his whistle. Brendan and the others pumped their arms and legs high and fast. When Brendan thought he couldn't pump anymore, the coach blew his whistle again. Eighty players dropped to the ground and sprang back up, pumping their arms and legs higher and faster. Again and again and again, the coach blew his whistle. For a brief moment, exhausted, Brendan contemplated what would happen if he stayed down. But he knew the answer: He'd be off the team. So he pushed through the pain in his arms, legs, and lungs until it was over.

The drills grew more brutal as the days dragged on. Between practice sessions, players struggled to control the pain shooting up and down their thighs, calves, and hamstrings with every step, limping between the dorms, dining hall, and practice field, bitching all the way. Brendan dreaded the moment when the coach blew his whistle in the morning, signaling the start of another practice session.

After three days of relentless conditioning, something shifted within Brendan. The coach called out the names of eleven offensive and defensive players and lined them up for the first time to engage in live hitting. Brendan felt a surge of adrenaline and started salivating. It was the reason he loved football—the return to a primal state. On the first play of the scrimmage, he lined up against the top wide receiver on the team, a college senior who had earned all-league honors the year before. Brendan backpedaled as the receiver sprinted toward him and cut sharply to the sidelines in a down-and-out pattern. The ball was in the air as Brendan closed in. Just as the receiver extended his hands to catch the ball, Brendan, running at full speed, lowered his shoulder and drove his helmet into the receiver's spine, causing his head to snap back as he lost control of the ball and fell limp to the ground. Coach Smith rushed over to help the fallen receiver to his feet. Then he turned to Brendan.

"Come over here, O'Shay," he shouted.

Brendan hurried over to the coach.

"What the hell do you think you're doing?"

"Playing football, sir," Brendan said.

"He's the best goddamn receiver we've got," the coach shouted.

"He'll think twice about lining up against me, sir."

Coach Smith pressed his nose against Brendan's face mask. He was sure this was the end for him. "That was one hell of a hit, Brendan," the coach whispered, flashing a wink that only Brendan could see. Then the coach resumed his shouting. "Get back to the huddle, O'Shay."

After practice, Brendan sprawled with the other players under the shady maple trees outside the dorms, enjoying a teammate's boom box. He found it amusing that they were listening to Diana Ross instead of AC/DC, preferring "Love Hangover" over "It's a Long Way to the Top (If You Wanna Rock 'n' Roll)." The players sang out the lyrics and ogled photos of girls in the freshman pig book.

The only player missing was the starting quarterback, Jake, whose girlfriend had arrived on campus that morning. The dorm rooms were hot, and Jake left his window open a tad too wide. As the shrieks grew louder and more frequent Brendan glanced up at Jake's window. So this is what it's like to be the senior captain and team star, Brendan thought. Eventually the shrieks subsided, and a few minutes later, Jake sauntered on the lawn with his girlfriend strutting barefoot behind him, wearing a wrinkled white halter-top and Daisy Duke cutoff denim shorts. Her tousled blond hair cascaded over her deeply tanned shoulders. She stopped in front of Brendan. "My name's Candace, but you can call me Candi," she said. "What are you reading?"

"I'm not reading," Brendan said. "I'm dreaming."

She took the pig book from him, glanced at it, then handed it back. "You got a girl back home?"

He thought about Emily. "Had one," he said, "but not anymore."

"Don't worry, handsome," she said. "There'll be plenty on campus soon. I'm sure you'll be just fine."

Brendan smiled as she strutted away, leaving the whiff of sex in her wake. He hoped she was correct.

"Guys, listen up," Jake said. "Got some good news." The music stopped. "Coach just called me. Said we've done so well this week that he's giving us the afternoon off. You're free!"

The players hooted like Marines given a weekend pass to Bangkok. They piled into cars, raced to a cold mountain stream a few miles from campus, stripped down to their gym shorts, and plunged into the icy water. Drinking beer and sunning themselves on the river boulders, they reminisced about hometown girlfriends, summer jobs, and anything else that wasn't football. As Brendan tilted his head back to take a swig of beer, he heard a Tarzan-like cry from above. Standing on a rocky outcrop forty feet up, Jake launched himself into the air and performed two backflips before slicing into the water through a small gap in a circle of boulders. Brendan and the other seventy-nine players held their collective breath. When Jake surfaced unscathed with a broad smile, they let out a cheer that echoed up the sides of the rocky ravine and dissipated in the Vermont sky. Brendan finished his beer, swam alone downstream, and sat on a rock in the middle of the river, contemplating his good fortune. He was sure these guys would be his friends for life.

●

When classes began, Brendan thought he'd hate it, and for the most part, he did—until his American literature professor assigned Henry David Thoreau's essay "Civil Disobedience." Thoreau's words were dry, but his message struck a chord, railing against a socioeconomic system that upheld the status quo, empowered the wealthy, and crushed the dreams of the working class. He connected Thoreau's themes to his own family's experiences. When his dad dropped him off at Painter, he immediately turned around and drove five hours home because he had to work at six the next morning. His dad was forty-eight years old, struggling with booze and earning five bucks an hour cutting meat at In-Out Groceries despite his thirty years of experience as a butcher. He noticed how men like his dad, who did the most physically demanding jobs, earned the lowest pay and were the first to get fired. Thoreau called working-class men "the masses of men lead[ing] lives of quiet desperation."

Thoreau didn't let workers entirely off the hook, though. He criticized them as working stiffs who accepted a system rigged against them. Brendan had always blamed his dad for losing jobs and drinking too much. But perhaps his dad was a victim of a system that wore him down. He began to see his dad in a more forgiving light.

At the same time, Brendan recognized that capitalism provided industrious, risk-taking individuals the opportunity to create jobs for the working class and to make a lot of money for themselves. Even the indigent could achieve the American dream. He was living this economic divide at

Painter, where rich kids drove BMWs to get to college while he hitchhiked. Rich kids summered in Nantucket. Working-class kids hardly knew that "summer" could be a verb. Rich kids skied in Colorado. Working-class kids couldn't afford skis. Rich parents stayed at the fancy Painter Inn and took their sons and daughters to expensive restaurants. Working-class parents stayed in no-name roadside motels ten miles off campus and ate ham and cheese sandwiches on white bread in their rooms.

Somehow, Brendan's working-class ambition—to play college football—had thrust him into a world of privilege that he both resented and yearned to join, to be a "have," not a "have-not," to exploit the socioeconomic system that had exploited generations of O'Shays before him. The exploitation had to end somewhere. If he was going to break the chain, he had to take his fight from the football field to the classroom, to be a doer *and* a thinker, to become something more than he had ever believed he could be. To never, ever give up on his dreams. To trust himself.

For most of the fall semester, he struggled, earning C's in his classes and sitting on the bench in football. His break came on the Monday before the last game of the season when the starting cornerback twisted his knee while playing beer pong in the dorms. Coach Smith called Brendan into his office and delivered the news. "You're starting against Northfield U. You know how important this game is. It's a long, bitter rivalry. Make sure you're ready."

"Success happens when preparation meets opportunity," Brendan said, echoing his high school coach's mantra. "I'm ready now."

He shook Coach Smith's hand and left the office, stopping at a pay phone to make a collect call home, hoping his news would bring a moment of good cheer to his dad, who had been fired from his job at In-Out Groceries for, of all things, trying to unionize the workforce. "We'll be there," his dad replied, a response Brendan hadn't expected. Every player had his parents in the stands for at least one game, and some players had entire families—fathers and mothers, brothers and sisters, aunts and uncles, second cousins twice removed—attending every game. Brendan's parents had only visited the college when they dropped him off in August. While he envied his teammates, he felt secretly relieved that his parents hadn't shown up.

He couldn't imagine his parents participating in the weekend ritual of the wealthy, who rose early in their rooms at Painter Inn, packed knapsacks with fresh mozzarella, basil, and tomato sandwiches on French bread drizzled with olive oil, tossed in bottles of cabernet, and drove their Volvos to Long Trail for a five-mile hike. Afterward, they returned to campus to indulge in canapés at pregame tailgate parties before cheering for their boys. They'd eat with the other parents, dissecting the game, questioning coaching decisions, and praising one another's boys. Gradually, after a few scotches, the conversation drifted to John Anderson's disruption of the presidential race between Jimmy Carter and Gerald Ford, as they subtly slipped their professional success stories as lawyers, doctors, and businessmen into the discussion or described "the Donald Ross track" at their country clubs while exchanging handicap indexes. He'd heard it all while quietly sitting at these dinners as a guest of the parents he both admired and resented.

Rick and Rose O'Shay arrived at Painter the night before the Northfield game. Brendan borrowed a teammate's car to visit them at a roadside motel ten miles from town. As he entered their tiny room, a wave of scorching heat and cigarette smoke rushed out into the cold night, hitting his face like a blast furnace. The thermostat was set to eighty, and his dad lay sprawled on the bed, snoring, with half a dozen butts in the ashtray on the nightstand. His mom sat in a frayed puke-green armchair, intently watching *Sanford and Son* on a thirteen-inch black-and-white television. Their clothes were scattered in open suitcases on the floor. While Brendan was away at college, his mom had stopped dyeing her hair, and her gray roots resembled the stripe on a skunk's back. The hem of her brown rayon pants clung to her swollen calves and ankles. Brendan found a spot to sit at the edge of the bed next to his dad's gnarly bare feet and long toenails, listening to him snore. He asked his mom about the ride from Nehoiden to Painter, but she was too engrossed in her show to respond. An hour later, he gently shook his dad to say goodbye but couldn't wake him up.

The next day, on the football field, Brendan heard the public address announcer call out the starting lineups as the team went through its pregame drills.

"And starting at cornerback is Brendan O'Shay. Brendan is the first freshman to start for Coach Smith."

Brendan looked into the stands and winced when he saw his dad stumbling up the stadium steps. The last thing he wanted was for other parents to gossip about his dad having whiskey breath. He searched for his mom, but she wasn't there.

On the opening play, Brendan dropped into coverage, reading the eyes of the Northfield quarterback. Just as the quarterback released the pass, Brendan stepped in front of the tight end, intercepted it, and returned it eighty yards down the Painter sidelines for a touchdown. Amid the cheers of the hometown crowd, Brendan spotted his dad, surrounded by strangers in the stands, clapping and wiping his eyes. Were those tears of pride, or was the cold wind making his dad's eyes water? For the rest of the game, the announcer repeatedly said, "Tackle by O'Shay," "Pass broken up by O'Shay," and "Interception by O'Shay." When the game ended, his dad hobbled onto the field, rubbing his bare hands together to stay warm.

"The fans were talking about you before the game," his dad said. "Some bigmouth claimed Northfield would target the freshman O'Shay until he cracks. You shut him up with that touchdown of yours." Then, his dad did something he had only done when his grandfather had passed away. Wearing a thin orange windbreaker, with his head and hands bare and his eyes full of tears, he embraced his son. Brendan's uniform was caked in mud, his jersey number obliterated, and dirt streaked down his face as he smiled. A woman snapped a Polaroid and handed the photo to his dad. He folded it and tucked it into his wallet.

"There's a party for players and parents at a frat house," Brendan said. "Why don't you get Mom to come with you?"

"I need to get home," his dad said. "Have a job interview tomorrow."

"That sounds promising, Dad. Drive home safely," Brendan said, aware that his dad couldn't afford two nights in a motel and wouldn't have a job interview on a Sunday. "Thanks for being here. I'll always remember this."

●

What began as a team gathering devolved into a blowout college party. Brendan and his buddies were downing beers and shots of Jack Daniel's, high-fiving, laughing, and singing along with the music. Suddenly, someone rubbed the small of his back. He turned to see Candi dressed in sheer tights, a black leather miniskirt, and a sleeveless pink top. She leaned in close and offered to fetch him a beer. The scent of her cherry lipstick sent shivers through his body.

"Dance with me, Brendan," she said, grabbing his hand and pulling him toward the dance floor, only to be intercepted by her boyfriend, Jake.

"You played well today, O'Shay," he said, "but not well enough to dance with my girl." Jake tugged Candi onto the dance floor, leaving Brendan alone in the crowd.

Brendan felt a light touch on his forearm. "You don't know me. I'm Heather," she said. "We're in Geography 101 together. I saw you playing today. Were you nervous out there?"

He knew her but only in his fantasies. Overwhelmed by adrenaline, beer, and newly acquired attention from girls who had largely ignored him, he babbled incoherently until the DJ changed the song to Tavares's "Heaven Must Be Missing an Angel."

"Let's dance," he said, leading Heather to a gap beneath the disco ball.

A teammate next to him elbowed Brendan in the side. "Hey, O'Shay. What a difference a day makes. You're hot shit now."

"I'm the same guy I was yesterday and the same guy I'll be tomorrow," Brendan said, his head spinning. "Except tomorrow, I'll be hungover."

Brendan reached out his hand, and his teammate slapped him five.

As he twirled on the dance floor with Heather on his arm, he realized that despite his denial, he was changing.

Brendan

Painter College Late Fall 1976

Brendan trudged to the college library, hoping to finish three days of homework in one afternoon. But his mind drifted from reading *The Great Gatsby* to his last football game as he tried to understand how a single moment could impact the future.

Had his life trajectory changed because the cornerback ahead of him on the depth chart had a freak accident? Would his future have shifted if he had stumbled on the field and allowed his opponent to score early in the game? Where would he be if his high school coach hadn't motivated him to trust himself? He had even taped the phrase "Trust Yourself" to his bedroom mirror. Would he have attended college or ended up as a construction worker? Would pretty girls have been asking him to dance at fraternity parties? How much did success depend on luck, and how much on preparation? He thought about his teammates. Most of them were bigger, faster, stronger, and more coordinated than he was, yet they didn't get the opportunity he had. Were the essential life lessons found in college classes or the moments in between? Did he control his destiny, or was life just a series of interconnected events?

He had read ten pages of his book in three hours but remembered nothing. He stuffed his books into his backpack and headed to the library's basement, hoping a change of scenery would help him focus. The place was crowded, but he found an empty chair opposite the most beautiful girl he had ever seen, sitting beneath a flower print by Georgia O'Keeffe. The girl's amber hair flowed off her shoulders halfway down her back.

Brendan bent down and picked up a red puffy vest beside her on the floor.

"Is this yours?" he asked.

She accepted it with a smile, her teeth flawless. He breathed in the enticing, lemony scent of her hair.

"This place is packed to the guts. Do you mind if I sit here?" he asked.

"The gills," she stated.

"Huh?"

"The idiom is 'packed to the gills,' not 'guts.'"

"Sorry," he said. He must have sounded so stupid.

"There's nothing to apologize for," she said as she stood up to collect her books from the table. She must have been six feet tall.

"Don't move your stuff," he said. "I only have this book to read. It doesn't take up much space."

She nodded and pulled out a pair of tortoiseshell glasses from an embroidered pink and green case with the initials "L.T."

He opened *The Great Gatsby* and, while sneaking glances at her, read the same sentence over and over about Jay Gatsby springing from his Platonic conception of himself.

"What are you studying?" Brendan asked, setting down his book.

"Piaget's cognitive theory," she said.

"Memory is a reconstruction of the past, a narrative," Brendan said, pulling the quote from thin air.

She scrunched her nose. "You know Piaget?" she asked, her tone causing Brendan to doubt himself.

"I had to memorize that line for a multiple-choice psych quiz in high school. Don't ask me why it stuck."

"It's common sense," she said and went on to explain the theory, yet all Brendan could hear was the melody of her voice.

"You've got that one nailed pat," Brendan said, unsure of what she had said or what he was referring to.

"I suppose I do," she said. "Sorry to correct you again, but it's 'down pat.'"

Brendan felt his face redden. "Duh," he said. "I'm so dumb."

"Anyone who memorizes Piaget isn't dumb," she said, extending her hand. "I'm Laura. Laura Taylor."

"Brendan O'Shay. Friends call me Bren."

"Nice to meet you . . . Brendan."

"You can call me Bren," he said.

"We're not friends . . . yet," she said, smiling.

They sat together at the table for the next two hours, with Laura never once looking his way and Brendan stuck on the same paragraph about how Jay Gatsby, a seventeen-year-old boy, had invented a conception of himself to which he was faithful to the end.

Finally Brendan had had enough. "Are you hungry?" he asked. "The dining hall will open for supper soon."

"'Supper'? That's an archaic word," she said. "Where are you from?"

"Just outside Boston," he said, utterly self-conscious about his choice of words.

"*Bah-stan*? That makes sense. Where I'm from in Connecticut, we call it 'dinner.'"

"Dinner. Supper. You say toe-mah-toe, I say toe-mae-toe," Brendan joked to hide his embarrassment. "So, do you want to go to dinner?"

She nodded yes.

They walked up the snow-covered path, past the chapel steeple silhouetted by the setting sun and entered the dining hall. Brendan made a peanut butter and jelly sandwich while Laura loaded her plate with vegetables. They sat alone at a table in the middle of the expansive room.

"I read *The Great Gatsby* in my junior year of high school," she said. "But I'm sure college discussions are much more sophisticated." She popped a piece of carrot into her mouth. "Where have I seen you before?"

"I play football."

"That's not it. Football isn't my thing," she said, tapping her fork on the table. "I remember where I've seen you." She pointed at the student waiters moving through the dining hall. "You clear tables."

Brendan nodded, knowing this would likely be his last supper with Laura. "I worked the lunch shift today."

"I'm impressed," she said. "You're not freeloading off your parents like the rest of us."

Since he'd always tried to hide his poverty, the compliment caught him off guard.

"I haven't seen you in the library before," she said.

"I mainly study in my room," he said. "The library has too many distractions."

"I hope I didn't distract you," Laura said, skewering a grape tomato with her fork.

Before he could reply, Laura's friends sat in the four empty chairs around the table.

"Who's he?" one of them asked.

"Brendan, though his friends call him Bren," Laura said.

"What do you call him?" another asked.

"Brendan," Laura said with a smile. "For now, at least."

●

For the next two weeks, Brendan secluded himself with Laura in the library basement, studying harder than ever to raise his C average and avoid academic probation. On the final morning before Thanksgiving break began, he handed Laura a fresh Boston cream doughnut and a hot cup of coffee.

"For *me*?" Laura said, sitting up, smoothing her T-shirt. "You're a considerate guy."

Brendan's stomach tightened as he took the leap. "I'm heading to the Igloo for a few beers tonight with a friend. Do you want to join?"

"Of course. I'll bring a friend along, too."

"All right," he said, grinning as the knot in his stomach relaxed. "It's a date."

"A date?" Laura asked.

"Oh . . . well . . . it's not a date. It's just an expression."

"I know," she said, patting his forearm. "See you tonight."

Brendan arrived at the Igloo with his roommate and looked for Laura, but she wasn't there. What had he expected? She was so far out of his league that it was pathetic. He and his friend wandered over to the pool table.

"We own the table," said a hippie guy with shoulder-length hair and an unkempt beard, leaning against his cue stick. "Challengers pay for the rack. Rolling Rocks to the winners. Those are the rules."

Brendan nodded, slid four quarters into the coin slot, and pushed the lever. The pool balls crashed into the open bay, and the hippie guy racked them. Brendan lined up his cue stick and felt a tap on his shoulder.

"Sorry we're late," Laura said. "I owe you one—for being late and for the coffee and doughnut this morning."

"That's three," Brendan said, proud that he had caught her in a verbal misstep.

"If you win this game, Marilyn and I will challenge you and your friend."

Brendan sank eight balls in a row, and the hippies handed their cue sticks to Laura and Marilyn, then left briefly and returned to give Rolling Rocks to the winners.

"Shall we play mixed doubles?" Laura said. "I'll partner with Bren."

She called me Bren, he thought, and she wants to be my partner. Now we're getting somewhere.

By midnight, Brendan and Laura had won five bottles of Rolling Rock.

"Where'd you learn to play pool?" Brendan asked.

"My dad built a pool room in our basement," Laura said. "I'd challenge him for extra awake time on school nights."

"'Awake time'? Did you need permission to stay up at night? That's funny," Brendan said.

"It's called parenting," Laura said, her expression serious this time.

When the Igloo closed at midnight, the temperature outside was below freezing. Brendan held Laura close to keep her warm. When they arrived at her dorm room, she gazed into his eyes and kissed him softly. Then they kissed deeper and longer. A girl passed by and whispered, "Get a room." Laura and the girl laughed, and Brendan gave Laura a sad-dog look while waiting for her to invite him inside.

"I had fun tonight," Laura remarked. Then she opened her door and slipped inside. Gone.

When Brendan returned to campus after Thanksgiving break, Laura was nowhere to be found. On his third day back, he spotted her alone in the far corner while he was clearing lunch tables. Her eyes were swollen and red, and she appeared sickly thin.

"Can I join you?"

"I want to be alone," she said with a frown.

"Did I do something wrong?" he asked.

"It's not about you, Brendan. I just need some time alone."

"Okay, I'm out of here. See you later," he said, trying to sound like he didn't care, but he was heartbroken. What had gone wrong? Had he been too bold or not bold enough, too friendly or not friendly enough? His football success had made him so cocky that he'd thought he could land a girl like Laura. No way. He had misread her. What a fool he was. She'd gone home to her fancy house and rich Connecticut friends and came to her senses. She wasn't going to hang around with a table-busing dumb jock like him. He had to forget about her.

The next day, while studying in a different spot in the library basement, he sniffed a lemony scent. His mind was playing tricks on him. He waited for the smell to fade, but it only intensified.

"Hi, Bren," Laura said, motioning to an empty chair. "May I join you?"

He noted her use of the nickname, but before he could reply, she sat down and clasped her hands in prayer.

"I have a confession," she said, "but not here. Come outside with me."

As he put on his coat to go out into the cold, he thought of all the reasons she didn't want to be seen with him.

"I spent the entire Thanksgiving break with my boyfriend—day and night. We shared something special, something I had never shared with a guy before. We were in love," she sighed, wiping her mouth. "At least I thought we were."

He placed his hands over hers. They felt cold.

"When I saw you in the dining hall yesterday, he had just broken up with me . . . on the pay phone in the dorm hallway."

He wanted to thank her for confiding in him, yet at the same time he wondered why she hadn't told him she had a boyfriend. He'd thought they had something good going. Was she just toying with him before Thanksgiving break? The thought of being played hurt him, and the way his family expressed hurt was to hurt back. But he didn't want to hurt her. He really liked her and wanted to be with her. How could he express these ambiguous feelings without sounding foolish? "I'm sorry," he said. "I hope you feel better soon." Those were the only words he could muster.

"Thanks for listening," she said. "You're a nice guy."

After that moment, Brendan spent so much time with Laura that his friends thought he had flunked out. She was insatiably curious about Brendan and his family. What did his father do for a living? What was his mother like? Where did his sister go to college? The questions made him uneasy. He didn't want the truth to scare her away. Could he plausibly say his dad was in the grocery store business, implying that he owned or managed one? Could he plausibly say his mom was currently at home, suggesting she had done other things when she hadn't? Could he plausibly say that Cassie was working to earn tuition money, implying that college was in her future? But in the end, he decided to be honest. "My dad's unemployed. My mom's a housewife. And my sister's a veterinarian's assistant." He waited for Laura's judgment.

"I look forward to meeting them," she said.

"Cassie is coming here for Winter Weekend in a couple of weeks."

"I can't wait. Tell me more about her."

"Cassie. Cassie. Cassie. How can I describe Cassie?" he said. "Adventurous. Fiercely independent. An enigma. There's no simple way to describe her." He decided his best move was to change the subject. "Tell me more about yourself, Laura. What do you enjoy besides playing pool, drinking beer, and skipping football games?"

"I don't *like* beer," Laura said. "But I absolutely love hiking."

"I enjoy walking in the woods too," Brendan said.

"Let's snowshoe to Abenaki Falls on Sunday. I'll drive to the trailhead, and you can buy the gorp."

"Sounds cool," Brendan said. He'd only seen snowshoes hanging above fireplaces and in his roommate's closet.

When he got back to his dorm room, he asked his roommate if he could borrow them.

"Snowshoeing? You must really like that girl," his roommate joked. "But you two are as different as Eliza Doolittle and Henry Higgins."

The reference flew over Brendan's head. "Show me how to strap on these contraptions so I don't fall flat on my face."

●

On Sunday, Laura drove along the winding mountain pass beside Painter River, where frigid water flowed steadily beneath a thin layer of ice. When they reached the trailhead,

Brendan strapped his snowshoes to the wrong feet. Laura corrected him and led them through the woods and across a pristine, snowy expanse marked with animal tracks.

"Grizzly bear tracks," Brendan said nervously. "Let's get out of here."

"Those are deer tracks, Dan'l Boone." Laura chuckled.

They settled into the rhythmic swoosh of the snow-shoes as the trail reentered the woods and climbed through a pine forest up the mountainside. Brendan asked Laura about her family and why she chose Painter over Harvard, Princeton, or Yale. She was smart enough.

"Dad grew up in a three-family house, and my grand-father worked at the post office in Brighton, Massachusetts. Dad worked hard to pay his way through college and law school, and eventually became a corporate attorney in New York City. When I was in ninth grade, he won a significant concession from the UAW on behalf of General Motors. His career took off, and soon we moved from our small ranch house in Norwalk, Connecticut, to a Frank Lloyd Wright home overlooking Long Island Sound in Westport, and they enrolled me in Westport Academy."

So that's how things are on the right side of the tracks, he thought.

"Everything was going perfectly. Then came the summer before my senior year." Laura paused and turned to Brendan. The smile faded from her face, and her eyes teared up. "Dad bought a fishing boat. He loved fishing. But Mom and I didn't care much for it. He would go out on the water with Chris, a boy from the neighborhood. Dad was obsessed with safety. Whenever a line got tangled in the engine, he would cut the motor and snip the line, losing the lure to the sea and dealing with the tangle when he returned to shore." Laura wiped her eyes. "As Chris recounted, Dad had given him a brand-new, shiny popper that day, so when it got caught in the engine, instead of following his safety protocol, Dad leaned over the engine to untangle it."

Laura sighed.

"A boat filled with rowdy teenagers sped past Dad's boat, and it made a massive wake. Chris stumbled backward, hit the shifter, and accidentally knocked the motor into gear."

Laura shut her blue eyes for a moment. When she opened them again, they were gray. "Dad didn't make it."

Brendan wrapped his arms around her. She leaned into him, and the sun reflected off her amber hair as she buried her face in his chest. She continued when she composed herself again.

"Mom stayed strong, and the school rallied to support us. Halfway through my senior year, I started dating a freshman at Bowdoin, so I applied there to be with him and at Wesleyan to stay close to my mother. Painter was the only college I applied to strictly for myself. I was accepted by all three and chose Painter. So, here I am."

"Here you are," Brendan said, "walking through the woods with a kid who had never read *Gatsby*, gone snowshoeing, or tasted Brie cheese before coming to Painter. Do you want to rethink the time you've spent with me?"

"You're so much more than that," Laura said. "Have faith in yourself." She held him close.

They continued snowshoeing quietly up to Abenaki Falls as elusive woodland creatures stirred a few yards away. He followed her, admiring how the sunlight shone through the diamond-shaped gap in her upper thighs. He felt more alive than ever. When they reached the falls, he settled onto a flat rock and opened the bag of gorp. She nestled onto his lap, took a squirt from a bota of red wine she had brought along, then passed it to him.

"Your legs are longer than mine," Brendan said, taking a swig and passing the bota back to her.

"Don't remind me that I'm five foot twelve inches tall," she quipped, swigging from the bottle.

"No, no. They're beautiful. You're beautiful."

"Shut up and feed me," she said playfully, opening her mouth. He dropped a few peanuts in. She washed them down with another squirt. He dropped in more, and she washed them down again. This time, his fingers lingered a split second too long, and she closed her lips around them. He let the bag of gorp fall to the ground, took the bota from her, and tossed it in the snow. They kissed until his lips went numb, then he looked into her eyes and put his hands under her baggy sweatshirt. She nodded yes, so he ran his hands up her warm back and snapped open her bra. Her breasts were soft and warm against his cold hands, and her heart beat fast as he kissed her lips, face, and neck. He shifted on the rock as his erection pressed against his jeans and his ass went numb.

"That's enough for now," she said, rubbing her nose against his, gazing into his eyes, and smiling softly.

He stood and snowshoed to the edge of the falls, broke off two long icicles, returned to the rock, and handed one to her. Soon, snow clouds obscured the sun, and the wind picked up.

"We should leave," she said, and they hiked out of the woods and drove back to campus.

That night, Laura's roommate was visiting her boyfriend at Dartmouth. Brendan and Laura sprawled on her bed in their underpants, kissing until their lips were numb, pressing their bodies against each other and falling asleep on the covers. He woke up in the middle of the night and saw the moonlight illuminating her face, her amber hair draping across her breast. He admired the shape of her sharp, pink nipples against her slender biceps and the curvature of her hip bones. He stroked her cheek. She opened her eyes and gazed into his, slipped off her underwear, and pulled him on top of her.

Cassie

Winter Weekend 1977

I had been working hard at the animal clinic and was bored out of my mind living at home. I needed to blow off some steam. I was psyched when Bren invited me to his college's Winter Weekend, and Dad let me borrow his car for the trip north. The sun shone brightly through the dirty windshield, but in my rush out the door, I'd left my sunglasses at home. Four hours later, as I walked into Bren's dorm, my eyes felt like they were soaked in battery acid, and my head throbbed. There was a note on his bed: *Sorry, Cassie. At a high school wrestling meet. See you at the ΣAE frat house at eight.*

I dropped my bag of clothes in the corner of his room and searched the hallways for his girlfriend's room. Laura's roommate said she'd left suddenly to visit her sick mother. Too bad. I wanted to meet her to see if she was anything like Emily. Maybe we'd meet on my next visit to Painter. I was hungry and hoped there'd be food at the frat party, so I washed up in the dorm bathroom, changed into some fresh clothes, and walked down a long path in the snow to the frat house. There must've been four feet of snow on the ground, and I had forgotten my winter boots. My toes were frozen when I reached the frat.

The place was packed, and the kids were totally wasted, even though it was only six o'clock. Suddenly, a massive guy with a shaved head blocked my path. My nose barely touched his chest. "Welcome, lovely lady," he bellowed. "My name's Hugh. Identify yourself."

Who says that shit? I wondered, but I played along. "Cassie O'Shay. I'm meeting my brother here later . . ."

"Brendan's sister?"

"Do you know him?"

"Everyone knows Brendan. He's our star freshman football player."

Oh, brother, I thought—more of this nonsense.

He smiled and raised a finger high above the crowd. "Bring a beer for this damsel in distress," he said, "and make sure it's from the good keg." I followed the other guy to the keg, filled a plastic cup, and gulped it down. There wasn't any food, so I filled up on beer and mingled around the frat, squeezing between groups of bodies, glancing at the door, waiting for Bren to show up. Each time it swung open, Hugh turned away the guys trying to enter and let in the girls.

I refilled my cup and stepped outside for a smoke. It was freezing out there. Two girls in pink and green sweaters approached the main door as I dragged on my cigarette. One had blood-orange hair and was built like a jockey, while the other had a large chest, wide hips, and soft black hair that resembled the mane of a prize mare.

"Remember our plan," the jockey said. "Have fun, but don't go overboard. These guys can seem friendly, but deep down, they're pigs. If you're invited upstairs, check in with me before you head up."

"Good plan," the horsey one said, stroking her haunches as the frat door swung open. I didn't understand why the girls thought they needed an exit plan. The college guys seemed harmless to me. I flicked the cigarette butt into the snow and headed back inside when the friendly bouncer dragged out two preppy guys by the collars of their ski jackets.

"Get in your daddy's BMW and get outta here," Hugh shouted menacingly.

"It's *my* Beemer," one guy grumbled, "not my dad's."

Hugh didn't seem as friendly anymore. When he spotted the jockey and the mare, his scowl transformed into a wolfish smile. "Welcome, lovely ladies. Identify yourselves," he said, raising two fingers above the crowd. "Two beers for these damsels in distress," he added, "from the good keg." I suddenly realized why the girls had an escape plan.

Back inside, I refilled my cup and leaned against the wall, watching the show. Before long, the horsey girl was pawing at Hugh and kissing his neck. He caught me watching. "Hey, Brendan's sister, want to come to the concert at the field house with us?" he asked. "Your brother can track you down there."

I was tired of waiting for Bren, so I nodded and squeezed into the back seat of his car next to a bag of dirty laundry. The two girls with an exit plan piled onto the lap of Hugh's friend in the passenger seat while Hugh swerved down the road like a blind man, sliding into the parking lot before skidding to a stop in a snowbank.

I squeezed out of the car and stumbled toward the main entrance, trailing behind the others as the two guys pushed through the crowd and got us so close to the band that I could touch the lead singer's shoes. I was having a blast for the first few songs, but the music was so loud that I thought my skull might burst. I needed fresh air, so I wriggled through the crowd and stepped outside, hoping to clear my head before Bren arrived. Feeling dizzy, I sat in the snow, wishing my head would settle. Hugh and the horsey girl came outside and lit a joint, but they didn't notice me sitting a few yards away, half buried in the snow and drifting in and out of consciousness. That's all I could remember from the night.

Brendan

Winter Weekend 1977

As Brendan was about to enter the field house, he heard a cry for help. He dashed toward the voice, slipped on the ice, and fell hard on his back before reaching the girl hunched over a body lying face down in the snow. He knelt and turned the limp body over. Her face was swollen and frostbitten. His heart stopped.

"Oh my God! Cassie, not again!" he shouted.

She didn't move.

He tore off his coat, wrapped it around her, and sent the other girl inside to call an ambulance. Then he hoisted Cassie onto his shoulder, carried her inside, and put her down on the floor of the field house foyer. Moments later, medics arrived and secured her to a stretcher. He climbed into the back of the ambulance with her, praying. "Please, God, help us. Please, God. Let her live." He wasn't sure he could endure an injured Cassie again. But he had to.

The medics rushed Cassie into the emergency room while Brendan paced in the waiting area, bargaining with

God to save her life, hardly noticing the other people there for their loved ones. Finally, a tall, middle-aged doctor in a blue cardigan and brown wide-wale corduroy pants approached him.

"Are you here for Cassidy O'Shay?"

He studied the doctor's sullen eyes for clues. "I'm Brendan, her brother."

"Her face, hands, and arms are frostbitten, and her body temperature was dangerously low. But she's stable now," the doctor said.

"Thank you, Doc. I really appreciate it. I'm not sure what else to say."

"I'm glad you're here for her," the doctor said. "She needs someone. And I'm glad you're sober. You're probably the only sober student on campus tonight."

"I was assisting at a high school wrestling meet and arrived late to the concert. A stranger discovered Cassie in the snowbank. She disappeared before I could get her name."

"A guardian angel," the doctor said. "They're out there." He grasped Brendan's forearm. "Cassidy might disagree with me when she wakes up, but this was her lucky night. You and her guardian angel saved her life."

●

Brendan slept in a chair in Cassie's hospital room that night, and the next morning, he walked to the frat house to get answers from the guys at breakfast.

"Your sister was on a mission to get fucking wasted," Hugh said. "She must be sleeping it off this morning."

"She's in the hospital," Brendan said. "She nearly died. Why didn't you cut her off?"

"Girls are on their own in this frat house," Hugh said. "Even sisters."

Brendan clenched his fist, but before he could throw a punch, Hugh hit him hard in the gut, knocking the wind out of him and pushing him against the wall. "I'll let this go, Brendan. But if you try to throw a punch at me, you'll find yourself in the hospital room next to your drunken sister."

Humiliated, Brendan stumbled out the door and crossed the snowy fields to the hospital. When he arrived, Cassie was sipping orange juice and chewing on ice. Brendan didn't even ask her how she felt before launching into her.

"I've been looking forward to Winter Weekend all year, and you ruined it. How could you get so wasted?"

Cassie sank low in the bed, tugging the sheets over her head. He threw his arms in the air and walked out.

The next day, he picked up the shopping bag filled with her clothes that she had left in his dorm room and drove their dad's car to the hospital to pick up Cassie. In a calmer tone this time, he asked her once more if she always got that drunk.

"I have a headache that could take down an elephant. I don't need lectures, superstar," she said. "Not right now, anyway."

"All right. Listen, stay in my room until tomorrow and take it easy. It's a long ride home."

"I can't do that, Bren. I have work tomorrow, so I need to leave now. I'm sorry I missed Laura and that I ruined your weekend."

"It's not just that you ruined my weekend," he said. "I'm worried about you. This is the second time in eighteen months that you've ended up in the hospital after a night of partying." He still hadn't admitted he'd caused her first accident. He wasn't sure he ever would.

"Did you bring my clothes?" she asked as she slid behind the wheel.

He pointed to the bag in the back seat.

"Sorry again, Bren," she said. Then she rolled up the window and left.

Brendan watched her drive off into the distance, catching the lingering scent of gasoline exhaust as he wondered if he could ever help her and contemplated the notion that a fluke incident had saved her life. If her guardian angel hadn't been there . . . if he had arrived just seconds later . . . would she still be alive? He shuddered. It was the same question he'd considered after his football game. How much of success depended on preparation, and how much on fate, luck, God, or whoever or whatever else was out there? He was damned if he knew.

Cassie

Canada 1984–85

Bren had moved to New York City after college, and I was itching to escape too. My opportunity arrived unexpectedly. I was thumbing through the want ads in the back of *Dog Fancy* magazine during my coffee break at the animal clinic where I'd been working for nine years. A kennel in Canada was looking for a helper and my credentials fit the bill. Desperate for a change—a big change—I called the number and shared my credentials with the kennel owner, Chester Nelson.

"You sound perfect for the job," Chester said. "Can you be in Winnipeg by the summer solstice?"

"Yes, I can," I said, and only after hanging up did I realize that Winnipeg was halfway across Canada. But I loved the way he said "summer solstice." No one talked like that in Nehoiden. The next day, I gave Dr. Johnson my two weeks' notice. He said I was being rash, but I didn't care.

When I told Mom about my new job, she cried and said it was a daughter's duty to care for her parents, not to take a risky job in another country. They were in their fifties; Dad was losing his battle with stomach cancer, and Mom didn't want to bear the burden alone. I don't blame her for wanting to keep me close, but I had my own life to live, and time was slipping away. As for Dad, he gave me the silent treatment, which felt even worse. Still, I was determined to go.

Three days before the summer solstice, I packed a large green trash bag with my belongings—two pairs of blue jeans, six sets of underwear, five flannel shirts, five pairs of wool socks, blue Chuck Taylor sneakers, one braided cloth belt, and two T-shirts. I tucked it under the tarp covering the bed of my Datsun pickup truck and hit the Mass Pike heading west to a small town just south of Winnipeg, eighteen hundred miles away, with my cat, Misty, a stray who had wandered into the clinic, by my side. I enjoyed gazing at the unfamiliar landscapes of rolling farmlands, listening to the accents on local radio stations, and exploring diverse musical styles as I drove through various regions of the country. When I grew tired of the radio, I chatted with Misty. I ate at roadside diners and slept in truck stop parking lots with the doors locked.

North Dakota was the starkest of all the places I traveled through—flat, grassy, and treeless. The wind whipped and pushed my truck across the highway. It was exhausting keeping the vehicle in its lane. Upon entering Canada, it felt like crossing a state border—there were no border patrol, fences, checkpoints, or even a noticeable road sign marking the boundary between the two countries. As I traveled through Manitoba, I spotted occasional stands of elm trees framing lonely farmhouses every few miles; otherwise, the landscape resembled North Dakota, with vast fields of waving grass beneath the expansive blue sky that stretched to the horizon in all directions. This stood in stark contrast to Massachusetts where trees, fences, stone walls, buildings, crisscrossing roadways, bridges, rivers, and hillsides interrupted the horizon.

I drove the last dusty quarter-mile of my journey down a hard-packed dirt road that led to Chester Kennels as the sun dipped below the outstretched plains, painting the undersides of wispy clouds violet. Finally, I arrived. The small white farmhouse with a wraparound porch and a red barn in the distance reminded me of an Edward Hopper painting I'd seen in an art class book. The dogs yelped loudly as I got out of my truck, stretched my arms, and inhaled the scent of clean earth and freshly cut grass. Misty jumped out of the cab, and when she spotted the chocolate Labrador retriever tethered to a column on the front porch, she dashed beneath the truck. I knelt to reach her, and when I stood up again, a man and woman were on the porch staring down at me.

The man was tall, with a deeply tanned face that appeared weathered by the wind. His blond mustache curled down over his upper lip. His grayish-blond hair was cut in a mullet and spilled out from under an olive green baseball cap with the silhouette of a white Alaskan Malamute stitched on the front. The visor was stained with sweat. His T-shirt hugged his muscular shoulders and chest and draped loosely over his slim waist.

The woman had a similar V-shaped figure, with thick brown hair cropped at the nape of her sinewy neck. Her high cheekbones sloped into a small, dimpled chin, and her lips seemed awkwardly plump for her narrow face. Her indigo blue T-shirt scooped low across her chest and the hem rested just above the waistband of her frayed cutoff shorts. She peered at me with deep blue eyes.

"You must be Chester," I said, smiling and waving at him.

"Yes, and you are . . ."

"Cassie O'Shay. We spoke briefly a few weeks ago about the job."

He took off his hat and scratched his head with the brim. "Cassie. From Massachusetts. We talked on the phone, and now you're . . . you're here."

"You said to be here by the summer solstice."

A puzzled smile crossed his face.

"This is Jessica," he said. She nodded at me and wrapped her arms around herself as if the temperature had dropped below freezing.

"Well, come on in," Chester said. "I'll help you with your luggage."

"I've got it," I said, reaching into the back of my truck and lifting the green trash bag over my shoulder. "But you can help me with my cat."

Misty jumped from his arms when he crossed the porch and hissed at the chocolate Labrador. Jessica stepped in front of the dog and tried to kick Misty away. I rushed over and scooped her up before any trouble started. I couldn't believe she tried to kick my cat. Chester led me through the kitchen, and I noticed the dishes drip-drying on a wooden rack on the counter. I guessed they'd had supper without me.

I dropped my bag on the bed, and a cloud of dust rose from the bedspread. I washed up in the bathroom and changed into a clean T-shirt, then noticed them outside my bedroom window standing halfway between the house and the red barn, shouting with their arms waving. The wind blew away from the house, so I couldn't hear what they were saying. I just hoped they weren't talking about me, because judging by how they were acting, I didn't think they had been expecting me.

I returned to my room, closed the door, and flopped onto the bed, stirring up another cloud of dust. I took off the bedspread and tossed it into the corner and lay down again. Despite being dead tired, I couldn't fall asleep. My mind was racing. After a few minutes, the rocking chairs on the porch started creaking. The wind shifted toward me and carried their whispers through my open window.

"What's she doing here?" Jessica asked.

"I don't know. We talked once. I mentioned she'd be great for the job, but I never hired her. I don't even have a work permit for her."

"Impulsive," Jessica said, her voice trailing off as the wind shifted again.

I probably should've confirmed the job with Chester before driving up here. Yet, as I sprawled on that soft bed, with the cool breeze caressing my tired body and enjoying the first bathroom I could call my own, it felt like my dream had come true. I'd show them that being here was the right move for all of us.

The next morning, I greeted Chester and Jessica with the aroma of freshly cooked bacon, eggs, and hash browns. "I hope you're ready for a big breakfast," I said, handing them their plates and pouring coffee.

"Good start," Chester said, nodding at Jessica.

"I see you've found your way around the kitchen," Jessica said, her tone a blend of sincerity and sarcasm. After breakfast, they led me across the field of tufted grass to the red barn, where twenty dogs yelped excitedly. Chester demonstrated the dogs' morning feeding, cleaning, walking, and training routines.

"What are their names?" I asked.

"We've named the alpha dogs Simba and Kiska, but the others are named after their functional positions on the gangline. They're here to work," Chester said.

"Functional positions? That would be like naming you *Boss*, and Jessica *Wife*, and me *Helper*. They need real names," I said. "Dogs are a lot like people, only better. They need personal identities, and it all starts with a name. Give me a local map and some time alone with the dogs."

Chester pointed to one tacked on the wall and walked back to the house.

I spent the rest of the day playing with the dogs and learning their personalities before bringing Chester and Jessica to the kennel to suggest the names. "I'd like to name them after the local towns," I said. "This one is the most obedient dog, so we could name her Saint after the town of that name. That one is the smartest, so we could name him Crystal. And this one is so regal. He could be named Kingsley."

Chester and Jessica glanced at each other hesitantly, then Jessica nodded in approval. It was still early, but they seemed to be warming up to me.

●

In the following weeks, Chester taught me how to train the dog team on dry land using a steel sled mounted on thick bicycle wheels, which ran on a quarter-mile circular track in the open field behind the kennel.

"The first step is determining where each dog fits into the lineup. The alpha always leads the pack while the others follow. You can't effectively command the team if you can't identify the alpha dog. Each position in the lineup must align with the dog's personality, and the dogs must get along with their neighbors. Otherwise, they'll bicker, the team will fall apart, and the sled will stall."

He reminded me of what Brendan used to say about a football team. The entire team suffered if one player didn't do his part, missed a block, fumbled the ball, or went offside. Before long, I understood these dogs' strengths and weaknesses better than Chester did.

"Kiska is the lead dog. And Mariapolis always nips at Kiska's heels, so we'll keep them away from each other," I said.

"The last two dogs in line must be workhorses," Chester remarked. "They're closest to the sled, so they load up first."

I developed the best configuration after a few days of trial and error. Then Chester taught me the universal commands of dog mushing: "Hike!" means go, "Whoa!" means stop, "Gee!" means turn right, "Haw!" means turn left, "Easy!" means slow down, and "On By!" means ignore the obstacle ahead. I learned that a good musher gets off the sled and pushes it when the dogs struggle uphill. You throw the snow hook if the sled needs to be stopped quickly when the "Whoa" command isn't enough.

"Once you master the technical side," Chester said, "relax and appreciate nature's beauty. Give it a shot. I'll be here to help you."

I grabbed the handles and stood on the short platform behind the training sled. Chester jumped behind me on the platform, pressing close and reaching around my hips to grasp the sled handles. His chest pushed against my shoulder blades, and his hips pressed into the small of my back. His breath brushed over my head, carrying a sweet-and-sour scent. He was too close, but I pushed that thought aside and focused on mushing. After a few laps around the quarter-mile track, he stepped off the platform and stood in the middle of the dirt ring, barking out directions to me as I ran the dogsled. Soon I was gliding along without his help. The dogs thrived under my command. Chester called me a natural. I hadn't received that kind of praise since Teacher Dave. It felt like a lifetime ago. Living where the air was clean and the countryside breathtakingly beautiful, I experienced a sense of completeness I had never felt before. I set my mind on an impossible dream—to train the dogs for the Iditarod in Alaska.

It took a few months, but Jessica gradually warmed up to me. After supper, while Chester played hockey with his friend in town, we sipped wine in the rocking chairs on the porch, bundled in warm wool blankets, and talked a mile a minute. I shared my whole history: my car accident, Dad's drinking and his tendency to get fired from jobs, Mom's unhappiness, and the hopelessness I felt in Nehoiden. She let me talk uninterrupted for hours. "No one's ever listened to me like you do, Jess, except maybe my brother, Bren, when I was recovering from my car accident."

"You never mentioned that you have a brother," Jessica said.

"He's in New York City . . . in high finance," I said. "We haven't spoken or written since I left home last June."

"Are you friends?"

"I admire him. I despise him. Sometimes we're friends; other times we're not. It's complicated."

"You've left all that negativity behind you, Cassie," she said, resting her hand on mine. "We're glad you're here."

I had longed to hear those words. I rose from my rocker, embraced her, and asked her to share her story. We went into the kitchen, where she traced her finger along the rim of her wineglass, staring out the window. "My story's complicated too. I'll admit I wasn't exactly thrilled when you showed up. I'd been trying to get pregnant for a couple of years, but it just wasn't happening. We weren't directly blaming each other, but let's just say things were tense. I understood why Chester didn't hire a man; in this line of work, men can often be unreliable—mostly drifters and drunks who work hard until they get their first paycheck. We've seen our share of bad ones. But the last thing I needed was a beautiful woman moving into our spare bedroom."

"What happened to the beautiful woman?" I asked.

"Look in the mirror, you dummy."

I honestly hadn't thought she was talking about me. Sure, I'd received compliments on my emerald green eyes, but when I looked in the mirror, I saw yellowed, bonded teeth and a jagged purple scar on my forehead. I felt ugly.

"Chester and I tried various experimental methods to conceive. Hormones. Thermometers. Needles. Stirrups. It took a toll on me. It was expensive, but my parents left me a trust fund when they passed away. We spent most of that money to purchase this kennel. It should be named Jessica Kennels, not Chester Kennels, because I'm the owner, not him. But you know how a man's ego can be. The remainder of my trust fund went toward IVF treatment. It's ironic. I spent my teens and twenties on birth control pills to avoid getting pregnant. Now, when I want to have a baby . . ." Jessica's voice trailed off as she set down her glass, leaned against the counter, and buried her face in her hands.

"I think I know what you're going through," I said.

"How would you know?" she asked.

I wished I could snatch those words from the air and shove them back into my mouth. But they were irretrievable, so I tipped the last slug of wine from the chardonnay bottle and revealed the secret that only Mom, Dad, and my doctor knew. My words spilled out awkwardly. I shared the stomach pains, the bleeding, the hospital trips, the tests, why Mom had taken diethylstilbestrol, the consequences, and the diagnosis: DES syndrome. I said that Dad called me "damaged goods." Salty tears rolled down my cheeks and pooled in the corners of my mouth. "The joke is that my eggs are fertile, but my uterus is shaped like a *T*, which means I can get pregnant, but my uterus can't carry the embryo to term. Instead, the embryo lodges in the fallopian tubes in what's known as an ectopic pregnancy. It's deadly." I spoke about my organs as if they were separate, distinct entities—third-party actors on a side stage of my life. Jessica straightened up as she connected the dots.

"My God," she said. "I have the opposite problem; my marriage is falling apart because of it. Chester desperately wants a boy to teach him how to play hockey. You know . . . the Canadian male dream. And I'd love to have a little girl who grows up to despise hockey players." She frowned and rubbed her belly.

"My girlfriends have adorable little Lucys—pink dresses, Barbie dolls, and tea parties. They flaunt baby photos in front of me. It hasn't been easy. They mean no harm, but their happy stories crush me." As Jessica shared her sorrow, I reflected on how I had never wanted a child—an easier thought to hold on to than the reality that I couldn't have one.

Jessica suddenly embraced me, pressing her chest against mine and kissing my forehead. We rested our heads on each other's shoulders, holding on for so long that I worried Chester might walk in on us and think we were lesbians. We loosened our embrace, and she held my hands tightly. No longer seeming vulnerable, she became fierce and determined.

"We've done a lot for you, haven't we, Cassie? A job. A home. You're the happiest you've ever been. You just said that, right?"

She was manic, and I didn't know what she would say next.

"Separately, we're broken. Together, we can be whole."

Where was she headed with this? I dreaded to find out.

"Could you ever find a place in your heart to consider giving . . . offering . . . donating . . . or selling . . . your eggs to me?"

My eggs! Jessica was rambling nonsensically.

"Chester and I could have our child. You'd be a part of that child . . . a part of our family. We'd be forever connected and forever grateful to you. And one day, I could return the favor when you meet the right person. I could be your gestational surrogate and carry your and your husband's embryo to term if and when the time comes."

I straightened up. What kind of fucked-up bargain was Jessica proposing? "That's insane," I said. "Can that even be done?"

"I suppose it sounds insane," Jessica said, "but yes, it can be done. It's not something that's done every day, but it's doable. Is it crazy to think we can get what we want without hurting anyone? It'd be a win-win situation."

My head was spinning. I needed to lie down. She released my hands and warned me we'd discuss it again in the morning.

●

The next morning, I was cooking bacon and eggs when I heard Jessica and Chester arguing in their bedroom.

"Did I hear you right?" Chester yelled, hitting the wall so hard I flinched. "That's sick. What are you thinking? I want you to have our child, not Cassie's."

They came flying into the kitchen.

"You don't understand," Jessica pleaded. "I can't have our child. I'm barren, goddamn it! As barren as that tundra outside." Jessica swept her arm toward the landscape and burst into tears. "This is the only way!" She collapsed into a chair and buried her face between her knees. Suddenly, as if possessed by the God she had just cursed, she rose and shouted, "Look at Cassie.

Pretty. Funny. Passionate. Athletic. We share the same coloring and stature. She's the perfect match." Chester scanned me from head to toe like I was a prize dog at the Winnipeg County Fair. Jessica slowed her pace, enunciating each word as she tried to convince him she was right. "We'll have a child. Our child. A little boy. Your son. Your genes. You'll skate together. Coach his hockey team." She turned to me. "Cassie, tell him I'm not crazy."

Chester shook his head and stepped onto the front porch. Jessica chased after him and wrapped her arms around his waist from behind, planting her forehead between his shoulder blades. Chester turned and embraced her. It was difficult to watch them. I felt envious that they had each other while I was alone. In my heart, I longed to be part of their embrace. In my mind, I wanted to play with the dogs and forget this had ever happened. Chester pressed his lips to Jess's forehead.

"I'm gonna be in the kennel with the dogs," he said. "I'll think about it."

I decided to go to the kennel, too. At that moment, he seemed slightly less crazed than Jessica.

Fortunately, when we arrived at the kennel, the loud chorus of twenty barking dogs kept us from talking. After feeding them, we used a flat shovel to scoop up their mess and toss it onto the dung pile.

"This is a crazy pile of shit," Chester said, interrupting the silence. "Jess's baby idea, I mean."

"Either of us can squash the idea with a single word—no," I said.

"If it were that easy," Chester said, "I would've ended it by now."

He didn't elaborate, but I understood what he meant. It had taken me months to endear myself to Jessica, and her kennel gave me a sense of purpose for the first time in my life. I didn't want my time there to end. But to have my eggs harvested and given to her? To have a biological child who would legally belong to someone else? It was incomprehensible. Still, I wanted to continue working and living at the kennel. I was happy there.

For a week I avoided Jess and ate supper alone in my bedroom, with Misty purring beside me. I woke up in the middle of the night with stomach pains and wicked headaches as I tried to decide what to do. My indecision ended one morning when Jessica met me at the threshold of my bedroom, arms crossed, glaring coldly into my eyes, demanding the answer she sought. I pushed past her on my way to the kennel, but she followed me closely, grabbed a shovel, and shoveled dog shit alongside me, relentlessly pushing her desire onto me.

"It's just a simple medical procedure," she insisted. "That's all it would be. Your eggs would become mine. It'd be my baby. I'd bear the consequences, not you. What harm could it cause?" Finally, Jessica sank to her knees in the dung and mud, clutching my thighs, supplicating herself like a captured soldier on the battlefield, begging for mercy. I finally gave in. She quickly stood and dashed to Chester, kneeling before him. He bent down and wrapped his long arms around her head. I stood alone next to the shit pile, watching them from afar.

Ten days later, we walked through the unmarked black steel door of the Winnipeg Fertility Clinic. I watched the local traffic report on the small television secured to the waiting room wall until a tall, thin man in a white lab coat extended his long manicured fingers and beckoned me into his office for my initial in vitro fertilization consultation. He explained how the IVF process worked—a complete physical examination, checking for signs of infectious diseases, screening for familial and genetic disorders, assessing my psychological state, and evaluating my body's likely response to the ovulation induction medication. When he asked for my medical history, I held nothing back, hoping he'd find a reason to stop this idea.

"There are no medical reasons why you can't donate your eggs to the Nelson family, but it's a serious commitment, and you've been through a lot of physical and emotional trauma. If the process succeeds, how will you feel about Jessica being the mother of your biological child?"

"It all happened so quickly," I said. "But the Nelsons have always treated me well."

"If you want to repay them, buy them a nice bottle of whiskey and some flowers," said the doctor.

"I know what I'm getting into," I pretended.

"All right, Ms. O'Shay. Let's go over the consent form." He slid it across his desk and walked me through it.

"Do you agree to have your reproductive eggs fertilized with Chester Nelson's sperm?"

"Yes."

"Will you grant Chester and Jessica Nelson full legal control over the resulting embryos?"

"Yes."

"Do you grant Chester and Jessica Nelson full legal authority over the remaining reproductive eggs?"

"I won't need them," I said.

"Egg donors usually answer no to this question," he stated. "It stops the recipients from using them in a way that would be unacceptable to you."

"Then destroy what's left," I said.

"Things might change in your life," he said. "Don't close yourself off from possibilities."

"Okay, then my answer is no."

"In the event of your death or incapacitation, who would you designate as the custodian of your remaining reproductive eggs?"

At that moment, I realized my eggs weren't just objects to give away; they were a living part of me. I was stumped. Dad and Mom would freak out if they ever became custodians of my eggs. I thought of my long-lost friend, Emily. She was so compassionate, but we had drifted apart and hadn't talked or written in years. I didn't even know where she lived.

"Ms. O'Shay, triggering the custodian clause is highly unlikely. However, the clinic is legally obligated to have a custodian named on the paperwork. Choose a reliable family member."

The only one left was Bren. We had drifted apart too, but I could rely on him to do the right thing. I held my breath and said, "My brother, Brendan O'Shay."

"Please sign the form, and remember that you can change your mind about this entire procedure until the last possible moment. If you have no other questions, I'll see you and the Nelsons next week."

A week later, we returned to the clinic, and for the first time I noticed that the waiting room walls were painted in soft hues of pink and blue, adorned with posters of smiling parents holding chubby, bright-eyed babies. I trembled as the nurse demonstrated how to inject the ovulation induction medicine into the fleshy part of my thigh. In another room, Jessica was receiving estrogen and progesterone injections to stimulate the lining of her uterus in preparation for the embryo that would be created from Chester's sperm and my egg. For the next several weeks back at the farmhouse, Jessica and I coordinated our injections to synchronize our ovulation cycles.

During my third and final visit to the clinic, the nurse explained the procedure that was about to begin. She aimed to calm me; instead, my palms sweat. Then she swabbed my vagina with a sterile solution, inserted an ultrasound probe to observe my follicles, and stabbed a long needle through my vaginal wall into each follicle, removing fluid.

As I gazed at the ceiling, my mind filled with the image of Dr. Horowitz from the Boston Hospital for Women's Dysplasia Clinic when I was sixteen, his slick hair and thick glasses, as he diagnosed me with DES syndrome. Then the embryologist entered the room, searched the fluid for eggs, placed them in small collection dishes, and enclosed them in an incubator. I was officially harvested.

"Congratulations," said the embryologist. "Twenty eggs! That's far more than usual. You're a fertile myrtle."

She said those words. I was stunned. I expected her to be serious like Dr. Horowitz. Then I thought about Mom. If she hadn't taken diethylstilbestrol, my life could have been different. I might have had a family. Who knows what direction my life would have taken? Maybe I would have worked harder in school. Maybe I would have tried more to find a guy and have a long-term relationship. There were countless maybes to consider. The embryologist left the room to mix Chester's sperm with ten of my eggs, each in a separate petri dish. The ten unused eggs went into cold storage, in my mind never to see the light of day again. We drove home exhausted, sore, and anxious.

Three days later, the clinic called with the news: The ten attempts resulted in two viable embryos. Jessica jumped for joy, hugging Chester and me, exclaiming how the pain was all worth it and their dream was coming true. I congratulated them and slipped outside to be alone with the dogs. The next day, Chester drove Jessica to the clinic. When she returned home, she told me everything went fine. But her expression revealed a different story. She reminded me of an eerie painting I had seen in my high school art class book, called *The Scream*, of a man standing on a bridge, his eyes shockingly wide open and his face distorted—wavy lines of red and orange, black and blue.

After supper, Chester went outside with a can of beer while Jessica headed to bed. When I peeked in on her, she was curled up in a fetal position, covered by a heavy comforter. I wanted to hide under the covers too, but something compelled me to the porch, where Chester had moved on from drinking beer to whiskey, smoking a cigar, and rocking in a chair with a wool cowboy blanket draped over his shoulders.

"How did it go today?" I asked, leaning against the porch railing.

"It's what she wants," Chester slurred.

"What do you want?" I asked.

"Doesn't matter," he said. "It's happening. We're gonna have a baby." He downed his whiskey, rattled the ice in circles around the empty tumbler, and then refilled it. His eyes crossed lazily, gazing off the tip of his nose. "How was your day, Cas?" he slurred. He had never called me Cas before. No one ever called me Cas.

"Nothing special happened," I said.

"Caaasss. Do you ever think you'll be a mother, too? This will be our biological child." He waved his burning cigar back and forth between us. "Yours and mine."

"I'll never see it that way," I said. "Never. This child belongs to you and Jessica. Not to me. Never to me."

"Yes," he slurred. "Mine and yours. Our genes. Yours and mine, even more than mine and Jess's."

The whole conversation freaked me out. I left him rocking in his chair and went to bed, unable to sleep a wink.

●

Jessica shuffled listlessly around the house in the weeks following the procedure. She didn't eat, help in the kennel, grocery shop, or read the newspaper. She told me she was having nightmares that made her reluctant to fall asleep. In one, she found Kiska's puppy dead in its cage, which made no sense because Kiska was a male. I told her to stay positive and send the baby good vibes.

Not that I believed in the whole power-of-positive-thinking nonsense, but it seemed like something that might calm her down. I never confessed this to her, and I hated myself for thinking it, but deep down, I hoped she didn't have the baby. Chester's drunken words haunted me. I couldn't bear the thought that their kid would be my kid. The whole idea felt like a terrible mistake.

The following week, Jessica's premonition came true. Her body rejected the embryos. I went overboard trying to console her and hide my relief, even foolishly offering her the remaining ten eggs, which would've put me back in the same predicament. "I'm not meant to be a mother," she said, her face ashen. "I tried to fool fate and got what I deserved. A child isn't in the cards." Then, as if she had swapped a mask of grief for one of stoic resolve, her tears disappeared and her eyes hardened. "I've had enough. Enough." She swept her arm wide as if to encompass the entirety of her existence.

I stayed out of Jessica's crosshairs for the next few months, starting and ending my days working with the dogs outside during the brief daylight hours. I crouched with my back to the cold, steady wind that whipped across the plains, tossing the top layer of snow into a white fury of swirling flakes that targeted every nook and cranny of exposed skin on my body.

My cheeks and nose chafed. I thought winters were cold in Boston, but Canada made Boston feel like Miami Beach. I dreamed of lying down with the dogs beside a roaring fireplace, bundled under six wool blankets, hibernating until spring.

●

But I loved my job, so instead of giving up, I confronted the cold head-on, mushing the dogs for miles daily to keep warm and bond with them. I would get off the sled's runners and plod through knee-deep snow alongside the sled whenever the trail went uphill, using all my strength to keep the sled upright when the dogs pulled hard around sharp corners. At night, I enjoyed long, hot baths to warm my bones and relax my aching muscles, wrapping myself in a towel as soon as I stepped out of the tub. Then one night I left my towel on my bed, so I hurried out of the bathroom buck naked to grab it, dripping water onto the hardwood floor, stopping in my tracks when I passed the full-length mirror on my bedroom wall. I stared at my reflection, wondering who was looking back at me. My thighs rippled with tiny movements. My stomach was a flat washboard, and my butt was a taut, round ball of muscle. My chest, shoulders, and arms were slim and strong. I looked like a racehorse. I thought back to when I was ten and could outrun and outwrestle Bren, how I had neglected my athleticism to hang out with the cool kids in high school, most of whom turned out to be aimless nobodies. I didn't want to be an aimless nobody. It was my turn, my time, my chance to show Bren, Chester, Jessica, Mom and Dad . . . to show myself . . . to show the world . . . who I was and what I could become.

My progress built upon itself. The stronger I became, the stronger I wanted to be. I dedicated myself to training hard and preparing for a sled dog race. But I needed Chester's and Jessica's support to make my dream come true. Otherwise, my opportunity would slip away. I couldn't let that happen the way I had let my chance to go to college pass me by.

One night at supper, I brought up the topic. "I read about the Canadian Challenge Dog Sled Race in February," I said as Chester stuffed a red potato in his mouth and Jessica nibbled on a piece of lettuce. "There's a women's division. I'm planning to enter it. Is there any chance the kennel will sponsor me?"

Chester and Jessica paused midbite. "This is completely unexpected," Jessica said, elbows resting on the table, her eyes narrowing.

Chester grimaced. "Slow down, Cassie. The Canadian Challenge is a huge deal up here. It's a qualifying race for the Iditarod: two hundred miles, eight dogs, the sled, and you against the relentless forces of nature. No outside help is allowed on the trail. One mistake . . . you could be in over your head."

"I'm talking about the open race, not the main event," I said. "It's a five-dog race covering sixty-nine miles from Prince Albert to Anglin Lake to Elk Ridge.

There's a twenty-four-hour time limit, and then the organizers sweep the trail for stragglers. I can do it, but I need your sponsorship and help with training." Chester tugged on his thick blond gray-flecked beard, which he had been growing since early fall.

"This is out of the blue," Jessica said. "Out of the fucking blue."

It was the first time I'd ever heard her swear.

"Is it more out of the blue than what you asked of me?" I blurted.

Jessica turned completely cold, but I didn't care.

"Look," I said, "if I'm successful, it'll be great for the kennel. And the dogs will love the challenge." I pushed away from the table and eyeballed both of them. "Sleep on it," I added. "I want this."

I don't know what was said after I left the room, but Jessica came into the kitchen in the morning and stared me down. "You can do it," she said. "My debt to you is paid." Then she left. The interaction chilled me. I understood why Jessica was so depressed, losing the baby and all, but I couldn't understand why she took her anger out on me. I suspected it was about Chester.

I was almost ready in early February, two weeks before the race. I had chosen a spring distance sled with seven-foot-long metal runners that generated good speed on snow-packed straightaways and was easy to maneuver around woodland trees and along steep, narrow riverbanks, where a loss of balance could mean a watery death for me and the dogs. The sled's basket was large enough to hold clothing, a headlamp, matches, medical supplies, food, and blankets.

Selecting my dog team took some skill. Kiska, a natural alpha, was my lead dog. Baldur and Snowflake, the swing dogs responsible for initiating left and right turns, were next in line. Mariapolis and Pilot were the wheel dogs positioned just before the sled. Kingsley served as the backup, riding in the sled's basket and ready to substitute for any dog that came up lame.

I had to be a physical specimen to survive out there, and my toughest challenge was getting in even better shape. I remembered Bren's summer training for college football. He'd tape his workout log to our refrigerator—a matrix of dates, exercises, repetitions, times, and weights, and an upward-sloping chart recording his progress. He was a stud. No wonder Emily had begged me to set them up. I needed to be the female equivalent of a stud on the trail. I adapted his routine to dogsledding, mushing for three hours a day, jogging in snowshoes across the tundra for an hour, and maxing out on sit-ups, push-ups, and pull-ups to finish the day. It was amazing how much easier the workout became as the race date approached.

After supper one night, Chester passed around three shots of Jack Daniel's. I took in the smoky warmth, breathing it deep into my lungs, tempted to swallow it. Instead, I pushed the shot glass back to him. "I'm in training," I said.

"Relax, Cassie. Have a drink." He slid the glass back toward me.

"I have something to ask," I said, ignoring the whiskey. "I need to do a sixty-mile training ride next Saturday, starting at dusk and finishing around midnight."

"Go for it," Chester said, downing the whiskey in one gulp and then taking my shot glass to finish it. "What do you need from me?"

"Follow me on the snow machine."

"Sure will," Chester replied without hesitation as he poured another shot.

"Are you forgetting something?" Jessica asked, scowling.

"Crap, Cassie, next Saturday is our wedding anniversary. Can you do it another night?"

"I need to stick to my training schedule," I said. "Can you help me?"

Chester looked at Jessica, who shot him a glare.

"This is ridiculous," Jessica said, rising from the table. "Spend the entire night out on the trail together. Keep each other warm."

She tipped her glass of Jack Daniel's back, swallowed hard, and walked out.

"Jessica, it's not like that," I said, chasing after her, but she slammed her bedroom door in my face. I knew my words were pointless. I returned to the kitchen to wash the dishes while Chester watched me with a smug half-smile. After that, I went to my room too. As I lay in bed that night, I contemplated Jessica's insinuation. She had confirmed my suspicions about Chester.

I began my training run at sundown on the following Saturday. Soon, the full moon rose on the horizon, and the temperature dropped below freezing. By eight, I was three hours into the sled run, and the moon hung high in the sky, illuminating my path with its yellow light. I balanced on the sled runners, sipped water, and enjoyed what Bren ate when he trained for football—peanut butter and banana sandwiches. I breathed hard, inhaling the scent of the dog's hot breath and sweat-soaked fur while my body odor leaked from my jacket. The unpleasant smells signaled that I was fit, excited, alive, and ready.

Throughout the night, the hum of Chester's snow machine reassured me. During a break to feed and water the dogs, he suggested ways to improve my mushing. He was all business until the last rest stop.

"My timing sucks," he said, "but I need to get this off my chest. Jessica and I aren't seeing eye to eye. The baby situation has been tough on her . . . and on me, too. I never thought we'd be without children. I figured she was such an athletic babe that she'd give me a team of hockey players. That dream is gone."

"I'm not interested in your marital troubles," I said as I climbed back onto the sled. "Your complaining to me won't make things better. Man up and move on with your life." Then I yelled "Mush!" and took off to finish the last leg of my training run. Instead of focusing on the dogs and my preparation, I thought about Chester crossing the line again. I hoped I had been harsh enough to send him a clear message. I didn't want to hear about his relationship with Jessica, and I definitely didn't want him to see me as someone to confide in, especially since I'd be spending several days alone with him on our way to and from the race. Maybe I should ask Jessica to come with us?

●

Two days before the race, we loaded Chester's truck with the dogs, sled, and equipment, then drove ten hours along snowy highways, passing deep crystal-blue lakes formed by receding glaciers eons ago, passing shiny-eyed wolves and lumbering moose, and traveling through the boreal forests of spruce, fir, and aspen that surround Prince Albert, Saskatchewan. When we finally arrived at the starting area, I went inside the log cabin to check in for the race, handing my US passport to an icy-eyed man sitting in a metal folding chair behind a plastic folding table.

The man scrutinized every page of my passport, flipping it over and rubbing it like it was an unfamiliar artifact from a distant world. Then he pulled my registration form from a file box at his side. My Massachusetts address was circled in red. He glanced up at me, took a bite of a half-eaten liverwurst and onion sandwich, and dialed a black rotary phone, saying my name, Cassidy O'Shay, grunting a series of *okays* and *uh-huhs* before hanging up and scowling at me, a piece of liverwurst stuck in his scruffy beard. He pointed his thick, nail-bitten index finger at my face.

"Off with your toque," he grumbled. "Not polite to wear it indoors."

I was confused.

"A toque is a local slang for a hat," Chester said.

My bad feeling about the situation intensified.

"We keep a tight grip on this event, Missy. This dogsled race is a point of national pride for us, alongside hockey and lacrosse. Your registration has been denied. The address from south of the border raised our suspicions. Ran your information through CBSA. No record of you entering the country. No work permit on file. Passport violation. You're in our country illegally. Here's your registration form and entry fee. There's the door. Go back to where you belong."

I swiveled my head between Chester and the icy-eyed man.

"What the fuck is happening here?" I said. "You're not making any sense. I've been working in Canada for over eight months. I don't even know what 'CBSA' means. I'm an American citizen. What do you mean I'm not welcome here? For crying out loud, Canada and America are practically the same country."

"That's the point, young lady. You're American, not Canadian, and they're not even close to being the same country." He narrowed his eyes. "And you better watch your foul mouth in this building."

"I'm sorry," I said, "but I don't understand what's happening. I've trained for months for this race!"

"CBSA—Canada Border Services Agency. Immigration. If you've been working here for eight months, you're breaking the law. Border patrol authorizes organizations like ours to apprehend illegals. You have been detected. Illegal migrants can't be in this race. It's that simple."

"Illegal? I'm not some Haitian boat person!" I said.

"Boat people are refugees," he said. "You're lower than that."

My body was suddenly on fire as tension built in my head and neck. Stupid tears rolled down my cheeks. "How can I fix this?" I said.

"You shoulda fixed it before you got to Canada," he said. "I'm surprised you didn't get a departure order long before you reached this point. The order gives you thirty days to leave. Inform CBSA when you leave the country, or they'll bar you from returning for years to come."

"How the hell . . . how could this happen?" I muttered.

"Sloppy or shady employer trying to dodge taxes. Speak with your boss. He should've known you needed a work permit. Every employer in Canada knows these rules. Keep Canada Canadian. That's the motto."

I turned to Chester, who had stepped back toward the door, staring at his feet.

"Chester!" I shouted.

He raised his palms toward the ceiling.

"I never expected you to show up last June," Chester said. "You caught us by surprise! I didn't realize they'd connect the dots like this. I'm in trouble for this too, you know. This comes with a steep fine."

"I heard you talking to Jessica about my work permit the night I arrived," I cried. "Why didn't you handle it?"

"If you knew about it," he said, "why didn't you push me to fix it? You were just as eager as we were to ignore it. You're at fault too."

"What kind of country allows an American woman to donate her eggs but not participate in a lousy dog-sled race?" I didn't get an answer, nor did I expect one.

Chester started with excuses, but his voice sounded like static from an AM radio. He'd trampled my dreams like the mud on the dirty rug beneath my feet. Just when

I thought my fortune had changed, Lady Luck said, "Hell no, Cassie. Hell no!"

I went outside, feeling angry and anguished. I fed and watered the dogs, then loaded the truck for our ten-hour drive home along barren wilderness roads. Chester was the last person I wanted to be with, but I had no choice. We were tired and hungry, so after a few hours on the road, we pulled into a roadhouse and sat at an oak-slab bar, surrounded by moose antlers on the walls and a black bearskin nailed to the ceiling. I ordered venison stew and a Molson beer. I hadn't had a drink in months, and after three brews and hardly touching my stew, my temples throbbed.

"My headache is unbearable," I said. "I can't drive any longer."

"The Mounties are out tonight, and with these snow flurries covering the road, we won't get very far," Chester said, finishing the rest of my stew and soaking up the juices with fresh sourdough bread and choke-cherry jam. "Hey, bartender, do you rent rooms?"

"Thirty bucks a night. The room is through that door," he said, pointing to the side of the bar.

Chester collected our duffel bags from the truck while I took the key and entered the windowless room. A blast of mold and mildew almost knocked me out.

"I can't sleep with this odor. And there's only one bed here."

"We don't have a choice," he said. "Don't worry, I'll stay on my side."

"You're sleeping on that chair," I said, pointing to the corner.

I lay down and wrapped myself like a mummy in the blanket, trying to fend off the evil I feared was closing in on me.

When Chester got in my bed, the evil arrived.

We left at dawn, and I drove all day, staring at the blurred landscape. Chester tried to make conversation, but he was dead to me. I was dead to myself. I couldn't wait to get back to the kennel, grab my things and Misty, and drive far, far away, never to see or hear from him or Jessica again. When we reached the kennel, I asked Jessica if I had received a letter from the CBSA. She pointed to a pile of mail in a basket on the counter. As I sifted through it, I found an official-looking letter postmarked from a month earlier, notifying me that I had less than two days to leave Canada. But the next day wasn't soon enough.

The next morning, I hugged the dogs goodbye, put Misty in the passenger seat of my truck, and waited for Jessica to pass me my pay through the driver's side window. When she handed me the Canadian dollars, I realized why they had always paid me in cash.

"You've been paying me under the table to keep the authorities out of it," I snapped at her. "You've known the whole time."

"We paid you in cash to protect you, Cassie. We did it for your sake."

I wanted to tell her that her husband had raped me, but what good would that do? She would blame me for sharing a room with him, just like Larry's friends called me a slut for going into the woods with him at Devil's Den in high school. Chester and Larry were guys being guys. I was a slut. That was the way of my world. Instead, I floored the gas pedal, spinning my rear wheels on the dirt driveway and kicking up a cloud of dust that shrouded them and their farmhouse. Hours later, I arrived at the unmonitored border between Canada and North Dakota, stopped at a roadside mailbox, wrote "DECEASED: RETURN TO SENDER" on the CBSA notification letter, and dropped it in. Gone.

Cassie

New Ash 1985–92

After being on my own in Canada, I couldn't stay with Mom and Dad in Nehoiden for more than a few weeks. So I drove to the Lake Ash region in central New Hampshire and looked around. The locals wore flannel shirts, dungarees, and work boots. The traffic was sparse, the sidewalks were empty, and the tallest building in town was a three-story country inn. It seemed perfect. I stopped by a Realtor to find a place to rent. The first place she showed me was a fixer-upper cottage with a stream running behind it. I loved it.

"How much?" I asked.

"It's listed at twenty-five thousand, but I can persuade the owner to accept twenty-two. He's a widower moving into a nursing home, with no family. He wants someone to give the place some care. He'll finance it for you; just offer to give him a note and pay five hundred dollars a month. He'll agree to it."

"Sorry," I said, "I'm looking to rent, but if he lowers the price to fifteen thousand and the monthly payment to four hundred with no money down, I'll take it." We headed to her office to call the owner.

"You have a deal, Ms. O'Shay." With that, I became a homeowner in New Ash, New Hampshire. I drove home, feeling exhilarated, but when I told my parents, I thought they might faint.

"If that isn't the most harebrained, impulsive decision I've seen since you moved to Canada! You never told me why you left, but I can only imagine why it didn't work out," Mom hollered. "I hope to God you didn't sign anything!"

It pained me that Mom couldn't be happy for me. But caring for Dad, who seemed to deteriorate every day, had worn her down. Still, I had to live my own life. A month later, I moved into my new home. It reminded me of the best parts of my time in Canada: waking at dawn, sipping coffee, watching mallards gently paddling on the pond, and observing the mist rising from the mountains in the distance. I worked from dawn to dusk, tearing down and replacing drywall, sanding and staining the oak floors, scrubbing the linoleum in the kitchen and bathroom, replacing rotted wood around the windows and doors, setting mousetraps, and scouring local yard sales for dishes and furniture. At five, I'd shower and head to the Red Oak Tavern for supper, sitting at the long oak bar with local plumbers, electricians, and carpenters who dropped in for a pop or two after work. I'd pick their brains on installing a new sink, window, or kitchen cabinet, and I'd be home and in bed by ten.

One night, a burly guy in a gray T-shirt walked into the tavern. He looked like a frontiersman straight out of a Frederic Remington painting, wild with a bushy reddish-blond beard and deep-set blue eyes. He sidled up beside me at the bar.

"I've seen ya in here before," he said. "The name's Warren. Warren Whitman. Mind if I sit here next to you?"

"Suit yourself," I said. We drank and talked until the bartender rang a handbell and threw us out at midnight.

"Mind if I follow ya home . . . to make sure you get there safely?" Warren said.

I smiled. "No thanks. I can handle myself."

Warren was at the Red Oak Tavern again the following night, occupying the same stool he had the night before.

"You're predictable," he said.

"That's the first time anyone's ever said that to me," I said with a laugh.

"If you don't mind me askin', whose house are you livin' in?"

"You followed me home?"

"Don't take it the wrong way," he said. "I was worried about you. You had a lot to drink."

I didn't want to listen to his nonsense about my drinking, but I was feeling lonely, so I played along. "It's my house," I said.

"You own a house?" he said. "How'd ya manage that?"

"That's my business."

"Your business, eh? Where do ya work?"

"Nowhere just yet. I'm fixing up my house for now. But I'm good at figuring things out and skilled with my hands . . . That's no lie. I'll get a job when the time is right."

"A jack-of-all-trades, eh? Good for you."

"What do you do?" I asked, suspecting he worked on a road crew. But he surprised me.

"Make custom entry hall staircases at a local manufacturing plant. The company sells them to McMansions in the Boston area. Business is boomin', and we're lookin' for jack-of-all-trades types."

The next day, at noon, I took a break from my home renovation projects and met with the plant manager, who hired me on the spot.

As I was working ten hours a day at the same company as Warren, our relationship quickly developed. We loved the same music—Dylan, Clapton, Grateful Dead, and the Allman Brothers. The list goes on. He was a self-taught singer with perfect pitch and a true gentleman, always holding doors for me and waiting to eat until I got my food. He even smiled at grandmothers in the grocery store. He was a gentleman in bed, too. He asked. I never knew guys asked until I met Warren. Once, I said no just to test him, and I was blown away when he actually stopped.

By midsummer, Warren had moved in. He worked hard, bought our food, made our breakfast, swept and washed the floors, and even made the bed. He showered and brushed his teeth every morning and night. It was nice having him around. As a moving-in present, he bought me an Alaskan Malamute puppy, which I named Nomad.

Mom and Dad were so angry with me for buying the house that it took them months to visit. Having Warren there felt awkward, but he was kind and respectful toward them. Dad's stomach cancer was worsening; he had dropped to a hundred pounds and walked with a cane. Warren knew how to help Dad without showing pity, and I appreciated that. Dad loved what I had done with my house so much that he joked about moving into my spare bedroom. I laughed it off, but I knew he was serious. Mom wandered around, picking up ashtrays I'd taken from bars, examining them from every angle before putting them back where she found them without saying anything.

Three months later, Warren proposed. We had a simple wedding in my front yard on a sunny late spring morning. A local justice of the peace officiated, and bluegrass musicians played *Pachelbel's Canon* on the banjo and harmonica. I wore an off-white peasant dress and carried a bouquet of wildflowers cut from the field where I walked Nomad. Dad was too weak to walk me down the makeshift aisle between two rows of folding chairs, so Bren stepped in. Laura, Mom, and Nomad were the only other witnesses. We had lunch at the Red Oak Tavern, where we ran into some of our new friends and acquaintances from town.

"When's the baby due?" someone shouted, and the crowd burst out laughing.

"We have Nomad," I said. That was all they needed to know.

For the next five years, until the fall of 1990, Warren and I had the time of our lives. He taught me how to backcountry ski, hunt deer, and fly-fish for brown and rainbow trout in the tributaries of Lake Ash. I received a promotion at work and hit the road making sales calls, pulling in a grand a week—more money than I had ever thought possible. I bought high-quality camping gear and a Winchester hunting rifle with the extra cash, taking long camping trips with Warren. I continued upgrading my house, replacing the old single-pane windows with double-glazed ones in my sunroom and swapping out the roof for architectural asphalt shingles. I bought a new red Toyota truck straight off the dealer's lot to replace the green Datsun truck I'd been driving since before I moved to Canada, locking myself into a five-year loan without worrying about making the payments. The headaches that had occasionally sidelined me since my car accident had all but disappeared. What a change!

Then came 1991 when I learned about economic cycles the hard way. America invaded Iraq, and somehow what was happening halfway around the world crushed the stock market at home, sending the economy into a recession and discouraging rich people in Boston from buying staircases for their homes. The staircase company laid off three craftsmen and reassigned me from sales to a part-time position in the woodshop. Things began to spiral out of control. Inhaling sawdust and industrial fumes triggered my brutal headaches. I started wearing a surgical mask over my nose and mouth and took a break every hour to breathe fresh air outside. The guys on the shop floor gave me a hard time about it.

"What ya wearin' that mask for?" one old-timer asked. "So we don't have to see your ugly face?"

I ignored the old pig.

Then something else happened that I couldn't overlook. Warren was good friends with the shop manager, Oscar, and we had a routine of enjoying a beer or two and playing pool at the Red Oak Tavern after work. I was one of the guys, as Warren liked to say. The problem was, I wasn't one. And Oscar knew it. He was the type of guy who liked to poke people in the ribs or slap their asses. The guys put up with it, but I was reaching my breaking point. One night, when Warren walked over to the jukebox, Oscar leaned in and cupped his hand over his mouth.

"Why'd you pick Warren?" he asked. "Why not me?"

I almost fell over. "Are you flirting with me while my husband, your best friend, is standing fifteen feet away?"

He scrunched his nose as if he smelled ammonia.

"What d'ya see in him that you don't see in me? I'm the one in charge."

"This conversation is inappropriate. End it before it gets out of hand," I said.

When Warren returned, Oscar smiled at him. They clinked bottles, and as Warren lined up his cue stick, Oscar winked at me.

I woke up the following day with the worst headache I've had since the night I was thrown out of Canada. I lay paralyzed in bed and told Warren to go to work without me.

"Oscar was with us last night, Cassie," he said. "You know how he feels about the Irish flu."

"It's not the Irish flu," I said, irritated by his accusation. I could handle my booze.

Still, Oscar exploded and told Warren that I was replaceable.

I went to work the next day, and my headache worsened. I chewed on aspirin and chugged water, but it felt like an axe was embedded in my skull. I told Oscar that I needed to leave early.

"You leave now and you're gone for good, Cassie. You're drinkin' too much and takin' too many breaks. And you're wearin' that stupid mask, acting like this is a lousy workplace. You're makin' the other workers anxious."

"It's not my drinking, Oscar. I've been struggling with severe headaches since my car accident in high school. They come and go in cycles, and I'm in a rough patch right now. The bad ventilation system here doesn't help."

"Like I said, if you leave now, don't come back. I'll give Warren your final paycheck."

"Screw you," I said, unhooking the shop key from my gun-shaped keychain and tossing it at him. It ricocheted off his pudgy nose and slid under the lathe. Warren merely watched from behind his workbench, not coming to my aid.

When Warren came home that night, I let him have it. "That bastard fired me because I wouldn't sleep with him. Did you know that, Warren?" I asked. "And he thinks I'm a drunk. I like to party, but that doesn't stop me from putting in a solid day's work. It's these damn headaches. I hope you're not planning to keep working there."

"Cassie, you're pissed off, but you've gotta think straight. You just lost your job, and you've got car and house payments, plus food, utilities, and whatnot, and you want me to be out of work too? I don't think you understood him right. He's overly friendly with everyone. You got fired because of his drinking policy. He doesn't respect people who can't handle their booze."

I understood why Warren shouldn't have quit, but I hated that he could keep his job while I lost mine. I didn't drink more than Warren or anyone else at the shop. The incident reminded me of Brendan's motto taped to his bedroom mirror: "Trust Yourself." I trusted myself, but Warren trusted Oscar over me. He let me down—big-time.

●

By the summer of 1992, Dad was nearing the end, so I hosted a Fourth of July barbecue for him and Mom, inviting Bren, Laura, and their two-year-old son, Shannon. Bren picked up Dad and Mom in Nehoiden and drove them to New Hampshire. Dad struggled to get from Bren's car into the lawn chair I had set up for him under a maple tree. I brought Dad a beer, but he waved it off and asked for water. I had never seen him reject a beer before. I removed his Red Sox baseball cap so the soft summer breeze could cool his brow while he watched Shannon play with Nomad. It saddened me that Dad would never see his grandson grow up.

While I grilled hamburgers and hot dogs, Bren wrapped his arm around Dad's shoulder. Usually, in these moments, Bren would make light of Dad's declining health, pretending it was merely a temporary setback and that Dad would be okay. But this time, Bren's eyes filled with tears, and Dad pulled him close, whispering that he didn't have much time left and asking him to take care of Mom and me when he was gone. Through my tears, I looked at Warren, but he didn't understand what had happened. For the rest of the cookout, I couldn't shake the feeling that Dad believed I would need Bren's help. That night, I resolved to show Dad I was responsible, and invited him and Mom to move in with me until Dad's end.

On July 5, Warren drove my parents to Nehoiden to collect their belongings while I prepared the guest bedroom for them. I also arranged hospice care for Dad through the Lake Ash Visiting Nurses Association. Although I expected him to resist, he accepted the nurse's assistance. He joked with her, laughing at his frailty and complimenting her new hairstyle, even though she styled her hair the same way every day. Near the end, he reached into his wallet for a five-dollar bill to tip her, and a photo slipped out.

"Who are these handsome guys?" she asked, picking up the photo from the floor.

"My son, Brendan, and me at his college football game in 1976," Dad said.

Dad kept a photo of himself and Brendan in his wallet, but he didn't have one of me. I didn't know whether to be sad or angry.

It didn't take long for Dad's breathing to become more labored, and his energy faded as New Hampshire faced its worst humidity on record. He sat on my back deck under an umbrella, where a breeze blew off Mount Krystal, crossed Lake Ash, and flowed up the tributary, passing through my backyard, to cool him down. While Dad napped on the deck, I quietly went into the garage to finish a wooden rocking horse I was making for Shannon. When I returned with a glass of water for Dad, I found him slumped in his chair. I didn't need to check his pulse. I fell to my knees and howled from deep within my soul, from a place I never knew existed. His pain was over.

●

Me getting fired, Warren siding with Oscar, and Dad's passing were a triple kick in the gut. And the bad news didn't stop there. A few weeks after Dad's death, a letter arrived from the fertility clinic in Canada. I sifted through the legal mumbo-jumbo and arrived at the simple truth: Chester and Jessica Nelson had prepaid storage fees for my eggs from 1985 to 1992. Since I held the legal title to the eggs, I was responsible for paying three hundred bucks a year or I'd lose control over them.

The situation messed with my mind. I hadn't thought about the eggs since leaving Canada and had no practical use for them, but something inside me kept me from letting go. So I skimmed money from the grocery, utility, and car maintenance bills and sent seventy-five dollars every three months to the fertility clinic. It felt like I was throwing money away, but I was compelled to do it.

Cassie must have run out of steam because her memoir abruptly ended. Brendan closed the moleskin notebooks and bundled them together with a thick elastic band before going upstairs and gently sliding under the covers beside Laura. He thought about what he had just read until, exhausted, he fell asleep. When he woke in the morning, he knew what he had to do.

PART THREE

Brendan

January 2008

"Good morning, Mr. O'Shay. I'm Maggie St. Jean, a case-worker at the Winnipeg Fertility Clinic. I received your request regarding the disposition of your sister's eggs. Do you have time to discuss it now?"

"Thank you for calling me," Brendan said. "I'm at my desk in the middle of the trading floor surrounded by other traders. I'll put you on hold and then pick you up in my office where I can talk in privacy." He rushed from his trading floor desk into his office and picked up the phone line.

"First, Mr. O'Shay, I'd like to extend my condolences for your loss." Her voice was warm and pleasant.

"Call me Brendan. The market's hectic right now so I'll get to the point. I'm way over my head with all this fertility stuff. What options do I have?"

"I must admit, Brendan, this is the first time I've worked with a sibling rather than the owner of the eggs herself. However, your options are the same as your sister's would have been, except, of course, for using the eggs for yourself. Donating them to an egg recipient who will use them to create an embryo as part of in vitro fertilization is a common choice. We can help find an egg recipient, or if you prefer, you can look for one on your own."

"I wouldn't know where to begin," he said.

"Most people ask us to conduct the search," she said. "But if you decide not to donate them to a recipient—and I fully understand that choice—the most common alternative is to donate them to medical research. Many find solace in knowing that the eggs will contribute to advancements in medical science."

"I like the idea of doing social good," Brendan said, reflecting that his job lacked social redemption.

"A third option is to destroy them."

"Destroying them feels dishonorable—legally, ethically, and morally." He liked that his words sounded righteous.

"It's honorable on all three counts," she said. "Eggs are not human life. Even the Catholic Church doesn't see them that way. Additionally, the fertility system is overwhelmed with eggs that are stored indefinitely in cold storage facilities, with no hope of ever being used by their owners, many of whom struggle to accept the decision to destroy them. We're getting to the point where we're beginning to question whether it's immoral or unethical *not* to destroy them."

Maggie was giving him the chance to destroy the eggs and move on with his life. But something inside him held him back. Was it regret for how he had treated Cassie in her final years? Was it sympathy for the cruelty she endured in life? Was it guilt over the opportunities made available to him as a boy but not to her as a girl? Was it the shame of what he had done to her in the Raven Bay parking lot back in high school? He had to bear that shame for eternity. Destroying her eggs was out of the question.

"I'm considering donating them to a deserving recipient," Brendan said. "What's the process like?"

"We will make Cassidy's eggs available to our list of potential recipients, and we will provide information such as her blood type, ethnic background, height, weight, eye color, and family medical history. You must sign a consent form allowing us to gather and share that information. Additionally, we will require you to send pictures of Cassidy from all stages of her life, as the egg recipients will want to see what she looked like. We don't share identifying information, such as her name, address, or phone number. Similarly, we won't disclose yours to maintain your anonymity."

"And what's the screening process for the potential recipients?" he asked.

"We screen them to ensure they show fitness for parenting, but it's done in a nondiscriminatory manner. Except for a history of criminally or psychologically dangerous behavior, the requirements are quite low. They come from various social, economic, racial, and religious backgrounds. Most are married heterosexual couples. Others include domestic partners; some are gay or lesbian couples, and some are single. The variations are as vast as humanly possible."

"I want a say in who gets Cassie's eggs," Brendan said.

"Unfortunately, you won't have that."

Brendan's temples throbbed. He reached into his desk drawer for an aspirin and swallowed it dry. "Maggie, I'm going to get philosophical for a minute. As humans, we have external selves that we show to the world and internal selves that we keep hidden from others. With that in mind, let me share about Cassie and my relationship with her. I thought I knew my sister, but she had given her memoir to me through a mutual friend right before she died. It revealed aspects of Cassie's external and internal selves that I never knew existed. In it, I found a woman with many diverse natural talents, yet her environment and life experiences hindered her from living a full, meaningful, and happy life. Her major obstacle was ... how do I put it ... the less-than-nurturing environment in which we were raised. I'm sharing this because I want to make a request that may sound politically incorrect to you."

Maggie sighed heavily into the phone. "We get all sorts of requests, but they usually come from egg recipients who must live with the outcome, not the donor. What is it that you want?"

"I'd like to donate Cassie's eggs to a well-educated, straight married couple with strong family values, good jobs, and high morals. Ideally, this couple would be well-established in life, living in a nice house, with a healthy bank account and a commitment to providing the best nurturing environment for this child. Perhaps you could find a couple who already has children and a proven track record of successful parenting. That would be ideal."

"That's quite a list, Brendan. Should they also be Ivy League graduates?" she asked.

"That would be a bonus," Brendan said, ignoring her evident sarcasm.

"I understand your concerns," she said, irritated, "but you're being unrealistic, Brendan. Furthermore, those attributes don't ensure that your version of the ideal egg recipient will achieve a better outcome than all the other potential family structures."

"There are no guarantees in life, but in my profession, I focus on probabilities—the odds, the risks, and the rewards associated with every decision I make. Naturally, I acknowledge that young, poor, uneducated, gay, lesbian, and unmarried couples can be wonderful parents . . . unfortunately, the odds are stacked against them."

"You're being a bit closed-minded," the caseworker groaned.

"Maybe so, but I'm trying to manage the process as much as possible to give Cassie's biological child every advantage to increase the chances of achieving a fulfilling life." He paused briefly to let his words settle in before making another request. "And," he said, "I want the anonymity clause waived."

"Oh, Brendan," she said, "requesting to waive anonymity will significantly decrease the chances that your version of the ideal egg recipient will want Cassidy's eggs. Most parents don't want strangers tracking their children."

"But I wouldn't be a stranger; I'd be a blood uncle."

"I presume you have kids, Brendan."

"A son named Shannon. He'll be attending Painter College next fall if everything goes as planned. We receive news from college admissions in April."

"Would you have wanted your sister Cassidy to interfere with how you're raising Shannon?"

"Of course not," he said. "But Cassie wasn't in a position to positively influence my son's life."

Maggie let out another sigh.

"Besides, I'm not talking about interfering with raising the child. I'm talking about observing. Why go through the effort of donating her eggs if I can't see how it turns out?"

"Donating eggs should be a selfless act of kindness, not a do-over for a life that you feel has fallen short of your expectations and values."

"A child is a do-better," he said. "Parents want their kids to do better than they did. That's part of the American dream."

"It's part of the Canadian dream, too," she said, "but you're not thinking clearly about what egg donation is for. It's for the egg recipients, not the donors. It fulfills a couple's desire to procreate and have a family. You're convoluting the intent of this endeavor."

"I'm sorry, Maggie, but this conversation has taken a wrong turn."

"There's a fourth option to consider, Brendan," she interrupted. "You can hire a private agency in America that might be more flexible to your needs and may be able to find what you're looking for. I can give you some names of agencies, and we can arrange to ship the eggs once you've found a recipient who meets your criteria. Given our discussion today, I suggest you take it."

Brendan heard a knock on his office door. He was needed on the trading floor. "Sorry, Maggie, gotta go. I'll get back to you."

"The sooner, the better, Brendan. The clock is ticking."

Laura

April 2008

"Shannon?" Laura hollered, leaning her rolled-up yoga mat against the kitchen wall. "Shannon? . . . Shannon?" She noticed a ripped admissions packet from Painter College on the countertop and peeked inside. He's in, she thought. Bren will be happy, but what about Shannon? Would he come around and go where his father wanted him to go? She went upstairs to look for him. His lacrosse gear was scattered on his bedroom floor, but he wasn't around. She went back to the kitchen and opened the French doors to the back patio, shouting for him, but he didn't answer. Where was he? He sometimes liked to chill down by the dock and watch Bren's forty-two-foot fishing boat rock in the waves. She hated that damn boat, unable to separate it from what had happened to her father on a fishing boat a mile up the shoreline. The wind had picked up, and misty rain started to fall. She wrapped her arms around herself and jogged down to the dock. Empty. She caught a whiff of pot smoke drifting from the direction of three white Adirondack chairs arranged in a semicircle at the opposite end of the lawn. He was smoking pot again. Damn it! He had promised to stop. She jogged over to the smell.

"Shannon! What's the matter with you? Get up off the ground. It's raining!"

He lifted his head toward her, his eyes red and puffy. "Dad got his wish, Mom. Painter accepted me. So did the other colleges I applied to. Now leave me alone."

"Are you high? Your father will be devastated if he hears you're smoking pot again." She could have kicked herself for saying those foolish words.

"We can't have that, can we, Mom? We can't upset Dad's plan for me. And we can't have the neighbors calling me a pothead."

"You're not a pothead," Laura said, instinctively glancing around for spying neighbors before realizing their houses were too far away for them to see him on the ground and her hovering over him. "It's cold and wet out here, Shannon. Please, let's talk inside."

"You go on inside, Mom," Shannon muttered. "I'm not moving."

Laura wanted to demand he go inside, but he wasn't a little boy who would obey her every command. She left and watched him from the kitchen window until the rain began pouring down. He finally stood up and stumbled inside, passing through the kitchen and ignoring her on his way upstairs. She followed him upstairs and lingered outside his bedroom doorway.

"Go away, Mom."

"I'm here to listen without judgment," she said, yet her words felt hollow and insincere.

"You want to listen, Mom? Then listen to me: Go away!"

Bren came home from work after ten that night and switched on the bedroom light. Laura was sitting on the edge of the bed with her hands covering her face. He placed his hand on her shoulder. "What happened? Don't tell me Painter rejected Shannon!" Bren slammed his fist into his palm. "After all the money we've given to that ungrateful college. After all the Painter grads I've hired at my bank. I'm calling my friend on the board of trustees right now. I don't give a damn how late it is."

"He got in," she said, lifting her face from her hands and glaring at him.

"What? This is great news! Why are you so upset?"

"He's also been accepted to Wesleyan, Bard, and Skidmore. He would rather go to one of those colleges."

"I don't understand," Brendan said, throwing his hands up toward the sky.

"You've never tried to understand him. He doesn't want to go to Painter."

"That's absurd. It's been the plan," he said.

"You don't have the right to dictate where he goes to college. You made your own college decision when you were his age. Shannon wants to make his own choice too."

"It's not that I made my own choice. It's that Painter was the only college that gave me the money I needed to go to college. In a way, the decision was made for me, and it turned out to be one of the best decisions of my life. I've always wanted Shannon to have the same great experience we had at Painter. He'd be a fool to pass up this opportunity. I won't let him."

Laura was about to tell Bren how she'd found Shannon earlier in the evening, but the last thing she wanted was for him to push his way into Shannon's room and lecture him about irresponsibility and ingratitude, and to somehow twist his argument into shoving Painter College down Shannon's throat.

"I'm going to talk to him," Brendan said. "Is he in his room?"

"Don't go in there," Laura pleaded. "Give him some space."

"I just want to reason with him."

"I'm begging you, Bren."

He turned and walked down the hall to Shannon's room. She jumped up from the bed and ran after him, ready to hold him back. The door was open, and the lights were off. "He isn't here," Brendan said.

"What?" Laura said. "I'm calling him." She dashed back to her room, grabbed her phone, and dialed his number. "Where are you?"

"At Ines's house," he said. "Her parents are away. She's scared of being alone. I'm spending the night."

"Good idea," she said, barely questioning herself for encouraging her drug-impaired high schooler to spend the night unchaperoned at his girlfriend's house. She went back into the hallway to confront Brendan. "He's with Ines. He'll be home in a few hours. In the meantime, for God's sake, cool off before you drive him away."

He brushed past her on his way downstairs. She considered following him but decided they needed to cool off in separate spaces. She returned to her room, tugged off her yoga top and bottoms, tossed them onto the floor at her feet, and climbed under the covers without washing up, hoping Bren wouldn't wait up for Shannon only to realize he wasn't coming home. An hour later, Bren entered the room, washed up, and got into bed beside her. She reached across the gap between them and held his hand.

"Please, Bren, don't force Painter on him. Call it a mother's intuition, but I have a bad feeling about him attending a college where he doesn't want to be."

"He's going to Painter," Brendan growled, pushing her hand away. "That's been the plan all along. We're not changing it now that he's in."

She turned away from him as tears streamed down her face onto the pillow. She wished she could call her mother for help, but there were no cell phones in Heaven. Instead, she prayed that Bren would somehow see the light.

Brendan

April 2008

"I believe this couple is the one," said the agent from the New York fertility clinic Brendan had hired to find worthy recipients.

"Tell me more," Brendan urged.

"A heterosexual couple living in Buffalo, both in their mid-thirties. Married four years. Husband works in logistics for Buffalo Transit and has excellent job references and a track record of steady promotions. Wife creates and sells homeopathic tinctures from their home. Caucasian. Neither has a criminal record or history of violence. Both the husband and wife hold associate degrees. This is a second marriage for both of them. Husband has children from a previous marriage—an eight-year-old boy and five-year-old girl. Been trying to conceive but no success."

"Anything else?"

"They're a wonderful couple, Brendan. You can't go wrong with them."

Brendan put the agent on hold for a minute to reflect on it. The couple had positive attributes but had faced challenges in their first marriages. Who was to say they wouldn't struggle in this one? They likely didn't have much financial stability, either. The last thing he wanted was a broken home with parents who could barely make ends meet and would have a hard time providing Cassie's child with every opportunity that money could buy.

"Thanks for showing me this couple, but there are too many red flags. I'm going to pass," Brendan said, sounding as if he were talking to a broker trying to sell him junk bonds.

"We're losing patience with you, Brendan," the agent said. "If you don't approve a recipient before year end, as per the custodial agreement, the eggs will be destroyed."

A tap on his shoulder pulled his attention. "Sarah wants to see you right away," her assistant said.

"Gotta go," Brendan told the agent. "Don't get discouraged. Keep at it."

He jogged to Sarah's office and found her leaning over her Bloomberg Terminal, hurling invectives. "The vultures are circling, Brendan. It's Armageddon time. Calculate our funding risk and report back to me. Stat."

Sarah was tough, but he had to admit she was brilliant and savvy despite her decision to fund Williamson Trust Financial. She'd grown up outside Detroit, the daughter of two high school math teachers, and worked her way through Princeton while playing field hockey and lacrosse. After that, she worked as a monetary policy research staff member at the Federal Reserve Bank of San Francisco before earning an MBA at Wharton. The head of the economics department at Wharton urged her to pursue her doctorate and teach monetary policy, but her parents served society as teachers, and she aimed to make money. Landing a job in the derivatives trading unit at Global Investment Bank's office in London, she earned three million dollars a year by age thirty and was likely pulling in ten million a year now. Brendan had never seen Sarah nervous—until now.

He sprinted to his desk to assess his risk. On his way back to her office, he noticed Gus hunched behind a stack of six computer screens, tapping his desk with a pair of drumsticks.

"I'm about to report my funding risk to Sarah," Brendan stated.

"Who the fuck cares?" Gus said without looking up.

"Just giving you a heads-up in case she begins to ask you questions."

"You're fucking joking, right? Sack-less O'Shay is giving me a heads-up?" Gus scratched his armpit with a drumstick. "I know you're slow on the uptake, O'Shay, but let me teach you something. My mortgages are in Arizona, Florida, and Nevada, where people retire to play golf, gamble, eat, and die. The homeowners work at resorts, restaurants, and hospitals. They're the heart and soul of America. They'll pay their mortgages. Because that's the American way."

"That makes sense in normal times," Brendan said, "but these times aren't normal, Gus. These homeowners will default when the teaser rate ends and their monthly payments triple. Senior citizens will be moving into their kids' basements or living in cardboard refrigerator boxes on the streets of Phoenix, Miami, and Reno," Brendan added.

"News flash, you stupid fuck, you're not the first one to come to that conclusion. But suppose you paid attention to the mortgage market like I do every day instead of tuning in to talking heads on cable news. In that case, you'd realize that mortgage volatility is decreasing and prices are increasing." Gus pointed at a chart on the Bloomberg Terminal. "You should spend less time worrying about me and more time joining the team, for once in your fucking life."

"What do you know about my life?" Brendan snapped, surprising himself with his anger.

Gus sprang up from behind his desk and puffed out his chest. The veins in his forearms bulged. He looked like he could still win the NCAA wrestling crown.

Brendan backed away, seriously afraid that Gus was about to rip his head off.

"Relax, hombre. It's a fucking saying," Gus said, smirking in a way that twisted his cauliflower ear. He glanced at his Bloomberg screen, waiting for the market to open in Tokyo, and softened his tone. "Look, as much as I hate to fucking admit it, I agree with you. Despite the positive signs now, this market is about to implode. But when the Four Horsemen of the Apocalypse ride in on their black horses, I'll be shorting the market with put options and derivatives. As for now, get out of my way and go build a new addition to your vacation home with the money I'm making for this bank."

A wide Cheshire cat grin crossed his face as Gus circled to the front of his desk and cocked his arm to slap Brendan on the back. Brendan braced for impact, expecting his ribs to crunch. But suddenly Gus's grin vanished and his face twisted into a menacing scowl. "O'Shay, tell Sarah your own risk. Keep your mouth shut about mine. Or I'll run you over."

Feeling winded and dizzy, Brendan headed to Sarah's office. Should he tell her about his suspicions regarding Gus? It was a no-win situation. She'd hold Brendan partially responsible for Gus's losses if Gus's trading book crashed and Brendan hadn't warned her. But if he was wrong about Gus's risk, then his career at Global Investment Bank would be over. He decided not to be Gus's keeper.

Brendan

August 2008

Brendan dressed in a loose blue tank-top and a faded pair of orange swim trunks, strolled down to the shoreline of Cape Cod Bay, and let the gentle waves lap over his toes as he inhaled the salty air. He reflected on everything that had happened since April. The mortgage market was imploding and his wife and son were barely talking to him after he had cajoled Shannon into enrolling at Painter. And nothing had come of the ten-thousand-dollar retainer he had paid to a fertility agent in New York to find a suitable egg recipient for Cassie's eggs. Suddenly two golden retrievers splashed in the water and pawed at his side. He bent down to scratch their necks when he heard a loud whistle. The dogs sprinted up the dunes and disappeared into the tall grass. He glanced at his watch—time to return to the cottage.

"Where have you been?" Laura asked. "The parking lot will be full if we don't get to the beach soon."

"Why do we need to go to a crowded beach when this empty one is right here?" he asked, but he knew Laura and

Shannon wanted to meet up with their summer friends at the ocean beach.

He loaded his old army surplus Jeep, a two-door relic bought from a local fisherman, with umbrellas, towels, chairs, a surfboard, and two lacrosse sticks. Maybe Shannon would play catch with him on the sand like they used to do. But when Laura and Shannon jumped in the Jeep, Shannon tossed the sticks on the driveway as they drove away, and Laura shot Brendan an *I-told-you-so* look. Their reconciliation wouldn't be today.

When they reached Benson Beach, Shannon tucked his surfboard under his arm and ran up the beach path. Brendan and Laura followed him, their feet sinking into the soft sand. Browned-out beach grass swayed alongside them as they crested the dunes. He gazed down at the pristine expanse of pale cream sand and the myriad greens and blues of the Atlantic Ocean spread before him and felt the soft, warm breeze against his face. He released a huge sigh as if the sun, sand, and sea were miraculously cleansing him of his troubles. Perhaps a new beginning was at hand.

He spotted the summer crew gathered in a circle of pink beach chairs, yellow umbrellas, paperback books, flip-flops, plastic coolers, and canvas bags. Laura made a beeline for them, and he slowly followed. Around the circle sat Dave, the geologist and storyteller; Scott, the aeronautical engineer and surf caster; Steve, the hairdresser and expert griller; Amy, the architect and color field painter; Bernie, the psychoanalyst and shell fisherman; and Joy, the yoga instructor and New Age philosopher. They adjusted their beach chairs to expand the circle for Brendan and Laura. She unfolded her chair while Brendan sat directly on the hot sand and hugged his knees to his chest. The hot sand against his feet felt like a long-overdue penance. He watched Shannon walking toward four blondes, dragging their toes through the wet sand, adjusting their bikinis at the water's edge.

"Glad you're here, Brendan. We're discussing the stock market. What kind of abomination do you and your fellow one-percenters have us in now?" Bernie asked.

"Financial markets are like waves," Scott interrupted, nodding toward the ocean. "Watch them roll in unceasingly from the depths, lapping the shore in sets, pushing higher up the sand, then retreating and settling lower on the shoreline. It's all quite predictable. You can chart it. Then an unexpected surge occurs—a rogue wave—and you have to grab your beach chair and run for higher ground. Anticipate the rogue wave and you won't get soaked. Understand ocean waves and you'll understand financial markets."

What little relief Brendan had felt on top of the dune vanished. "The problem with your analogy is that when you misjudge the waves, your chair gets wet," Brendan said. "When you misjudge the market, your net worth can be wiped out. Hedge funds have been devastated this year, and many more are on the verge of collapse. Don't be surprised if one or two global banks go under too."

"You're such a pessimist," Scott said.

"Hope for the best—prepare for the worst. For heaven's sake, Scott, you make helicopter engines. You should know that by now."

Brendan opened his book to signal he was out of the conversation. The words looked like strange black symbols on an off-white page. He dropped it on the sand and glanced at Laura, who was shrouded in a wide-brimmed hat and round purple sunglasses, her nose buried in Caroline Knapp's memoir, *Drinking: A Love Story*. He had once read the opening chapter after a guest had left it behind, but it reminded him too much of Cassie. He looked up at Shannon talking with the girls, their hair blowing in the onshore wind. In another month, Shannon would be at Painter, and Brendan knew in his heart that his son would be okay. Painter was where he belonged. Shannon would thank him one day.

The magic of Benson Beach was gone. He pushed himself up and brushed the sand off his backside. "I'm going for a bike ride, Laura. Call me when you want a ride home. Don't forget, we have dinner reservations at seven."

"Shannon and I will get a ride home from Joy," Laura mumbled.

He ran lightly across the hot sand and asphalt parking lot and hopped into his Jeep. His cell phone rang as he pulled away.

"This is Tom Gallagher, attorney for WTF," a raspy voice said.

Brendan reflexively thrust his hand out the window and gave the world the finger as he drove past a white-haired older gentleman and a gray-haired lady walking hand in hand along the roadside. The man shielded the lady's eyes.

"Sorry," Brendan called out.

"Sorry about what?" Tom asked.

"Nothing, Tom. What's up?"

"I've been reviewing the margin call fiasco we experienced eight months ago, and there have been some close calls since then with other banks. I'm proposing several mutually beneficial amendments to our legal agreement, and I'd like to discuss them with you."

Whenever Brendan heard a hedge fund lawyer say "mutually beneficial," he instinctively checked for his wallet to make sure he hadn't been pickpocketed.

"I'm all ears," Brendan replied.

"Let's meet in person," Tom said. "Your attorney, Bill, mentioned you're in P-town this week. I'm here for a few days as well. Is there any chance we could get together for dinner to discuss it? Feel free to bring your partner along."

"I'll bring my wife, Laura," Brendan said.

"Tonight at the Victory Café. My husband, Mark, and I will get there by seven. See you there," Tom said and hung up.

His day was officially ruined. He hoped Laura wouldn't castrate him when she heard about the change in plans.

At six o'clock, Brendan stood in front of a full-length mirror wearing a black polo shirt, comfortable dark blue jeans, black designer skateboard shoes, and aviator sunglasses. His dark hair, graying at the temples, was slicked back on the sides and tousled on top. He strode downstairs and stepped onto the deck, sipping sparkling water while waiting for Laura to join him.

Soon she emerged on the balcony outside their bedroom. Her amber hair was styled with bangs sweeping across her forehead. She wore pink lipstick, and her fingernails and toenails were painted red. Her white skinny jeans complemented a rose-colored sequined sleeveless top that hugged her midriff and lifted her breasts. A wide, gold-embossed belt with an oversized silver buckle cinched her narrow waist. She carried a sunflower-yellow Chanel purse. Fifty was the new thirty-five.

"Aren't you going to shave that thing?" she asked, frowning at his day-old beard, speckled with gray.

Brendan shrugged. "Let's get going. I don't want to keep them waiting."

"Keep who waiting?" she asked.

"We have a slight change of plans," Brendan said. "A business associate and his husband are joining us for dinner."

"You must be joking," she said. "I thought this was *our* vacation."

"I'm really sorry. I know this isn't ideal for you, but the guy is the lead attorney for my biggest client. We've had a rocky relationship, and now he seems eager to make things right. Your presence and grace will be a huge help in smoothing things over."

"Let's go before I change my mind," she said.

They drove to Provincetown in silence, navigating a long sandy causeway between the turbulent ocean and the tranquil bay. Brendan gazed at the pale dunes, imagining himself soaring high above his speeding car, watching it take him to a better place, which was anywhere but where they were going. Walking into the restaurant, Laura patted his shoulder, signaling a truce for dinner. The interior of the Victory Café featured a mix of male and female nude oil paintings on the east wall; German Expressionism in bold reds, yellows, and greens with strong brushstrokes and simplified human forms on the north wall; and expansive windows facing south and west toward the sea. The tables were packed closely together, and the crowd's noise made his ears pulse.

"I'll be right back," Laura said as she walked toward the restroom.

Brendan glanced around the room, imagining what Tom might look like. They had never met in person.

"May I be of assistance?" the maître d' said.

"A reservation for four at seven o'clock under the name Tom Gallagher."

"You're the first to arrive," the maître d' said and led him to the table.

While Brendan waited for the others to join him, his eyes lingered on a redhead and a brunette perched on stools at a high-top table across from him. The redhead's white halter-top hugged her designer breasts, and her legs were parted. He was reasonably sure he spotted a bulge in her strawberry-red thong beneath her black leather miniskirt. He glanced at her companion, whose chestnut brown hair was tied back in a ponytail. The neckline of her sheer fuchsia blouse plunged to her belly button. A phallic-shaped silver pendant dangled in her tanned cleavage. The redhead winked at him. Flustered, he glanced away at another table, where five men in drag wore lavender "Bridesmaid" ribbons running from shoulder to waist, surrounding a bearded man clad in a lacy white wedding gown. They belly laughed above the noise, sipping scotch, devouring juicy steaks, and belting out show tunes in deep baritone voices.

Laura returned from the restroom and sat down.

"I think they're here," she said. A tall, fit, dark-haired man and a short, chubby, balding man approached the table. Brendan stood. "I'm Tom Gallagher," the taller man said as he shook Brendan's hand firmly. "Glad to finally meet in person."

"Likewise," Brendan said. He hated when he said "likewise." It made him feel submissive.

Tom's husband lightly grasped Laura's fingertips in his and kissed the back of her hand. "I'm Mark O'Donoghue," he said, smiling warmly. "You must be Laura."

Brendan couldn't remember the last time he'd seen Laura blush. During appetizers, she smiled and laughed at Mark's quick wit, nibbling on crudite and sipping Chardonnay.

By the time the main course arrived, Tom's raspy voice had softened and become less irritating, and Brendan began to admire his savviness. In business, Tom had out-maneuvered him and gone for the kill like a mongoose attacking a rattlesnake. Yet at dinner, he displayed perfect social grace—talking, listening, laughing, and smiling with elegant timing, never once mentioning the legal agreement they were there to renegotiate, always attentive to Laura's needs. And when the waiter brought the check, Tom reached across the table and took it.

"This dinner's on Williamson Trust Financial," Tom said.

"It's been wonderful," Brendan said, "but we never discussed the legal agreement."

"Come back to our place for a nightcap," Mark suggested. "You and Tom can take care of your business in the library while Laura and I stargaze. The view is truly spectacular."

Laura nodded her head in agreement.

"We'll stop in for a quickie," Brendan said. "We don't want to keep you guys from bed." He wondered if his remarks sounded awkward.

After a short drive, they found themselves in the foyer of Tom and Mark's gray mid-century modern beach house on Pilgrim Hill, which overlooked Herring Cove.

"Nice place," Brendan remarked. Once more, he regretted sounding so crass.

"It's a Gropius. We've added a few contemporary touches."

"Functionality dictates form," Brendan said. He'd read about Walter Gropius, but he'd never been in a house designed by the Bauhaus architect.

"Well done, Brendan. Now come with me, Laura," Mark said, gesturing toward his recent remodel: new granite countertops, a stainless-steel refrigerator, bamboo floors, and custom windows imported from Portugal, tinted to reduce ultraviolet rays and glare, along with electronically controlled window treatments. Two white armchairs flanked a life-sized purple porcelain greyhound figure across from an angular navy-blue sofa. A red squeeze ball rested at the center of a glass and chrome coffee table. "Step out onto the balcony, Laura," Mark said. "I'll make whiskey sours to enhance the moment."

"You're coming with me, Brendan," Tom said, his raspy voice in full force. Inside the library, Brendan browsed Tom's collection of books, neatly arranged on the mahogany shelves—*Moby-Dick, The Brothers Karamazov, Remembrance of Things Past, Les Fleurs du Mal,* and *A Portrait of the Artist as a Young Man.* Melville, Dostoevsky, Proust, Baudelaire,

Joyce. *The Hours, Middlesex*, and *Interpreter of Maladies* lay on a separate table, anchored between two crimson leather bookends embossed with the Harvard Law School crest.

"You have excellent taste in literature: French symbolism, nineteenth-century Russian works, Joyce, the Great American Novel, and authors trained right here in Provincetown," Brendan said. He thought he might be sounding like a dilettante and wondered why he was trying so hard to impress this adversary.

"Novelists aren't trained," Tom said. "They simply are."

Brendan attempted to recover from Tom's slap by discussing the book he was reading (though he was still on the first page), eventually admitting he was too busy to read fiction.

"Sad," Tom said. "In our line of work, it's crucial that we compartmentalize and safeguard our personal time."

"Compartmentalizing isn't easy to do."

"I'm a gay corporate attorney representing the brightest minds in the most type-A, male-dominated, macho-oriented industry in the world," Tom said. "I don't do what's easy; I do what's best." He handed the contract to Brendan. "The red sticky notes highlight the changes in black," Tom explained. "You'll find that the changes are mutually beneficial."

"Whenever I hear that oxymoronic phrase, I wonder how I'm getting screwed," Brendan said, attempting to gain the upper hand. He quickly skimmed through the black-lined changes and found nothing particularly egregious. "In principle, I can accept this. But I'm tired right now. Send it to Bill, and I'll discuss it with him when I return to work next week." Brendan handed the document back to Tom.

"The world doesn't stop while we're on vacation, Brendan," Tom snapped, slapping the document down on the edge of his desk.

"Look, Tom, I canceled date night with my wife for dinner with you and Mark. I refuse to spend the rest of my vacation working."

Tom shook his head as they left the library and rejoined Mark and Laura in the living room. Brendan sat beside Laura on the edge of the blue sofa as she sipped a second whiskey sour from a crystal tumbler. Tom and Mark settled into the white armchairs. Mark stroked the purple porcelain greyhound figure while Tom squeezed the red stress ball so hard that his fingers turned white. The decor, stunning views, and whiskey sours seemed to have fueled Laura's curiosity.

"Where did you grow up? How did you two meet?" she asked.

Mark finished the last of his drink. "We met at a Harvard–Yale football game four years ago, in 2004. Tom was the backup quarterback when he was at Harvard and has attended every Harvard–Yale game since graduating. I went to the game with colleagues from McLean Hospital. We sat beside each other and immediately hit it off. We dated for a few months, moved in together, and married in P-town. It's a haven for us and keeps improving every year. It has become much more family-friendly for gay and lesbian couples."

"In what ways?" Laura inquired.

"For one, I'm sure you've noticed the baby carriages," Mark said. "Many of these children are biologically related to one of the parents. And the more we saw these happy families, we thought why not us? So we researched IVF and gestational surrogacy. Tom handled the legal work while I explored fertility clinics and looked into our options. It's a complex web and a big business. The range of choices is astonishing. It's similar to finding the right college for your high-schooler. You visit a website, check the desired characteristics, and let the computer algorithm find a match: race, ethnicity, gender, height, athletic ability, musical talent, and family health history. It's a complete circumvention of chance—a brave new world."

"Any prospects for you?" Laura asked.

"Not yet," Mark replied, "thanks to Tom. He tends to focus on the things that can go wrong."

"From a legal perspective, Tom, what worries you the most?" Brendan asked, thinking about Cassie's eggs languishing in the fertility clinic, with time running out before they would be destroyed.

"Custody battles," Tom said. "One case in California stands out as particularly alarming. You may have heard about it. The Los Angeles Lakers drafted a seventeen-year-old high school prodigy and signed him to a thirty-million-dollar contract. The prodigy's parents underwent IVF treatments using the husband's sperm and eggs from an anonymous donor. It turned out that a six-foot-two

Lithuanian woman in UCLA's premed program had sold her eggs to fund her tuition. Fast-forward eighteen years from the time she sold her eggs; she's now a gynecologist in Santa Barbara. She spotted a front-page photo of the basketball prodigy in the *LA Times* next to Magic Johnson. The kid bore a striking resemblance to her, prompting her to hire an aggressive lawyer, who discovered that the player was her biological son. She ultimately secured kinship rights. It was a warning about the fraught custody law."

Tom stood and paced the living room, squeezing the red ball so hard that Brendan thought it would bleed.

"I've thoroughly researched Massachusetts case law regarding gestational surrogacy and child custody, and I found a troubling local case where a married couple used their own sperm and egg to create an embryo. After the child was born, the surrogate sought parental rights despite having waived all her rights in a legally binding surrogacy contract. Ultimately, she was denied parental rights because she was unmarried and had not used her own egg. But the judge said that had the surrogate been married, or if the married couple had used donor sperm or donor eggs instead of their own, he would have ruled in favor of the surrogate. The judge's opinion was blatantly antigay because gay men obviously must use donor eggs. We're left in a conundrum. Our egg donor will have a custody claim that even extends to her husband upon her death. The only scenario that ensures gay men have uncontestable custodial rights is if the egg donor is deceased *and* was single or divorced at the time of her death, and the gestational surrogate is single."

The red stress ball bulged between Tom's fingers.

"We know the odds are slim, but we still have hope," Mark interjected. "And if anyone can untangle this complicated mess, it's Tom."

While Tom paused and met eyes with Mark, Brendan thought about how Cassie's eggs fit into this puzzle.

"We're looking for a single woman from Massachusetts who will agree to our surrogacy contract," Mark said. "We'll pay for a luxury apartment in our building in the South End, just a short ride to Brigham and Women's Hospital, where she'll give birth. We'll compensate her generously and cover the expenses for uterine preparation, embryo implantation, doctor visits, and prenatal exercise classes. We'll even provide her with groceries, which is the least we can do considering that she must follow the strict diet we'll set for her."

"I can't believe surrogates aren't clamoring to sign up," Laura said.

"They are, but we haven't found anyone who's emotionally intelligent, physically fit, and willing to accept our drop-and-run provision," Mark said.

"Drop and run?" Laura asked, setting her drink on a coaster.

"Slang for carrying a child to term, cashing the check, and vanishing," Mark said. "We're in regular contact with local doulas, but we haven't had any success so far."

Doula? Brendan immediately thought of Emily, with whom he had spoken once since Cassie's funeral eight months earlier, to finalize the sale of Cassie's house.

"And, of course, we need to find the right egg donor," Mark said. "Tom is being a bit too legalistic about this. I'm afraid we've missed several good opportunities."

Tom frowned, and the conversation paused for a beat too long.

"Is it already midnight?" Laura asked, nodding at Brendan. "We've overstayed our welcome. We should head home to wait for our teenage son." Laura stood up and ran her palms down her thighs, smoothing the nonexistent wrinkles in her white jeans before giving Mark a playful hug. "Thank you for your hospitality. I hope we see each other again," she said with a smile.

●

"Why did you suddenly decide it was time to leave?" Brendan asked during the drive home. "I was curious about their story. It offers a different perspective on IVF than mine."

"I'm tired and a little tipsy, and I wanted to talk to you privately. I realize I haven't shown much interest in what you're facing with Cassie's eggs, but they're always on my mind. Her eggs could solve Tom and Mark's conundrum."

"It would be a good fit, but even with the shift in how America views gay marriage, it would be hard for a child to grow up with two dads. It wouldn't be what's best for Cassie's child," Brendan said.

"First, these eggs won't result in Cassie's child," Laura said, tapping her fingernails on the dashboard. "Second, it's time you look beyond gay and straight. Tom and Mark will be nurturing, protective, and loving parents with plenty of financial and emotional resources. Plus, they live in the South End and Provincetown, two of the most LGBT-accepting communities in America."

"I don't know, Laura. Mark's a nice guy, but Tom can be a jerk," Brendan said.

"He's strong-willed. Focused. A lot like you, to be honest."

"Me?" Brendan exclaimed, slamming on the brakes to avoid a coyote crossing the road. "Tom and I don't exactly see eye to eye."

"That's because you have conflicting interests," she said. "You might see things differently if he was on your side."

Brendan had reluctantly arrived at the same conclusion about Tom when they faced off against each other in business several months earlier, but it hurt to hear Laura say it. He was about to tell her so when his phone rang.

"Hello. Yes, I'm Brendan O'Shay. Yes, Shannon is my son. What's this about, Officer? Is Shannon okay?"

"What happened to Shannon?" Laura shouted. "Not a car accident. Oh God. Is he okay?"

"Yes, Officer. We'll be there in ten minutes." He hung up the phone, glanced around, and made a sharp U-turn.

"Is Shannon all right?" Laura yelled again.

"He's in jail, Laura. Shannon's in jail."

"Jail!? Behind bars? How could that be? Shannon's not someone who goes to jail." She grabbed Brendan's arm and tugged hard. The car swerved across the road. He turned the wheel just in time to avoid an oncoming pickup truck.

"Laura! Calm down! You could've killed us!"

"What's he doing in jail?"

"He got into a bar fight," Brendan said.

"A bar fight? What's he doing in a bar? He's underage. I hope he's not hurt."

"He's not hurt," Brendan said, "but the other guy is—pretty badly. The police are calling it a hate crime."

"Hate crime? That's ridiculous! Is that what the cop said? Shannon doesn't hate anyone."

"Call Tom," she said. "We'll need a good lawyer."

"Not Tom," Brendan said. "I don't want to owe him anything."

"Our son is in jail for a hate crime! Tom is a great lawyer, or so you say. Call him. Now."

●

It was nearly three in the morning when Tom stepped out of the police holding cell, with Shannon shuffling a few steps behind him, staring at the gray linoleum floor tiles. His knuckles were scraped raw. Brendan reached out to hug his son, but he slouched away from him. Laura rushed to embrace him, and Shannon wrapped his arms around her. She glanced over Shannon's shoulder into Brendan's eyes and shook her head.

Brendan reached out to shake Tom's hand, but Tom ignored him. "I've worked this out with the authorities," Tom said. "The victim is an acquaintance of Mark's from the Gay Men's Health Crisis Center. He's the town libertine, and that says a lot around here. His story lines up with Shannon's. He thought Shannon was one of his regular hookups, so he gave him a reach-around at the bar. Shannon coldcocked him. Broke his jaw. He wants money. The police know the situation and have agreed not to prosecute as long as Shannon stays out of town for the rest of the summer."

"Phew! I owe you big-time," Brendan said.

"Actually, you owe the libertine. Bring me a check in his name for twenty-five grand tomorrow. I'll make sure he gets it. And a twenty-five-grand donation to the Gay Men's Health Crisis Center would be a meaningful way to show your gratitude."

"Done," Brendan said. "I'll bring you the checks in the morning. Thanks again, Tom."

"Take the kid home and clean him up," Tom said, dismissing Brendan's words of thanks.

Brendan turned to Shannon, who was leaning against the wall with pale skin and bloodshot eyes. "Are you okay, Shannon? What the hell happened? How'd you even get into a bar?"

"Not right now, Dad," Shannon said through clenched teeth. "Let's get out of here."

Brendan woke up at nine, wrote out two checks, tucked them into the tiny side pocket of his black Lycra bike shorts, gulped down a black coffee, and hopped on his bike, pedaling toward Provincetown under the translucent morning light. The sun-bleached pavement unfurled beneath him as he passed a series of small white cottages strung neatly along the shoreline of Cape Cod Bay. He reached the Province Lands Bike Trail and rolled through a beautiful wasteland of sand dunes, beach grass, and twisted pines. The longer he rode, the more he relaxed.

He turned onto Commercial Street and coasted past the bar where Shannon had fought the night before. Brendan thought about Tom and Mark's efforts to have a child of their own, free from the burdens of an unpredictable legal system regarding child custody rights. He reflected on how they had saved Shannon, whose life would have been ruined if he had been convicted of a hate crime. Painter College would have revoked Shannon's acceptance, creating a lasting curse for his son and a stain on him and Laura as parents. He stopped his bike at a café, sat on the bench outside, and sipped an espresso. That was the moment he decided to offer the men Cassie's eggs. But first he called Emily.

"I thought I might eventually hear from you. Is this about the eggs?"

"You knew about them," Brendan remarked.

"Of course I did. Cassie told me everything about them when she asked me to give you her memoir."

"You can only imagine how difficult these eggs have made my life," Brendan lamented.

"Cassie had a knack for complicating things," Emily said. "But as you remember from the crowded funeral mass, she made an impact on people."

Brendan paused, reflecting on how he had avoided Cassie over most of their adult lives, how she had been too much for him, and how he had let her down. He didn't want to let her down now.

"I found a possible recipient for her eggs," he said. "Two men who live in Boston and Provincetown. They're married. One is a lawyer, and the other is a mental health counselor."

"That's nice. But why are you telling me?"

"You're a doula, and if they take Cassie's eggs, they'll need a gestational surrogate. Do you know one in Massachusetts?"

"If you give them the eggs, also give them my number," she said. "If they call me, I'll help them."

"And Emily . . . I'm not sure how to put this . . ."

"Just say it," she urged.

"I don't think anything good can come from death, but in this case, reconnecting with you has been good."

Emily sighed deeply, then fell quiet. He immediately regretted his confession.

"Have them call me," she said, her voice breaking. "Goodbye, Bren."

He hopped back on the bike and rode to Tom and Mark's house where he handed the two checks to them.

"I'll send my bill to Shannon when I return to Boston," Tom said.

"Send it to me," Brendan said. "I'll pay it right away."

"No," Tom said. "Shannon is my client. I want him to understand his responsibilities in this matter. If Daddy keeps protecting him, how will he become a man?"

It stung Brendan to admit it, but Tom was right. No one had ever bailed him out when he was a teenager, so why was he coddling Shannon instead of making him face the consequences of his actions? Still, Brendan hated Tom for rubbing his nose in his shit. He fought his instinct to leave without discussing Cassie's eggs.

"May I sit down and rest for a minute?" Brendan asked.

"Of course," Mark said. "You've had a tough night, and you look tired and sweaty. Come to the kitchen table. I'll get you some water."

The three men sat at the table. Brendan took a long gulp of water before setting down the empty glass and leveling his gaze at Tom and Mark. "Your story last night touched me," Brendan said, "the challenge of finding the right situation to suit your circumstances. You need a Harvard law degree to navigate the IVF, egg procurement, and surrogacy issues."

For the first time since the previous night's dinner, Tom smiled.

"I believe I can help you have a child," Brendan said.

Tom and Mark exchanged glances. "How can you possibly help?" Mark asked.

"My sister Cassie passed away last December. She was fifty years old and died from cirrhosis of the liver. She lived an eventful life filled with extraordinary adventures and terrible heartbreak. It was painful and frustrating to watch the alcohol erode such a beautiful person."

"I'm sorry about your sister, but how's that relevant?" Tom said.

"Unbeknownst to me," Brendan said, "she had frozen her eggs while living in Canada during the eighties. When she died, I became the custodian of her eggs."

Tom gestured with his hand, signaling Brendan to continue.

"That's not all. A girl I dated in high school who was Cassie's best friend—her name is Emily—is a doula living in New Hampshire. She understands the inner workings of the gestational surrogate community in Massachusetts. I've been collaborating with an agent in New York to find egg recipients, but I haven't had any luck so far. If you're interested in exploring the idea of taking Cassie's eggs and talking to Emily, I can help you."

"This is so out of the blue," Mark said.

"I feel the same way," Brendan said, "but there are people who think the world works this way—guided by some unknowable force. I have to admit, even though it defies rational thought, I've felt that force a few times in my life. Both Laura and I felt it last night right here in your house. Unfortunately, I felt an opposite force when I had to bail out Shannon."

"Some call it God, others something else," Mark said, touching Tom's hand. "I felt it the time I met Tom at a random Harvard football game."

"Cassie wrote a memoir that you're welcome to read. I'll do my best to answer any questions you might have about her, but it's an understatement to say that we weren't close for most of our adult lives. That's something I regret."

"Could you give us a moment to talk about this privately?" Mark asked. "Please take a seat on the balcony. The morning sun's reflection on the salt marsh is beautiful. I'll get you another glass of water."

Brendan went outside and watched the white egrets stepping cautiously through the thin layer of water surrounding the marsh at low tide. He hoped he hadn't been rash. Fifteen minutes later, Tom and Mark came out to him, holding hands.

"Send us a copy of the fertility clinic's custodial agreement, your sister's memoir, and the doula's contact information. We'll do our due diligence. As you can imagine, with all these hedge funds struggling to secure bank financing, I don't have much free time right now. It might take a month or two to respond."

"I'll mail both documents when I get back to Connecticut. Give me a pen and paper and I'll write down Emily's number."

Brendan rode his bike to his cottage, eager to tell Laura all that had happened, except for the doula part. But when he arrived, his family was gone. On the kitchen table, he found a note: *I'm sorry, Bren, but last night's encounter with the police was too much to handle. Shannon and I are heading to Westport. Please close up the house and come home as soon as you can. Take the old Jeep; I hope it makes it back. We have work to do on this family.*

●

The army surplus Jeep was ideal for a quick trip to the beach and a romp over the dunes, but it was a miserable ride on the highway. He couldn't push it past fifty miles per hour without the wheels shimmying and the wind whistling through the canvas top. As he rattled down the highway, his thoughts lingered on Laura's last line: *We have work to do on this family.* Why? Because Shannon had gotten into a bar fight? Big deal. When Brendan himself was a teenager, he'd been in plenty of fistfights. It was part of growing up in America. Why was Laura making it into a crisis? He was about to dial her number to try to talk her back from the edge of the cliff, but he realized it had to be a face-to-face conversation. Instead, he called Emily.

"Two phone calls in one day?" she asked. "You're forming a habit."

"Is that a bad thing?" Brendan asked, his voice wavering. Before she could reply, he added that he'd given her number to the guys. "Will you tell me if you find a surrogate for them?"

"I work under a confidentiality agreement," she said. "But if those guys choose to take Cassie's eggs, you can assume they've found a surrogate. And Bren, just try to relax. You sound hyper-stressed."

"I thrive under stress," he replied, his voice shaking.

"That's not true, Bren. You thrive despite the stress, but it's not healthy."

"After thirty-plus years, you still know me pretty well," he said.

"I know you better than you think."

Brendan

September 2008

Brendan's parental dream had finally arrived—taking Shannon to Painter, watching the college president greet his son at the convocation ceremony, and affixing a PAINTER COLLEGE PARENT sticker to the rear windows of his cars. Shannon loaded his Gladstone bags into the back of Laura's Range Rover. This was a far cry from when Brendan brought his clothes and a clock radio to Painter in green trash bags in 1976.

As he backed out of the driveway, his phone rang.

"Brendan, it's Sarah."

She only called with bad news.

"John Smart just called me," she said. "He wants me to meet him at the Fed ASAP. Things are getting serious—crisis shit, Brendan. The problem is I'm in Miami. Put on your suit and get to Lower Manhattan immediately and cover for me. It's your area of expertise anyway, Brendan. Smart wants to know our firm's funding position. No one understands that better than you. It's your time to shine.

But don't speak out of turn with Smart. If you do, he'll tear you apart. My pilot's preparing my Gulfstream for takeoff in a few hours. I'll call you when I land at LaGuardia."

Brendan wondered why John Smart, the CEO of Global Investment Bank, was at the Federal Reserve Bank of New York on a Sunday and what Sarah meant by his speaking out of turn. He had spent his career biting his tongue.

"How soon can you get there?" Sarah asked.

"Sarah, I'm dropping off my son for his first year of college."

"Are you in New Hampshire?"

"His college is in Vermont."

"Whatever. Are you in Vermont?"

If Brendan said no, Sarah would force him to head to Lower Manhattan. If he said yes, she'd find someone else to fill his shoes, rendering him irrelevant.

"No," Brendan said, "I'm still in my driveway in Connecticut."

"Have Laurie take him," Sarah said.

"You mean Laura," Brendan said. Sarah had met Laura countless times over the years.

"Yes, yes, of course. Laura. I'm sorry, Brendan. I'm just stressed. Can you have Laura take Shannon . . . That's his name, right? How soon can you get to the Fed?"

"At most, two hours," Brendan said, unable to glance in the rearview mirror, too ashamed to meet his son's eyes.

"I'm sorry, Shannon, but this situation is out of my control. The world's on fire."

"No need to explain, Dad. You're an important guy. Go save the financial system," Shannon said, tugging his black and red Wu-Tang Clan baseball cap down over his eyes. "Mom and I have been handling things without you. We can handle this one, too."

He turned to Laura. "It's out of my control, honey. It sounds like the world is about to implode. Why else would our bank's CEO summon Sarah and me to the Fed on a Sunday?"

"I understand, Bren," she said, "but that doesn't make me happy, and it doesn't make it right, nor does it mean I have to pretend it's okay." Brendan stepped out of the car as Laura crawled over the center console to take the driver's seat. Shannon jumped into the passenger seat. Brendan stood by the driveway while Laura threw the car in reverse and pulled away with tires screeching. He couldn't blame them for their anger, but what choice did he have?

He rushed into the house and donned a dark gray suit, a white shirt, and a blue striped tie. He had been to the Fed hundreds of times to meet with government officials responsible for open market operations, an arcane function used to adjust the money supply and daily liquidity in the financial system. He had also served as the Chairperson of the Funding Division executive committee of the Bond Market Association, an industry trade group aimed at influencing government policy. Additionally, he had visited the Fed during emergencies, most recently following the September 11, 2001, terrorist attacks that disrupted funding systems in the global financial market. But even during that tragic event, he had never been to the Fed on a Sunday, nor had he been summoned there as Sarah's surrogate to talk to John Smart. For the past few Fridays, rumors had circulated that a major investment bank was on the verge of collapsing, yet the subsequent Mondays revealed that the financial system remained intact. It felt as though the day of reckoning had finally arrived.

He contemplated his work-life dilemma as he navigated the dreadful traffic on FDR Drive. He had busted his ass his entire adult life to be in a position to afford private school to prepare his son for Painter and to pay full tuition once he was accepted. Now the career that made it possible denied him the satisfaction of taking Shannon there. A cabbie cut him off, jolting him from his thoughts. He exited the chaotic highway into the cavernous, empty streets of Lower Manhattan, parked the car, and jogged past two fat gray rats gnawing a loaf of raisin bread over a sewer drain. Breathing heavily, he reached the Fed and emptied his pockets into a plastic basket before walking through the metal detector. A large security guard with a holstered gun and nightstick escorted him to the three-story mahogany and marble banquet hall.

The CEOs of every major Wall Street firm gathered with the heads of their government bond trading and funding departments—men and women from rival banks Brendan recognized from his years on committees in the trade association. He marveled at their power; these CEOs collectively controlled more assets than the combined economies of Japan, China, and Germany. They appeared deadly serious, as if on the verge of losing their mansions, vacation homes, Maseratis, country club memberships, and eight-figure sums in their personal investment accounts. He spotted John Smart leaning against a massive marble pillar, chatting intensely with a suave colleague. Brendan hurried over to him.

"Brendan, I'm glad you're here," Smart said. "You won't believe this. The Treasury secretary just announced Lehman's insolvency. Normally I'd be thrilled to see Lehman fail, but this could be disastrous for every bank. Brendan, from a funding perspective, are we safe?"

"Yes," Brendan said emphatically. "Our funding plan is invulnerable. We can weather a perfect storm."

"Can we weather a massively overvalued mortgage portfolio?" Smart retorted. "That's what brought down Lehman. Their mortgage traders overlooked the liquidity premium."

His June argument with Gus popped into his head. He should have disclosed his suspicions to Sarah, and it was time to confess to Smart.

"You're hesitating," Smart remarked. "Why are you hesitating?"

"Last June, I asked Gus Marchetti about the value of the mortgage book, but he reassured me everything was fine and told me to mind my own business."

"He told you to mind your business? That's the reddest of red flags. Did you inform Sarah?"

Brendan shook his head no.

"Call Sarah. Right now. Get her on it!" Smart slammed his hand against the marble column he was leaning on.

Heads were about to roll. Brendan knew he had messed up. Sarah had warned him not to speak out of turn to Smart. Yet he had. And Smart was tearing into him. His confidence crumbled to the floor. He slinked to the corner of the banquet hall and called Sarah.

"I'm about to land," Sarah said. "What's wrong?"

He fessed up.

"Oh, Brendan," Sarah said, "this is a total disaster. First I asked you to keep me informed, so you should have shared your concerns about Gus's book in June. Second, I researched the mortgage book myself, and it's flawless. Gus used derivatives to short the market. He's going to make billions for us when this mess is over. Why you told Smart something different is beyond me. What were you thinking?"

"The world is on fire, Sarah. He asked me a direct question and I told him what I knew."

"You're losing it, Brendan," Sarah said. "You should have called me first. I'll call Smart and straighten him out. You head back to the office and update our funding plan. I'll let Smart know you're out the door."

"Out the door?" Brendan said.

"Leaving the Fed for the office," Sarah said, exasperated.

As he raced to his Midtown office building, he passed groups of parents dropping their children off at NYU, couples strolling hand in hand through Washington Square Park licking ice cream cones, and street musicians entertaining the crowd. They were blissfully unaware that every retirement plan, home, and stock portfolio in America was about to lose half its value the next day. He wondered if Laura and Shannon were attending the parent-student orientation lunch on the campus lawn. He remembered how his dad had dropped him off at college before turning around to get back to work the next day. At least his dad had gotten the chance to take him to college. Brendan wondered, despite the money he earned, how much real progress he had actually made.

When he reached his desk, Gus Marchetti was strutting around the trading floor, barking orders at his traders. They looked like frat boys, sitting at their desks in cargo shorts, ripped T-shirts, and flip-flops, watching the New York Giants crush the St. Louis Rams on the television sets mounted to the ceiling, but they were working hard positioning the bank to withstand the financial Armageddon that was about to unfold. Gus spotted Brendan across the floor and charged at him like a mad bull.

"You fucker," Gus shouted. "I just spoke to Whetstone. I told you to mind your own business. I should body-slam you right now!"

"Gus, I meant to protect the firm."

"You'd better protect yourself. Whetstone's going to shoot you for this fuckup."

"She'll fire her funding manager during the biggest financial liquidity crisis since the Great Depression? I doubt it, Gus."

"Death by a thousand cuts. You'll bleed out within a year."

"That gives me plenty of time for redemption," Brendan said.

"Redemption?" Gus chuckled. "Redemption? This is Wall Street, dude. There's no redemption here. You're either in a state of grace, or you're disgraced. Consider yourself the latter." Gus flipped him off and swaggered away.

Brendan's hands trembled as he operated his computer, running worst-case scenarios through the advanced funding system he had developed, which Sarah had ridiculed for costing too much. He focused intensely on his work, determined to prove his worth to her. Moments later, she burst onto the trading floor and headed straight for his desk. "The firm is safe," he said, handing her his spreadsheet.

She snatched it from his hands. "I don't need you anymore," she said. "You can go."

As he exited the building, he bumped his thigh against a concrete pylon designed to protect against truck bomb attacks and limped to his car, unable to shake Gus's and Sarah's words. He would redeem himself. They would be grateful to him one day.

Laura

October and November 2008

"Shannon's in college. Bren works day and night, and hot yoga isn't cutting it for me anymore, especially after this morning's class," Laura complained to her friend Dianne. "The guy next to me was shirtless, dripping his gross sweat on my mat." Laura cradled her latte. "I need to do something meaningful."

Dianne had been an empty nester for five years. She understood Laura's struggle with adjusting to a home life without a child to care for. "Laura, you once mentioned that the Columbia School of Journalism accepted you before you had Shannon. Columbia might readmit you, and Yale is just down the road if you don't want to commute to Morningside Heights. You have so much to offer the world."

"At fifty?" Laura asked, gazing at her reflection in the mirror that lined the walls of the French bistro. The wrinkles at the corners of her eyes seemed to have deepened overnight.

"If that feels overwhelming, maybe you'd be open to a less daunting reentry into the workforce. We're looking for a copywriter for our development materials at FirstStep, especially in light of the financial crisis. This has been our worst fundraising year since the Latin American and Asian debt crisis triggered a huge sell-off in the US stock market ten years ago."

Laura had been to several of FirstStep's fundraising galas and had written substantial checks to support the nonprofit over the years. She admired the nonprofit's success in bridging the educational gap between students in Bridgeport and Westport, and the idea of working there intrigued her. But she was hoping her friend would just commiserate with her, not offer solutions. Dianne's ideas were coming at her too fast. "I'm not sure I understand the rules of the game these days," Laura said, seeking reassurance. "Do I want to punch a clock, meet deadlines, wear the right clothes, say the right things, think the right thoughts, analyze, evaluate, and recommend ideas at the risk of having them dismissed?" Her words reminded her of Brendan's constant complaints of how much his work sucked.

Dianne patted Laura's forearm. "Fear is a natural reaction after years on the sidelines. It's time for you to take your first step. I'm good friends with Randy Bauer, the executive director of FirstStep. You've seen him speak at our events. I'll tell him about you."

Dianne worked fast. The next day Randy's assistant called Laura to arrange an informational interview. Laura skipped her yoga class, showered, applied makeup, and begged the hair salon to fit her in for a color, cut, and blow-dry at noon. Afterward, she met her personal shopper, Marcia, at Mitch's clothing store.

"Darling," Marcia said with a rich Hungarian accent as they air-kissed near each other's cheeks. "Which gala are you attending?"

"I'm looking for a very professional business outfit, Marcia. Are you familiar with that product line?"

"But of course, darling. I have several senior executive women as clients. Do you watch the evening news?"

"Sometimes," Laura said.

"Then you must know . . ." Marcia leaned in and whispered the name of America's most famous news interviewer. "But a business outfit for you? This is surprising. Come with me."

Marcia guided Laura on a three-hour journey, and at the end, her assistant loaded massive shopping bags filled with shoes, jackets, blouses, skirts, belts, scarves, and jewelry into the back of Laura's car. The day had worn Laura out, but she still had homework. She drove home, dropped the bags in the entryway, and opened her computer to FirstStep's website. She reviewed its Charity Navigator quality rating, downloaded five years of tax returns, and sifted through its marketing materials. Equipped with data, she designed a mock fundraising brochure, printed it out, and held it up to the light. "This will blow Randy away," she said aloud. Then she checked her watch. Nine p.m. Twelve hours until her interview. Her stomach growled. She hadn't eaten all day but had one more thing to do before grabbing a handful of carrots from the kitchen. As she pulled a skirt, blouse, stockings, and shoes from the bags on the floor, the sales receipt slipped out—ten thousand dollars. For the last ten years, she'd felt a sense of decadent satisfaction spending Bren's hard-earned money on herself. Her entire walk-in closet was filled with shoes that attested to it. But after reading about FirstStep, for the first time, she felt almost nauseated by the waste of money. She neatly folded the clothes and placed them back in their bags. She would shop her closet for the interview, return the clothes to Mitch's, and donate the money to a worthy cause. Finally ready, she grabbed a handful of carrot and celery sticks to snack on and called Bren.

"I'm still at the office," Brendan said. "Crazy day."

"When is this crisis going to end?" she asked.

"It's more like 'how will it end?' Another bank went belly-up today. The Fed is pulling out all the stops to save the world financial system," he whispered.

"It can't be that bad," she said. "Mitch's was packed today."

"Dancing on the deck of the *Titanic,* Laura," Brendan said. "I sold all our stocks and put the money into T-bills today."

"Are we going to be okay?" Laura asked, contemplating whether to cancel some of their magazine subscriptions.

"We'll survive," he said. "I prepaid Shannon's college tuition. That's the most important thing. By the way, why were you at Mitch's? We don't have any galas on the horizon, do we?"

"I have a job interview," she said. "It's a copywriter position at FirstStep."

"This is out of left field," he said. "Are you bored with Shannon out of the house?"

"It's more than that," she said, irritated by his quick assumptions.

"When's your interview?"

"Nine tomorrow," she said.

"Don't stay up for me," he said. "Get some rest and blow them away. You can do it."

Laura ended the call with a new sense of urgency. It was no longer just about relieving her boredom or reasserting her value to the outside world; her family might need the money.

A few minutes before nine the next morning, she stepped out of the car and studied her reflection in the car window. A gray A-line skirt, a white silk blouse, a wide black belt with a gold buckle, a simple gold necklace with a pearl pendant, sheer stockings, and black pumps. Sharp. Modern. Confident. She walked tall into the main lobby, where a gray-haired woman in a knee-length red plaid pleated skirt and black pashmina shawl led her to Randy's office. Laura worried that she was overdressed.

She extended her hand to Randy as she entered the office, but he blankly motioned for her to sit on the couch. How much had Dianne twisted his arm to agree to this meeting? She quickly adjusted her approach, skipping the pleasantries and handing him her résumé and the example fundraising materials she had made.

"I did my homework, Mr. Bauer. I hope you like my work," she said. It felt strange addressing a man her age as "Mister."

Randy gathered the materials, settled into a beige wing-back chair across from her, and propped his black Chelsea boots on the glass coffee table. As he read through the materials in silence, her stomach twisted. Oh no, she thought. She was overprepared. He knew she was an impostor. After what felt like an eternity, Randy glanced at her and smiled.

"Very impressive," Randy said. "Phi Beta Kappa from Painter College in 1980, fast-tracked at your PR firm, accepted at Columbia. If you hadn't paused your career, I'd be working for you."

"I don't regret my choices," Laura said. "But I must admit that I have much to offer and hope to be a part of FirstStep." She hoped she didn't come across as too defensive or overconfident.

He rose from his chair, grabbed a list from his desk, and handed it to her. "These are the corporate philanthropies we're targeting," he said.

Laura recognized several hedge funds from the list; some were Bren's clients.

"They want to clean up their reputations, and there's no better way than to make a six- or seven-figure donation to charity. Our task is to ensure we're their charity of choice."

Randy did not present himself as the idealist she'd thought he was.

"Whenever board members such as Dianne recommend candidates, I expect to see charlatans in red dresses looking for any excuse to get out of the house. I'm looking for go-getters, not bored housewives."

"I'm a go-getter," she declared. "If you trust me with this list and are willing to give me a week, I'll create a plan of attack. If you like it, the job is mine."

"I'm looking forward to seeing your plan. Next Tuesday at nine a.m. sharp."

●

Laura shared the good news with Bren that night, but he smiled feebly. "Randy doesn't know how lucky he is to have you on the case."

Laura hugged Bren. "Why are you being so supportive?" she asked.

"I'm happy for you," he said. "And I'm so proud of you. You bring back memories of our college days and the early years in the city. You thrive in challenging environments where you can channel your intelligence and competitiveness into something positive instead of hovering over Shannon or trying to squeeze into the skinniest jeans on the planet. The business world suits you."

Laura released the embrace. Had he just complimented or insulted her? She tried to unpack his words. Sure, she had poured her efforts into being a room parent and social coordinator at Shannon's school, which benefited the whole family. Their family ski trips to Vail and Park City were built on the friendships she had nurtured. Her relationship with the head of the school allowed her to advocate for Shannon to get the best teachers, and those teachers went the extra mile for him, changing his grades from A-minuses to A's whenever she questioned them. Certainly, she worked hard to maintain her fitness, but Bren didn't grasp the pressure she felt to keep it up. Some of the other mothers at the school were former models; one was a former ballerina with the New York City Ballet. Nevertheless, she also knew when to step back.

"Are you suggesting I've wasted my life?" she asked.

"Absolutely not," Brendan replied. "I'm just saying this version of you is the one I fell in love with."

Laura was about to blow her stack.

"Please don't find insults in my compliments," he said. "I genuinely support what you're trying to do, and I'm truly happy for you. You'll kill it. I know you will."

Perhaps she *was* trying to find insults. Perhaps she didn't fully trust this version of her husband. But she didn't have time to dwell on it. She had a fundraising plan to develop, and it had to be great.

●

The following Tuesday, Laura styled her hair and applied her Foxy Lady lipstick, which was much more professional-looking than the name suggested. She arrived at Randy's office five minutes before nine—on time without appearing overly anxious. They spent the next hour discussing Laura's plan.

"I love it," Randy said.

"So, do I have the job?" she asked.

"You had the job when you left the office last week. I knew you would come up with a great plan."

●

During her first month on the job, Laura visited all of FirstStep's affiliated schools, sharpened her pitch, and met weekly with Randy to refine their strategy. They needed to strike between Thanksgiving and New Year's, when their target donors would finalize their philanthropic commitments. On the Tuesday before Thanksgiving, Randy stood by his office window, one leg on the sill, gazing at the fading cattails swaying in the marsh.

"We need to nail down this plan tonight. Let's have a working dinner at the new sushi restaurant on Post Road. It's getting rave reviews."

"Shannon is coming home from college tonight," Laura said. "I haven't seen him since I dropped him off in September. Bren and I are taking him to Pete's BBQ, his favorite rib joint."

"Okay. I'll see you in the office tomorrow," Randy said. Laura sensed his disappointment.

But later that afternoon, Bren called. He was stuck at work and might get a hotel room in the city that night. Then Shannon called about a campus party he wanted to attend. He would come home in the morning. She closed her office door and cried. She was anxious to see Shannon, who had become less communicative over the last month, and she needed to hug and talk to him to understand how he was truly doing. But she would have to wait another day. Wiping away her tears, she walked across the hall to Randy's office.

"My family canceled on me."

"I'm sorry about your family," he said with a weak smile. "I still have the reservation."

As darkness settled in, she trailed Randy's Volkswagen Jetta to the restaurant. It struck her as strange that he hadn't canceled the reservation. She parked beside him in the crowded lot, and he hurried to her car to open the door, insisting on carrying her briefcase.

"May I order for you?" Randy asked soon after being seated. He extracted ivory chopsticks from a satin bag tucked in his coat pocket. Laura ripped the paper wrapping off the wooden chopsticks on her place setting.

"You know your way around here," Laura said, "but I'd rather order for myself."

Randy lifted his chopstick to signal the waitress. "A tokkuri of sake and two ochoko, please." He turned to Laura. "I hope you like sake."

His actions irritated her. She remembered how indifferent he had been when they'd first met, and now all this over-the-top chivalry. "None for me," she said. "We have a plan to discuss." She pulled a presentation deck from her briefcase and flipped through it, pausing when the sushi, sashimi, and maki arrived.

"What happened to your family?" Randy asked while loading his plate with raw fish.

"Things came up," she said, stabbing her tuna maki with a chopstick but never bringing it to her mouth. "I'm curious . . . why didn't you cancel the dinner reservation?"

"I've noticed that you work late a lot and thought it might have something to do with things at home. I figured there was a good chance your family dinner would fall through. If you want to talk about it, I'm willing to listen."

Laura tugged at her pearl earring, wondering how he could be so audacious. Yet she had finally found someone who'd let her get her family troubles off her chest. "To be honest," she said, "the financial crisis is putting a strain on us. Plus, Shannon has gone silent with me, which is never a good sign. I don't think he's doing well in college." She explained the conflict between her husband and son.

"The battle between a father's desire for his son and a son's desire for himself is as old as time. Cat Stevens wrote a song about it," Randy said.

Wow, Laura thought, Randy is offering empathy instead of solutions. She didn't know men were capable.

He placed his chopsticks on his plate and waited for her to continue.

Laura told Randy about her troubles at home for the next half hour, and Randy's eyes didn't waver from hers, except to refill their ochoko.

Randy placed his hand on hers. "You're remarkable," he said. "Everything will work out for you. Trust me."

She slid her hand from under his and stood, retreating to a safe space in the restroom. Did he just hit on me? she wondered. She inspected herself in the mirror. The top four buttons on her blouse had come undone. She could see deep into her own cleavage and the inner edges of her bra. Did I invite his actions? Laura wondered, buttoning her blouse up to her neck and returning to the table, where the waitress was delivering a second tokkuri of sake.

"I hope I didn't give you the wrong impression," he remarked.

Now I know, she thought, he did hit on me. "It's been a long day," she said. "And we didn't get any work done here. I'll see you early tomorrow."

She left the restaurant quickly and pulled into her garage a few minutes later, surprised to find Bren's car parked inside. He had come home after all. She straightened her skirt and blouse. "Nothing to feel guilty about," she murmured and went inside.

Brendan

November 2008

Brendan's cell phone rang loudly in the dark. He glanced at the alarm clock. Three a.m. He picked up the phone and saw Shannon's number. This could only mean trouble.

"Why are you calling so late?" Brendan asked, groggy from sleep.

"Mr. O'Shay, this is Burton, Shannon's roommate. You need to help me, Mr. O'Shay. I'm standing over Shannon. He's catatonic."

"Catatonic? Where is he? What's he doing?"

"He went out drinking tonight. Alone. A few minutes ago, he stumbled into our dorm room and passed out on the floor. I can't wake him up. He wet his pants and is lying in a pool of vomit. He's not moving."

"Is he breathing? Burton, is Shannon breathing?"

"Let me check."

Burton went silent for what felt like an eternity.

"Yes, he's breathing."

"Call 9-1-1. I'll get there as quickly as I can. Figure five hours."

Laura was already standing, tugging on her clothes. "I can't believe this is happening again!" she screamed. "Get dressed! Let's go!"

They rushed to the garage and jumped into the Range Rover. "Where did all this snow come from in November?" Brendan asked. "It wasn't in the forecast." He barreled through the heavy, wet snow piling up in the driveway, sped down the street, and nearly fishtailed into the neighbor's mailbox.

"Don't kill us!" Laura yelled.

"I'm not trying to kill us," Brendan shouted. "I'm trying to save our son!"

Laura called the campus police. "My son is passed out on his dorm room floor. Gifford Hall, room 201. He might be dying. Please, please check on him," she begged. Then she called Shannon's phone, hoping his roommate would answer. "Burton, thank you for calling us," she said. "Did the EMT arrive?"

"Yeah, they are wheeling him out now," Burton said.

Brendan shuddered. It had been almost a year since Cassie was wheeled out of her house for the last time. And now, it was Shannon on a stretcher. But he had to get a hold of himself. It was a long way to Vermont and the roads were treacherous.

"Honk, Bren. Let them know to move over," Laura said.

"They'll just slow down if I honk," he said.

"Is every man in the world an asshole?" Laura asked, tears streaming down her face. "I can't handle this. Why is this happening to us? We're a good family. We try to do the right thing. Why are awful things happening to my baby boy?"

A few minutes later, the snowplow drivers pulled off the highway and Brendan hit the gas. He glanced at Laura; her head was in her hands. He turned on Bloomberg Radio, and a crackling voice reported that another bank had failed. He remembered he had scheduled a critical meeting with John Smart and Sarah Whetstone to review their bank's liquidity position. He couldn't miss it.

Laura called the college hospital, but the operator put her on perma-hold. She called back.

"Don't put me on hold again," she insisted. "What's going on with my son, Shannon O'Shay?"

The operator placed her on hold once more. Finally, a nurse picked up.

"They pumped his stomach, but he's still not out of the woods."

"Not out of the woods? What does that mean?"

"Ma'am, I need to hang up and get back to your son. He needs my help."

She turned to Brendan. "This is your fault," she said, pointing a trembling finger at him.

"How can you blame me for Shannon drinking too much at a party?"

"Can't you see? It's more than that," she exclaimed. "First, you made him go to Painter. Next, he smoked pot in the backyard. Then the bar fight. He's been spiraling out of control for months, and you've refused to acknowledge it."

"Pot in the backyard? What are you talking about?"

"Don't try to twist this. You made me dress him in a Painter College onesie when he was three months old!"

"Laura, I know you're freaking out. So am I. But we have to stay calm to get to Painter safely. Our son needs us. Please, as tough as it may seem, we have to work together and support one another. We can talk about everything else later."

Laura stared silently at the falling snow. Brendan squinted through the windshield, listening to the thumping of the wipers. The car's heater emitted a smell of burning metal—still another three hours to Painter Hospital. The last time he had been at the campus hospital was in January of his freshman year in 1977, when Cassie had nearly died visiting him during Winter Weekend. And now, Shannon was in the same hospital on a snowy night. He couldn't shake the terrible irony.

When they arrived at the college hospital, an elderly nurse led them to the room. A tangle of tubes and wires lay across Shannon's chest. Machines beeped and whirred. Laura pulled a chair up close to Shannon and held his limp hand. Brendan noticed the clock on the wall. Damn. He had missed his eight o'clock funding meeting and forgot to inform Sarah and the CEO about his absence. He left the room and called his boss.

"I can't believe you blew off this meeting," Sarah said. "Get your shit together, Brendan."

"My son almost died last night," he shouted. "Don't be such an asshole!"

After a long pause, Sarah finally spoke. "Take care of your son. We'll talk when you get back."

"I don't know when I'll be back. This situation is fluid." Brendan closed his eyes and took a deep breath. "I'm sorry for losing my temper, Sarah. Call me whenever you need me."

"We can manage without you," Sarah said.

"Are you threatening my job?" Brendan asked.

"You're not thinking clearly, Brendan. I'm telling you to take care of your son."

●

They stayed with Shannon all day and night, eating deli turkey on white bread in the hospital cafeteria on Thanksgiving Day. On Friday, Shannon sat up in bed for the first time, sipping ice water through a straw while watching college football on TV. Brendan popped in and out of the room, answering Sarah's questions about his funding plan. Despite her threat, she relied on Brendan's expertise; she could never fire him. He stopped worrying about his job and focused entirely on Shannon.

When the time seemed right, Brendan broached the topic shrouding the room. "How did you get so . . . so sick?"

"I have no clue, Dad. I went to a frat party. The punch must've been spiked."

"Are you sure? Your roommate said you were drinking alone."

"'Alone' means without him. He's such a tool. No one wants to hang out with him. I was at a frat party, Dad. Jesus Christ."

"So this was an accident," Brendan said.

"No. I tried to kill myself," Shannon said sarcastically. "Yes, it was an accident." He turned up the volume on the TV. "Give me a break, Dad. Why don't you ask me if I like being at Painter?"

Brendan ignored the question. "The doctor said you had a high level of Xanax in your system. Do you suffer from anxiety?"

"Seriously, Dad?"

"You were close to dying, Shannon. Please be honest with me."

"You want honesty, Dad? Fine, I'll be honest. You're my problem! You and Mom love this place, but it doesn't work for me."

"This college is tough," Brendan said. "You're feeling the pressure. It happens. I'll talk to the dean. I can help make it easier for you."

"No, Dad. You'll only make it worse. How many times do I have to tell you to stop controlling me?" Shannon fixed Brendan with a fierce gaze. He had Laura's eyes.

"Back off, Bren," Laura said, finally breaking her silence. She grabbed Brendan's arm and pulled him into the hallway. "You have to listen to him, or you'll lose him. We'll lose him . . . forever."

Laura paused as two doctors walked by in the hallway. "And another thing, Bren: If we get through this mess . . . when we get through this mess . . . we'll be going to family counseling. I've already gathered a list of psychotherapists. That's not negotiable."

Brendan felt his face flush. How could she drop this psycho-bullshit bomb on him now? He stomped outside through the snow to his car to try to find the college dean to straighten out this matter. Inside, his breath fogged the windshield. He was without a coat, but he didn't feel cold. On his way to the dean's office, he passed a pack of students who hadn't gone home for Thanksgiving break. They were horsing around, throwing snowballs, and pushing each other into snowbanks. He thought about Cassie in the snowbank again—it marked the beginning of their separation. He had failed her. He couldn't fail Shannon, too. He couldn't walk away from Shannon and expect him to follow. Laura was right. He had to listen. Instead of seeing the dean, he drove to Shannon's dorm room and loaded the car with his things, tossing out the drug paraphernalia he found in a desk drawer. He returned to the hospital room, where Laura was handing Shannon a cracker.

"I've packed your things," Brendan said. "You're coming home with us. And Laura, call the family counselor. I'll do anything to save this family."

Brendan

December 2008

The three men stood shivering on the deck looking down at the icy waves crashing against the shoreline. Three gnarled chokecherry trees bent in the unrelenting wind, reminding Brendan of *Macbeth*'s witches.

"Let's talk inside," Brendan said as he led them to the armchairs near the fireplace inside his house on Cape Cod.

"Where's Laura?" Mark asked as he looked around.

"She's working this weekend to meet an important deadline."

"We're sorry she's not here," Mark said, exchanging glances with Tom. "How's Shannon doing?"

"He hit another speed bump," Brendan said. "But he'll bounce back. Thanks again for getting him out of that skirmish last summer."

"It was more than a skirmish," Tom said. "He was facing three to five years in prison."

Brendan winced. Why couldn't Tom simply accept Brendan's gratitude without throwing daggers at him?

"Tell us about the speed bump," Mark said.

"He overdosed at college," Brendan said, lowering his gaze. "We pulled him out of school for the semester."

"That must be tough on you," Mark said.

Brendan nodded. He couldn't tell if Mark's words were sympathetic or meant to remind him that all was not well on the home front. "Would you guys like a drink? I have beer and wine and can probably scrounge up a bottle of scotch. I'm going to get a glass of water for myself," Brendan said, standing up to go to the kitchen.

"Make that two waters," Mark said.

"Three," Tom added.

Brendan left the room and went to the kitchen sink. His head spun as he gasped for air. He leaned against the counter. Why am I so nervous? he wondered. The guys wouldn't be here if they didn't want the eggs. Yet what did they want to talk about that couldn't have been accomplished over the phone? He closed his eyes and took a few deep breaths. Suddenly, he felt a tap on his shoulder.

"You've been in here awhile. Are you okay?" Mark said.

"Yes. Yes. Of course," Brendan lied. "I must be coming down with something."

"Let me help you with the water," Mark said, taking three glasses from the cabinet and filling them. Brendan gulped it down, then refilled it. They returned to the living room and settled into their chairs by the fireplace.

"I'm assuming you want the eggs," Brendan blurted out.

"Let's start by talking about Cassie's memoir; then we'll get to her eggs," Mark said.

Brendan suddenly regretted giving them the memoir. He feared they were put off by what they had read.

"From reading it, we feel like we know her. The tragic stuff—the effects of DES, her head injury, the physical, mental, and sexual abuse she suffered—saddens us. But she had so much spunk. I can only imagine the courage it took for her to leave her home in Nehoiden to venture alone halfway across the continent to live in a foreign country with strangers," Mark said. "And she almost fulfilled her dream of racing her dogsled team. She had wonderful character traits that we would love to nurture in our child."

Did the guys just commit to taking the eggs? Brendan wondered.

"However . . ."

Oh shit, Brendan thought.

". . . her alcohol abuse gives us pause," Tom said. "And Shannon's drug overdose suggests the gene is still strong in your family's DNA."

Why did Tom have to be such an asshole by dragging Shannon into this? Brendan thought.

"Tom and I talked a lot about her alcoholism," Mark said. "And, unfortunately . . ."

Here comes the rejection, Brendan thought.

". . . alcoholism runs strong in our families, too. There's no way to avoid it. The luck of Irish, I suppose. We'll just have to teach our child how to manage it."

Brendan felt the weight of rejection lift from his shoulders. He could breathe again. "So you want the eggs?"

"We're almost there," Tom said. "But we have a question, not about Cassie but about you."

"Me? What do I have to do with your decision other than signing the eggs over to you?"

"Cassie's memoir gave us a window into your sibling relationship and estrangement," Tom continued. "We have a good understanding of why you're so invested in finding the right match for your sister's eggs. It's admirable that you have taken your role as custodian so seriously, but frankly, it's unusual. Most people in your situation probably would've signed over the eggs to the fertility clinic or had them destroyed or donated to medical research. Your inordinate involvement in the process has raised our question: How much access to your sister's biological child would you expect?"

Yes, Brendan wanted access. He had so much at stake. It was his chance to rectify the debilitating effects of their family system on Cassie: the way she was disadvantaged compared to him, her lost opportunities, his survivor's guilt from the curse of alcoholism that ran through the generations and ensnared her while largely leaving him unscathed, except, of course, for the secondary scars of growing up with an alcoholic parent. And the rapes. He could not imagine how profoundly those unspeakable heinous experiences must have affected her. He wanted to make up for all of it through this child: showering the child with gifts, treating the child to an ice cream cone on a sunny afternoon, and sharing stories from Cassie's childhood, like when she brought home a guinea pig from the local pet shop, lined the pet's cage with wood shavings, and placed it beside her bed. When the time was right, he could share stories from her memoir—not the bad ones, but the good ones about training sled dogs and working with the local veterinarian. He felt that somehow, Cassie would know.

But he had to answer Tom's question carefully. The truth might scare the men away, yet downplaying his desire for a relationship with the child might seem disingenuous.

"A birth announcement, maybe invitations to the baptism or birthday parties, an occasional photo would be nice. Treat me no better or worse than a distant relative," Brendan said.

"We hoped you didn't want any access," Mark said with a frown. "We'll be honest with our child about the circumstances surrounding his or her birth, but we'll leave out details about Cassie, and we definitely won't mention the existence of a biological uncle, aunt, and cousin—at least not until the child is an adult and better equipped to handle such a revelation."

Damn, Brendan thought. He would be nearly seventy years old when the child might possibly learn about his existence.

"We simply don't want interference with how we raise our child," Tom said. "No letters, phone calls, stalking, or peeking at the baby around corners. If you see us walking the child in P-town, we expect you to ignore us. We'll ignore you."

Tom's words hit Brendan like a gut punch. He tried a different approach. "My main goal is to find parents who will give the child the opportunities Cassie never had," Brendan said. "You will be fantastic parents. You'll be nurturing, and you'll fight for your child. I want you to have these eggs, but I don't know if I can give them to you without having some way to know how things turn out."

"Give us a minute," Tom said. He and Mark stepped into the kitchen, out of Brendan's hearing range.

Brendan paced in the living room as the fire slowly burned down. He prayed the guys would reconsider and grant him some access to a child that existed only in the realm of possibility. Still, the child felt real to him. Fifteen minutes later, the guys returned.

"We want Cassie's eggs but not under your conditions," Tom said. "If you change your mind, call us. Meanwhile, we'll continue our search. I'm sorry we wasted each other's time. Just remember, whichever way you decide, you'll live with the uncertainty of never knowing the life this child could have had with us."

"This situation didn't turn out as I had hoped it would," Brendan said.

"I'm sorry," Mark said, embracing Brendan for a beat too long. "You've been searching for the perfect match for your sister's eggs for almost a year. Now you're letting the opportunity slip away just because it doesn't fit your idea of perfection."

"So, 'good enough' is good enough?" Brendan asked.

"'Good enough' is as good as it gets," Mark said.

After the guys drove away, Brendan turned off the lights in the room and gazed out the window into the darkness, reflecting on what had just happened. He believed they were the right guys for the eggs, and if he accepted their conditions, aside from a few administrative tasks, the journey would be over. But now he was at the beginning again. He'd have to negotiate an extension with the egg storage facility or the eggs would be destroyed, and he'd have to endure the long slog of finding the perfect fit. He didn't know what to do. He needed to discuss it with someone who knew him—someone who could help. He started to call Emily. As a doula, she had experience in these matters. But before he finished dialing, he hung up and called Laura. Laura deserved the first call.

"They want Cassie's eggs," Brendan said when Laura answered the phone.

"That's great news, Bren," Laura said. "I knew they would. They'll be great parents. You did a good thing giving the eggs to them."

"I didn't give them the eggs," Brendan said.

"Why?" Laura asked, sounding exasperated.

"They don't want me involved in the child's life. Knowing that Cassie's child is out there, I don't know how I will handle it."

"Bren," Laura said, "this situation isn't about making a right or wrong decision. It's about knowing right from wrong. Do the right thing, not for yourself, but for these guys who deserve to raise their child without interference. Most importantly, do the right thing for the child, assuming there is one, who deserves capable, nurturing, and loving parents like these guys will be."

He hung up and stepped outside onto his deck. It was pitch dark, except for the moonlight illuminating the shoreline. The wind howled in from the northeast, battering the beach grass and sending waves crashing against the dunes. In the sky above, the distant remnants of the Milky Way splattered the sky like a Jackson Pollock canvas—white on black. A cloud shaped like a fire-breathing wolf raced across the moonlit path. He pondered Laura's words. She was right; it was time to move on. He went back inside and called Tom.

"I've reconsidered," Brendan said. "I want you to have the eggs. I'll sign them over to you and instruct the fertility clinic to send the eggs wherever you want them."

Brendan heard Tom telling Mark the news. Mark snatched the phone from Tom.

"You're doing the right thing, Brendan," Mark said. "Thank you. Thank you. Thank you."

"You decide about my access. Wherever, whenever, however," Brendan said, making one last Hail Mary pass, hoping the guys would relent.

"We're sorry. There will be no access," Mark said. "None. Ever. But assuming we have a child, you can trust that we will do everything possible to provide him or her with a beautiful life. That is a guarantee."

Brendan sighed. "That's good enough," he said, but once he hung up, it felt like a lie.

Brendan

February 2009

On Wall Street Bonus Day, dreams come true, especially for the bond traders who have bought memberships in lavish country clubs and shares in Gulfstream jets—all in cash. But 2009 wasn't a typical bonus day. Instead, a grim procession moved in and out of Sarah's office as she handed out goose eggs. Membership at the Garden City Men's Club would be forfeited, and Gulfstream shares would be sold. One trader on his way out slammed Sarah's glass door so hard it shattered into a thousand pieces on her white Berber rug. The next trader out stepped over the crumbled glass, seized the nearest chair, and hurled it into a stack of computers worth a hundred grand.

Brendan bit his lip as glass crunched beneath his black tassel loafers when he entered Sarah's office. She droned on about the weak market performance, the bank, and the fixed-income department. To him, it was white noise. He only cared about one thing—his number. Sarah didn't share tales of woe when she distributed hefty bonuses. The more she spoke, the lower his expectations sank. Before she revealed his number, he made one last-ditch effort (he knew it would be futile) to spare himself from despair. "Look, Sarah, I get why you're cutting back. I won't claim I single-handedly saved us from bankruptcy, but I played a significant role. I hope you've been able to look beyond my John Smart snafu last fall to see that if it weren't for my funding plan, the chair you're sitting on would be in a dank warehouse, ready to be sold in a bankruptcy auction."

"Thank you for saving my chair," she said sarcastically. "That was noble of you." She broke her pencil in half and hurled the pieces across the room into a wastebasket. "You call what you said to Smart a snafu. I call it disloyalty."

"I was trying to be loyal to the the bank in the throes of an existential crisis," he pleaded. He loathed himself for pleading.

"Loyal to the bank?" she said. "People are loyal to people, not to things. I can't believe you've lasted this long on Wall Street if you don't understand that."

"I'm loyal to principles, honesty, and integrity," Brendan said. He had once believed in those words, but now they felt outdated, more appropriate for a bygone era. "Do you want me to pledge fealty to you?"

"That would be a start," she said.

"Is this about my leaving work early on Mondays and Thursdays for family counseling sessions?" He, Laura, and Shannon had been in family therapy since Shannon had dropped out of Painter. On Wall Street, no one gave a shit if your family life fell apart. Most guys were on their second or third marriages. But admitting that your troubled family life affected your performance at work contradicted the Wall Street credo. It showed weakness, and weakness was an unpardonable sin.

"Leaving early hasn't helped your cause," she said.

"I'm trying to do what's right for my family."

"Making money to provide for them is what's right for your family," she said. "Don't forget who pays you the money that allows you to be you." Sarah pointed her thumb at herself.

"Sarah, you don't have any kids, do you?"

"What does that mean?" she said.

"It means exactly what you think it means."

She handed him an envelope, then leaned back in her seat and crossed her arms over her chest. "It's a quarter of what you earned a year ago, better than some other traders around here. And it's deferred for two years. You get zero if you quit before the two years are up or are fired for cause." She formed a circle with her thumb and forefinger. "Zero."

"This is wrong, Sarah," he attempted to shout, but it came out as a whisper. "I've given my heart and soul to this place."

"Spare me, Brendan, and get back to work. There are others out there waiting to get theirs."

Brendan reflected on Sarah's harsh words as he went home that night: "the money that allows you to be you." She was right. He had chosen this career to support his family, but somewhere along the way, he had sacrificed them at the altar of Mammon. His pursuit of money was destroying him.

When he got home, he handed the envelope to Laura. She opened it and threw it to the floor. "How the hell did we end up here?" she exclaimed. "After all you've given to that godforsaken bank, how can they treat you so poorly?"

"My days are numbered. It's only a matter of time before they put a bullet in my head," he said.

"Maybe you should quit, Bren," Laura said.

He could only sigh at the suggestion. Leaving money on the table meant the bank had won. He couldn't bear to walk out the door without all the money he had earned. As long as he was unwilling to leave money behind, he would never quit. The price of freedom was simply too high.

Brendan

March 2009

"Don't tell me those fuckers missed another margin call?" Brendan shouted at an operations clerk in the money wire room, a twenty-two-year-old kid fresh out of City College.

"Please don't shoot the messenger, Mr. O'Shay."

Brendan mumbled "Sorry" and then called his attorney, Bill. "Come over to my trading desk as soon as you can. We have another problem with WTF."

They spoke on the phone with Trey Williamson and Tom Gallagher. When he heard Tom's deep, raspy voice, he was eager to learn the status of the eggs, but it wasn't the right time or place, and, as their written agreement specified, he couldn't even ask.

"WTF needs more than two business days to resolve this situation," Tom explained. "There simply isn't enough market liquidity to sell our collateral at a favorable price. I assure you, liquidating them in this market is the worst course of action you can take."

"You'll drive us to bankruptcy," Williamson shouted. He wasn't bragging about his tennis game or commenting on Sarah's athletic thighs this morning. "We'll take legal action against you for misconduct."

"You bankrupted yourself," Brendan said. "We're selling your collateral. I'll update you on the results when we're finished." He hung up on WTF and handed a list of collateral to the new head of mortgage trading who had replaced Gus shortly after bonus day. Rumor had it that Gus was pissed off about his five-million-dollar bonus, so he left for a bigger job at a rival bank and was pulling in ten-million a year. The new mortgage trading head sold WTF's collateral for $100 million less than the money Brendan had lent to them. WTF was gone, and so was Brendan's chance of earning a bonus next year. He felt sick to his stomach, knowing he had worked so hard, endured so much stress, and prioritized work over family with nothing to show for it—again.

He reported the WTF loss to Sarah. "I hate to say I told you so," Brendan said, "but I knew we made a huge mistake lending money to WTF."

"They'll rise from the ashes," Sarah said.

"All the jerks do," Brendan added. "And speaking of jerks, have you heard from Gus?"

"Fuck Gus," Sarah said.

"Finally, something we can agree on," Brendan said.

During his train ride home, Brendan received a call from Tom Gallagher. "That was a monumental mistake,

Brendan. You overreacted today. I can't believe you did that to my client after everything we've been through."

"A wise man once advised me to compartmentalize my work and personal lives. Have a nice evening, Tom." A smile crossed Brendan's face. He couldn't remember the last time he had smiled.

Brendan got out of his car and heard a thumping sound coming from behind the garage. He went to check it out and saw Shannon under a floodlight, bouncing a lacrosse ball off the wooden rebound wall Brendan had built for him years ago. He smiled for the second time that day; maybe things were improving. *Thump. Thump*. He went into the garage and came out with an old lacrosse stick. *Thump. Thump*. He stood on the edge of the floodlight's glow.

"Do you want to play catch?" Brendan called out.

"Not really, Dad," Shannon replied. "I'm working through some issues." *Thump. Thump*.

"Are you considering playing lacrosse when you return to Painter?" Brendan asked. "You could make the team as a walk-on."

"Dad, it's only been three months since I—"

"Quit," Brendan said, completing Shannon's sentence. "You can't be a quitter forever."

Thump. Shannon caught the ball off the rebound and, in one smooth motion, fired it at Brendan, grazing his ear.

Brendan fell to the ground and watched the ball roll all the way to the end of the yard into Long Island Sound. He thought of Cassie; she would have fired the ball at him too.

"I thought you wanted to play catch?" Shannon said, mocking his father.

Brendan stopped himself from retaliating and went inside, where he found Laura working at her desk in the study, her tortoiseshell Ben Franklin reading glasses perched on the tip of her nose. She glanced at him over her neatly organized stacks of paper.

"You have your look of shame. What did you do now?"

"I called Shannon a quitter for refusing to return to Painter," he confessed.

"After all the work we've put into family counseling, you regressed to that mindset?"

"Shannon fired a lacrosse ball at my head. He nearly killed me."

"If he wanted to hit you," she said, "you'd still be on the ground. He's reaching out to you. He's trying to break through your tough, demanding exterior. He wants you to open up to him on his terms, not yours. He doesn't want to go back to Painter. Get that fantasy out of your mind. He's been talking about seeing the country. Why don't you go on a road trip with him? You can satisfy your inner Jack Kerouac. It might be good for both of you."

When Brendan was Shannon's age, he read *On the Road* and dreamt about traveling across America on a motorcycle. But school turned into work, and almost thirty years later, he found himself trapped in a version of the American Dream that had turned into a nightmare. He pictured himself with Shannon behind the wheel of an Airstream RV, driving through the American Southwest, mountain biking on desert trails in Moab, Sedona, and Zion. Cold mountain waterfalls. Campfires. Cowboy coffee. Genuine conversations with his son. Had he ever actually listened to what his son was saying without formulating a counterargument to impose his parental will upon him?

"Shannon would never agree to that," Brendan said, frowning. "Plus, I'm overwhelmed with so much work that I'll never find a way out."

"You won't be getting a bonus next year, and they're threatening to fire you. We have money in the bank. Maybe it's time to think about resigning," Laura said.

"That's a major decision," Brendan said. "I want to leave, but can you manage having me around the house?"

"I love my new job, Bren. You should love yours too. We don't need this house or this lifestyle. We can downsize and still be happy. Change would be good for us."

It felt as though a thousand-pound weight had been lifted from his shoulders. Would he have the courage to quit in the middle of his career? If not now, when? "Let's sit with this idea," Brendan said. "If we still feel the same way in a month, I'll quit."

"I've already made my decision," Laura said. "But take your time until you feel ready. In the meantime, I'll try to persuade Shannon to take a road trip with you."

Brendan

April 2009

"I've spent my entire career at this bank," Brendan said, sitting on the couch in Sarah's office. "When my wife went into labor, I worked until the very last moment and barely made it to the hospital to witness the birth of my only child."

Sarah glanced at her watch.

"I'm resigning," he said.

"Resigning? We're in the worst financial crisis since the Great Depression, Brendan. Man up! You can't bail now. Did you get another job offer? From whom? We'll match it."

"I'm not leaving for another job. I'm just leaving. You ask for too much—my heart, my soul, my entire being. I've sacrificed too much for this bank at the expense of my family."

"For unto whomsoever much is given, of him much shall be required," Sarah said.

"I know my catechism," Brendan said. "But enough is enough."

"Take the day off," she said. "Reconsider what you're about to do. We'll talk again tomorrow."

"I've thought and thought and thought," he said. "I won't reconsider. I hope you have the decency to pay me my deferred compensation on my way out. I deserve to get what I've earned."

"Is that what we're talking about here—your deferred comp?" she asked.

"It's everything," he said. "It's about money. It's about dignity. It's about respect. It's about who I was, who I am, and who I want to be. I've never quit anything in my life— not junior high football, not a paper route, not school, not a team, not a job, not anything—even when I've wanted to. This is a difficult moment for me."

"I don't deal in sympathy, Brendan," she said. "It's not who I am."

"For unto whomsoever much is given, of *her* much shall be required," he said.

"Touché," Sarah said. She called John Smart and explained the situation.

"Sorry, Brendan. Loyalty has its rewards, and once again, you're being disloyal. We'll use your deferred comp to pay the people who aren't abandoning us. But if it's any consolation, I did try. You have an hour to pack your things and get out of the building. Have a good life."

Brendan knew his request would be dead on arrival, and it crossed his mind to threaten to sue the bank, but that would just prolong his agony. Instead he reached out his hand toward Sarah.

"I won't shake the hand of Judas," she said. "Leave my office now."

On his way back to his desk, Brendan brushed shoulders with his assistant manager, who was heading to Sarah's office. Out with the old, in with the new. He called Laura but got her voicemail. "It's done," he said. "They're not giving me my deferred compensation, but I'm free." He gathered his belongings in a small cardboard box—a photo of his wife holding their infant son, a paperweight celebrating his promotion to managing director, a worn-out black squeeze ball, and a couple of old neckties that he kept in his bottom drawer—tucked the box under his arm, and shook hands one last time with the people in his department. Then he walked out of the building for the final time. Twenty years. Gone.

Laura

Early May 2009

Laura sat on Shannon's bed, holding his sketchbook of the students at FirstStep. Randy Bauer had offered to show Shannon's artwork to his friend on the board at the Savannah College of Art and Design. She flipped to the first image, showing students gathered around a whiteboard filled with mathematical equations. The second depicted a teacher leaning over a girl's shoulder as she wrote an essay. The third captured students playing mixed doubles tennis on the playground. She wondered where her son had gotten his talent. She and Bren couldn't draw a stick figure.

As she turned the page, she was struck with the idea to use Shannon's sketches to promote FirstStep and persuade donors to become marquee sponsors of the upcoming fund-raising campaign.

She started opening desk drawers to see if Shannon had stored more sketchbooks in his room. They weren't in his desk drawers, so she checked the bottom drawer of his dresser. Isn't that where we hide things? she thought, but it was stuffed with old sweatshirts. The next drawer up was stacked with blue polo shirts and khaki pants, Westport Academy's student uniform in the spring. She stuck her hands under the shirts and struck something solid, pulling out a porcelain pipe and a plastic vial of marijuana buds. Damn! He hadn't stopped smoking. She closed the drawer and paused before moving up to the next one. Was she breaking one of the unwritten commandments between a mother and son—thou shalt not snoop? No, she rationalized. It was for his own good. His sketchbooks might be his ticket into SCAD.

The next drawer up held his athletic clothing. She lifted up a stack of gym shorts and out fell a pink yoga top, white leggings, and—oh, shit—a pair of black, sheer bikini panties. She pinched the panties between thumb and index finger and held them up, wondering how a woman—had she just called Ines a woman?—could fit into these tiny things. She sighed deeply and laughed out loud. They were in college. Of course they were having sex. She rummaged around some more. Ah, there it was, wrapped in Ines's Wellesley College T-shirt. Laura carried it to Shannon's bed and opened it.

The first page was a portrait of Ines, her brooding eyes, sculpted nose, full lips, and pointed chin framed by long curls cascading off the bottom of the page. How was Shannon able to capture the hue of her light brown skin with just a charcoal pencil? Ines seemed almost alive.

The next page showed Ines's hands—perfectly rendered tendons, knuckle creases, and a half-bitten nail on her ring finger, adorned with her grandmother's silver wedding band. Next page. The nape of Ines's neck with a yin-yang tattoo in the hollow between her shoulder blades. Next page. The curvature of her lifted breasts, dark nipples, and a barbell nipple ring. Is it real or artistic liberty? she wondered. Next page. Ines's flat belly with protruding hip bones tapering down toward her pubis. Next page. The sketch puzzled Laura. She turned it sideways. It portrayed Ines's leg from mid-thigh down, drifting at a peculiar angle, accentuating the bump of her kneecap and the flex of her calf. Her foot pointed skyward with slender toes spread wide. A tiny pair of bikini panties—the same pair I'm holding? she wondered—dangled from Ines's big toe. Next page. Laura nearly dropped the sketchbook onto the floor. Oh, boy. It resembled one of Georgia O'Keeffe's flower paintings, but it wasn't. The tufted flower trailed into muscular quadriceps that undulated like the foothills near Ghost Ranch outside Santa Fe.

Laura sighed loudly again. She found what she'd been looking for, a sketchbook with examples of Shannon's prodigious talent, but what could she do with it other than dress it back in Ines's T-shirt and, like a guilty thief, put it back in the drawer exactly how she had found it.

●

"I want to leave this dinner with a million-dollar pledge from Bigstar," Randy whispered to Laura as they entered

The Plantation, a mahogany and leather-clad dining club located in a converted mansion on the tip of Tod's Point in Old Greenwich. Bigelow Bigstar was the principal partner at Bigstar Capital, a hedge fund specializing in distressed debt, which meant it was a bottom feeder that bought delinquent mortgages from undercapitalized banks, evicted homeowners, and flipped those mortgages for a hefty profit.

It wasn't Laura's practice to notice the race, gender, or ethnicity of servers and patrons when entering an establishment, but The Plantation felt like the Antebellum South.

Bigstar greeted them at the table. It was the first time she had met him, and although she'd done her homework on him and seen his photograph in *Town & Country* magazine, his physical presence was overwhelming. He towered over Randy and her with broad shoulders like a professional football lineman, and had a tanned face and hands like a professional sailor. In all her years living around moneyed people, he stood out like a unicorn.

"I've already ordered for us," Bigstar announced. "Randy and I will be having steak cooked rare, and Laura will be having black sole with a medley of fresh vegetables."

Laura shook her head. "Bigelow, I appreciate your effort, but I prefer to order for myself."

"Don't be offended, Laura. I like to move things along," he said. "And my assistant did her research. I'm confident you'll be more than satisfied with my choices."

Not another one of these pompous turds, Laura thought. She excused herself to the ladies' room, where a Latina attendant turned the faucet and handed Laura a linen hand towel. When she returned, the meal had arrived and Bigstar had loaded his fork with a chunk of steak, a dollop of mashed potatoes, and a spear of asparagus.

"I can tell you're judging this place, Laura," Bigstar remarked. "And you're judging me."

"I'm not judging," she insisted.

"You are," he said. "And I'm glad you are. This place is deplorable. But it's where I can get business done, and I owe it to my investors to maximize profits. I know, I'm a member of the class that's been exploiting the weak since the Massachusetts Bay Company settled the land beneath us in 1640. I can't change that. But I have compassion in my heart, too. And that's why I agreed to this meeting after Randy sent me your brochure. Loved the artwork. I knew a little about your program, but I had my assistant do a deep dive on you guys. You're doing good work, and I want to support you. It'll make me feel better about myself." Bigstar turned to Randy. "Let's avoid the bullshit, 'cause I hate bullshitting. What's your ask?"

Laura kicked Randy under the table.

"Five large, Bigelow," Laura interjected. "You should be at the top of our donors' list, where a person of your stature belongs."

"I saw the kick, Laura," Bigstar said. "Great job reading the room. My guess is you came in here looking for a million bucks. Count me in for five." He stretched his arms wide, knocked a tray of bloody porterhouse steaks onto the floor, and ignored the waiter who kneeled to pick up the ruined food. Laura recognized the waiter as the father of a girl in the FirstStep program. She felt the urge to help him clean up the mess but averted her eyes instead and hoped he didn't recognize her. She didn't want to lose focus on Bigstar.

"For your generosity, you'll receive exclusive top billing in our marketing materials and media campaign," Laura said, glancing back at the waiter on his knees. No one was rushing to help him.

"I don't usually engage in win-win deals, but this looks like one," he said, raking his large, tanned hand through his long white mane. She noticed the diamond-encrusted 2008 New York Giants Super Bowl ring on his finger.

"It was a gift from the Mara family," Bigstar said. "We're old friends." Bigstar shoved his ring finger into his mouth, slicking it with saliva, then slid off the ring and handed it to Laura. "Try it on," he said.

She hid her revulsion and slid it over her ring and pinky fingers at the same time. There was room to spare.

"Keep it," Bigstar said, winking at Laura.

"This has to be worth . . ." she said.

"The cost doesn't matter," he said.

Laura smiled. She had no idea what to do with it, but she knew that if she rejected his gift, she'd bruise his ego, and so much depended on her stroking his ego.

"I'm looking forward to working together," he said, shaking Laura's hand and giving Randy a perfunctory nod.

"Let's toast to the deal with a bottle of Macallan Twenty-Five." Bigstar threw his paw in the air, and soon the waiter arrived with a bottle of scotch and three tumblers. Bigstar and Randy downed their shots and tapped their tumblers on the table, signaling the waiter to pour another round.

"Why aren't you drinking with us, Laura?" Randy asked.

"I'm toasting the spirit of the deal with good thoughts," Laura said, "but I know my limits when it comes to drinking brown booze."

"I like people who know their limitations," Bigstar said, nodding at Randy, who was pouring his fourth shot.

A few minutes later, the waiter arrived with the chit, and Randy reached for his credit card.

"My club, my dime," Bigstar said. "I don't want you getting fired for ordering a three-thousand-dollar bottle of booze." He signed the chit and handed the half-empty bottle to the waiter. "This is for your cleaning up my mess earlier tonight. Enjoy it with the boys in the kitchen."

The waiter smiled and walked away.

"Laura, you were troubled by my interaction with the waiter after I knocked his food on the floor."

"You ignored him," she said.

"Oh yes, I did," Bigstar said. "You see, we play a little charade, the waiters and I. I pretend to be a racist, and they pretend to tolerate it. But I want you to know that I pay his daughter's tuition at FirstStep, and I'll cover her tuition at Greenwich Academy, where I've already secured her admission. I'll pay for her college and graduate school education because she's a superstar, and I'm committed to ensuring she has every opportunity to reach her potential. So, Laura, as the old saying goes, don't judge a book by its cover."

Outside The Plantation, Bigstar's driver arrived in a blue Bentley, and Bigstar disappeared into the back seat. Moments later, a valet delivered Randy's Volkswagen.

"You ought to let me drive you home, Randy," Laura said. "I don't want to see your name in the police blotter for a DUI arrest."

The valet parked Randy's car and returned with Laura's. She helped Randy into the passenger seat. He chortled effusively the entire way home. "We bagged the white elephant," he kept repeating, sounding less coherent with every utterance.

Laura pulled up to Randy's townhouse.

"Come in for a nightcap to celebrate our win," he said, reeking of garlic and whiskey, apparently forgetting that Laura had abstained during dinner.

"Good night, Randy. And congratulations. We did it."

Randy opened his mouth as if to speak, then suddenly flung the car door wide open, leaned out, and vomited onto the pavement. He stepped out, landing in his own mess, and he stumbled to his front door. Laura wondered why her friend Dianne and the other board members tolerated his behavior. Before long, either she or Randy would have to leave. She'd be damned if it were her.

Brendan

June 2009

Sunrays poured through the window of the Airstream RV parked in the camping area of the South Rim of Grand Canyon National Park, waking Brendan. He stepped outside, where Shannon sat on a log, enjoying his coffee under the trees, sketching a red-tailed hawk perched on a nearby branch. The rich, nutty aroma mingled with the scent of fir and spruce.

"How about hiking the Bright Angel Trail to Indian Gardens?" Brendan suggested. "The trailhead's a short walk from here, then five miles down and five miles back up."

"Great idea, Dad," Shannon said.

Brendan felt Shannon becoming more receptive to him. He was profoundly thankful to Laura for proposing the trip.

"Mind if I peek at your sketches?" Brendan asked. Shannon handed him the sketchbook.

Shannon had filled a sketchbook with drawings from their three-day mountain biking trip along the hundred-mile

White Rim Trail in Moab, Utah, and hikes through Bryce Canyon, Zion, and the Escalante Staircase. His sketches of the rugged terrain, black-tailed jackrabbit, roadrunners, and bobcats could have been included in a naturalist's guidebook. The drawings of the wild-eyed people they encountered on the trails reminded Brendan of the Frederic Remington paintings he had seen at the Metropolitan Museum in New York.

"Where did you learn to draw so well?" Brendan asked.

"Whenever I needed to escape the pressure cooker you put me in, I sketched," Shannon said, sipping his coffee and gazing over the rim of his cup at Brendan.

Ouch, Brendan thought; his earlier conclusion that Shannon was accepting him had been premature.

"Do you remember meeting that old man with the gnarly walking stick and the prophet's beard at Bryce Canyon?" Shannon asked, shifting the topic.

"How could I forget?" Brendan mused. "I kept waiting for him to reveal his stone tablets."

"I walked with him on your day of rest. His name is Jim Merriman. He's an eighty-year-old artist who lives in a log cabin in Talkeetna, a town of seven hundred people about two hours north of Anchorage, Alaska, near Denali National Park. Before that, he lived in a mobile home in the Southwest, beach huts along the Northern California coast, and cold-water flats in Monterey and Santa Cruz."

"I've never heard of Talkeetna," Brendan said, noticing the calmness in Shannon's face and voice.

"He showed me photos of his charcoal sketches and watercolors displayed in small museums across the West—Tuba City, Arizona; Monterey, California; Bend, Oregon; and Talkeetna. Then he demonstrated techniques to bring my sketches to life, focusing on small details: the angle of the pencil and the sweep of the hand. He mentioned that I could contact him if I wanted to learn more."

"Cool," Brendan said, giving Shannon a friendly pat on the shoulder. "Tell me more about him on our hike into the canyon. Are you ready for it?"

"The question is, are you ready?" Shannon tucked his sketchbook into his day pack and stood up from the log he was sitting on.

Brendan noticed a friendlier shift in Shannon's tone. He hoped it would last.

They packed their knapsacks with energy bars, water, sunscreen, and extra socks and marched to the trailhead. Shannon rubbed beeswax balm on his lips and sunscreen on his face. He then put on his glacier sunglasses, which had dark lenses and leather sidewalls to shield his corneas from the reflective light. He adjusted his red and black Wu-Tang Clan baseball cap, the flat brim angled slightly off-center on his brow.

They were a few steps down the trail when Brendan put on his wide brimmed white canvas hat and threw his arm around Shannon's shoulder. When Shannon shrugged his arm away, Brendan realized he was trying to rush their reconciliation. Rome wasn't built in a day, he thought. They quietly descended the trail, passing layers of red, brown, green, and gray earth along five miles of switchback walls deep into the canyon. Condors glided in wide spirals in the vast expanse beneath the canyon's rim. A tourist helicopter swooped into the canyon, causing the condors to scatter. Three hours later, they arrived at the Indian Garden campground, sat in the shade of cottonwood trees, and refilled their water bottles.

"You're sweating, Dad," Shannon remarked. "Hand me your T-shirt."

They peeled off their shirts and Shannon plunged them into a crystal-clear babbling brook, wrung them out, and handed Brendan's back to him. The cold wet fabric made his skin tingle. "It feels great, Shannon."

Shannon pulled on his wet shirt, and it clung to his ribs. Brendan desperately wanted to tell Shannon to eat more and lift weights, but Laura had warned him not to judge.

"When Mom proposed this trip, I had serious doubts. Being alone with you in an RV for a month felt like a death sentence," Shannon said. "I mostly agreed to do it to please Mom."

Brendan winced.

"Honestly, Dad, I'm glad the way it's turning out."

Brendan felt like he was soaring with the condors. He resisted the urge to hug Shannon.

"Next time we're here, we should hike from the south rim to the north rim," Shannon said.

"Why not do it right now?" Brendan asked.

"Because we aren't prepared, Dad, but we didn't come this far to miss the Colorado River," Shannon said. "It's just another mile to Plateau Point. We'll get an incredible view from there—that's what Jim said after I mentioned we were coming here."

"Lead the way," Brendan said.

When they reached Plateau Point, a rocky outcrop that jutted out over the abyss, Shannon took out his charcoal pencil and sketchbook and began to draw. Brendan watched as his son brought to life on paper the lizards scurrying over rocks, the condors soaring on thermals, and the river winding through the canyon floor. When Shannon was done, they hiked up the canyon trail, arriving back at the south rim in the late afternoon. Shannon grilled hamburgers outside the Airstream while Brendan relaxed on a bench beneath the fir trees. A warm breeze brushed past him as he closed his eyes and breathed in the scent of the barbecue. They were taking baby steps together. It felt good.

Laura

August 2009

"Bigelow Bigstar here," the voice boomed through the phone and overwhelmed the steady drone of the air conditioner in Laura's office. "Let's have dinner. Tonight. To discuss your future." Laura hadn't seen or heard from Bigstar since he drove off in his blue Bentley after their closing dinner a few months earlier. She still had his Super Bowl ring in her safe at home.

"My future?" she asked.

"We'll talk at L'Ours. I hope you like wild game. My driver will pick you up at seven."

Oh great, Laura thought, more hunks of bloody meat and mashed potatoes, but this time au gratin. She tried to wiggle out of the invitation. "My husband and son are coming home from a long road trip tonight."

"They can wait a little longer. You won't want to miss this dinner," Bigstar said.

"I need to be home by ten," Laura said.

"Plenty of time," he said, and hung up.

Bigstar's driver picked her up at seven. As she settled into the back seat of the blue Bentley for the half-hour drive from Westport to Greenwich, she smelled the fragrance of orange and bergamot mixed with lavender and neroli. It was Floris No. 89, the cologne her father used to wear. She fidgeted with the television monitor in the back of the limousine.

"Would you like to watch Fox News, ma'am?" the driver asked.

"CNN," Laura replied.

She arrived at the restaurant during the anouncement that Senator Ted Kennedy had passed away. The driver opened the door for her and a petite French-speaking woman guided her to Bigstar's table overlooking a blooming perennial garden containing purple Russian sage, yellow goldenrod, purple New England aster, and lavender arranged between variegated hosta with a gravel path on the outside and aged stones along the border like a perfect French country garden. It reminded her of visiting Claude Monet's garden in Giverny when Shannon was still in a stroller. She sat down and the waiter poured her a glass of fine Burgundy.

"I'm happy with the FirstStep deal," Bigstar said. "It's rare that I'm happy."

"It's not a deal," Laura responded. "It's a long-term philanthropic investment to close the educational gap between the Black and Latino children in Bridgeport and the mostly white kids in Westport. It's a lifeline for their future."

"Everything's a deal for me. And another thing: We're both straight shooters. I appreciate that you say 'Black and Latino' instead of the meaningless term 'underserved.' You call a—"

"I call it as I see it," Laura said.

"That's right," he said with a nod. "I'll explain why you're here. FirstStep is in reasonably good hands with Randy. He has a drinking problem, but he's an adequate manager as far as I can see. You, however, are wasting your talents there. The ceiling is too low, and they're paying you squat. I never took a job where I was underpaid. It's un-American. I have a much better opportunity for you at my foundation, which sponsors Future Big Stars. Get it? FBS coordinates educational services with local school districts in dirt-poor Native American communities in New Mexico. The program teaches parents reading and math skills so they can read to their kids and help with math homework. The science behind the impact of positive parental role modeling is irrefutable. It's something we do for our kids without a second thought, but for these proud people, it's a systemic roadblock that's existed since the cavalry confined them to these reservations. I seeded FBS with twenty million a few years back, but the executive director struggles with fundraising and is a terrible administrator to boot. I don't tolerate mediocrity, not when my name's on it."

"Do you want me to help the executive director?" Laura asked.

"I want you to *be* the executive director," Bigstar said, taking a hearty sip of wine.

She thought she was there to discuss FirstStep, not to leave the nonprofit for a bigger job with Bigstar. Did she have the chops for an ED role? Did she want to invest the time and energy it would require? Would she have to relocate to New Mexico? Did she want to work for this character, Bigstar? He would be constantly in her face.

"I don't have any experience as an ED," she said.

"Bullshit. You already know everything you need to know. You know how to raise money. You have smart ideas. You've got what it takes. I need you to hold the ED title so you're seen as the expert when you're out raising dough. You can hire an assistant to backfill on the admin crap. Headquartered in Port Chester. Pays one-fifty. Chump change. I can't understand how people get by on that paltry sum, but it's not bad pay in your field. The job starts September 15. You can even bring in that graphic artist of yours. He's talented."

"He's my nineteen-year-old son."

"I don't give two shits about nepotism. I want quality."

Laura's gaze shifted past Bigstar to the mural of wrestling grizzly bears behind him. She needed to respond quickly and assertively. "Before we get ahead of ourselves, a few things are nonnegotiable. First, you can't interfere with me. Second, I want a salary of three-fifty, not one-fifty. If those requirements work for you, I'll consider your offer," she said.

"Done," Bigstar bellowed, wrapping his enormous paw around her hand as he stood up. "Dinner's over, Laura."

"We haven't even ordered yet," she said.

"I have another dinner tonight where I'll be taking money from investors instead of giving it to you. Trust me, I'm even better at that game. Feel free to order and take it home to your family." He dropped his white linen napkin onto the table.

"No thanks, Bigelow. I'll follow you out."

As they were leaving, the maître d' approached Bigelow, bowing. "Did we upset you, Mr. Bigstar?"

"Of course not. Charge me for two meals and a bottle of wine, and add 25 percent for my waiter."

The maître d' bowed once more and rushed off as Laura rummaged through her handbag, searching for the Super Bowl ring that Bigstar had given her during their first meeting.

"I'm returning the ring, Bigelow. I appreciate the gesture, but . . ."

"It was a gift, Laura. If you don't want it, auction it off at a fundraiser in your new job. Give the dough to the Native Americans you'll be serving," he said. "Or do with it whatever you want. It's yours. Now take the blue Bentley home," he said. "I'll take this one." He pointed to a yellow Bentley parked in front of the blue one.

She settled into the plush back seat and tried to make sense of Bigelow Bigstar. On one hand, he was a zealous, narcissistic, overconfident blowhard. On the other, he was a kind philanthropist aiming to make a real difference in the lives of those less fortunate than him. She pushed herself to look beyond his mannerisms and see the heart of the man. He said he would give her the autonomy and resources to succeed. And he believed in her. Her only question was whether she believed in herself.

When she arrived home, the house was dark and empty. She set her handbag on the counter and loaded that morning's breakfast dishes into the dishwasher. Then she heard car doors slamming in the driveway. She hurried to the front hall and opened the door to find Shannon and Bren on the front steps. She hugged her son until he wriggled free. "How was the trip?" she whispered to Shannon.

"Great," he replied softly. "Dad was great."

They stepped into the front foyer, and Bren kissed her cheek. "Put down your bags," she said. "Let me make you something to eat."

Shannon's cell phone rang, and Laura heard the faint sound of a girl's voice.

"I'm not hungry, Mom, and Ines wants to see me," Shannon said, hurrying out the door. She watched him speed down the street in his Jeep.

"Are you hungry, Bren?"

"We ate on the plane," he replied, "but I'll have a coffee."

She brewed a pot and poured him a cup. "Tell me all about the trip," she said.

"Let's go outside, and I'll fill you in," he said, holding her hand, leading her to the Adirondack chairs at the water's edge. He spoke for an hour, sharing every detail and summarizing it by saying, "I think Shannon might like me."

"Is there anything else about the trip?" she asked, not wanting to let a single detail slip by her.

"I'm too tired to talk," Brendan said. "Tell me your stories. Are you running the nonprofit yet?"

"Not FirstStep, but I might be running another one founded by Bigelow Bigstar."

"He's a caricature of a big swinging dick—straight out of a Tom Wolfe novel. But he has the Midas touch. How'd you get connected with him?"

"Networking," she said. "I told you about him last winter, but you were too preoccupied. He donated five million dollars to FirstStep, and tonight at dinner he asked me to run his nonprofit."

"What's the name? I might know it."

"It's called Future Big Stars," she said.

"Of course it is," Brendan said with a laugh. "In bold block letters at the top."

"I still have research to do, but I have a gut feeling it's making a positive impact. It supports education on Native American reservations."

"With Bigstar involved, you have power and money backing it—two key ingredients for success," Brendan said.

"I'm a little worried I don't have the skills to succeed," Laura admitted. "I haven't managed anything in my life."

"If anyone has the talent, you do," he said with a smile. "You can do anything you set your mind to."

The wind picked up. She wished she was wearing a sweater. Instead, she got up from her chair and curled up in Bren's lap. He hadn't been this supportive in such a long time.

"My other concern about leaving FirstStep is upsetting Randy. He's good friends with a trustee at the Savannah College of Art and Design and believes he can help Shannon get in."

"SCAD is an excellent school, but don't make the same mistake I did and try to force it down Shannon's throat."

"Are you my husband or did an alien snatch your body somewhere in the Southwest Desert and replace you with an empathic body double?" Laura asked, smiling.

"I learned the hard way," Brendan said. "I never want to put our family in that position again. It's his life, his journey."

"Wow," she exclaimed. "You *did* have an amazing trip."

Bren rose from the Adirondack chair, holding Laura in his arms. She could feel how his recent outdoor activities had made him lean and muscular. He picked her up and carried her across the lawn, her long legs dangling, her arms looped around his neck. She caught a whiff of his faint body odor. Her heart raced. Was she attracted to him because they'd spent a month apart, or was she reminded of the man she fell in love with at Painter? She tilted her chin up to meet his gaze, her mouth suddenly filled with saliva.

She parted her lips and kissed him as he carried her upstairs and gently placed her on the bed. She wanted to tug off his shirt and undo his belt, but it felt so out of character.

"I can't handle this, Bren," she said. "It's been a long day."

"It's been a long few years," he said.

"It's been a long few decades," she added.

"We need to find our mojo again," he said, smiling.

"Just because Ines gave Shannon a booty call doesn't mean I'm giving one to you."

"What's holding you back?" he asked.

Nothing, she thought. Nothing was holding her back. She wrapped her arms around his waist and pulled him on top of her.

Laura woke up and lifted the sheet. She couldn't remember the last time she had slept naked. She tugged the sheet up to her neck and glanced at Bren lying on his back. Shadows from the morning sun accentuated his shoulder and chest muscles, and his belly appeared thinner and tighter. In that light and at that angle, if not for the gray hair at his temples, he could easily have been mistaken for someone in his early forties—ten years younger than he had looked the day he left for his trip with Shannon. She sat up and studied his eyes to make sure he was asleep, then she scrambled out of bed to her walk-in closet, put on some underwear, a T-shirt, and a long satin robe, and headed downstairs to the kitchen. She poured herself a coffee and sat in the breakfast nook, watching the calm waters of Long Island Sound lapping against their boat, trying to sort through everything that had happened the night before. As she rose to pour a second cup, Shannon entered the kitchen from the garage, wearing the same clothes he'd had on when he answered Ines's booty call. She felt the urge to lecture him about unwanted pregnancy and how it could ruin Ines's dreams—and his, too—but she hesitated.

Shannon pressed a kiss to her forehead and took the cup from her. "Thanks, Mom. You timed that perfectly."

She smiled and poured herself another cup.

"Your dad said that you had a wonderful trip."

"It started off a bit rocky," Shannon said. "I almost bailed after the first few days, but we discussed things and set some ground rules. By the end of the trip, I was sure I had never met the version of Dad I was traveling with. He was so accepting and so much fun. Now I understand why you married him in the first place."

Strangely, Shannon's words brought her comfort. The Bren she had made love to the night before was the old Bren. She smiled.

"Your dad mentioned that you met an artist in Bryce Canyon and plan to keep in touch with him," Laura said.

"His name's Jim Merriman, an old Alaskan guy. As I rounded a dirt spire, he was on a rock with his sketchbook on his lap, capturing the sunlight with his charcoal pencil and putting it down on paper. It was magical. It reminded me of how Edward Hopper painted light, but Jim was doing it with charcoal instead of oil paint," Shannon said. "I watched him for an hour. We talked about art, travel, and life on the American road—topics you'd find in books by Kerouac or Steinbeck. Jim taught me some tricks."

Shannon dashed to the front hall, where he had left his backpack, and returned with a sketchbook. "Take a look," he said, handing it to her.

The sketches transported Laura to an unfamiliar world. She glanced up at Shannon, who was refilling his cup of coffee and topping off hers.

"You know, Shannon, I'm thinking about taking a new job and might have a freelance sketching opportunity for you in September."

"We'll see, Mom."

"You can earn good money," Laura said, wondering when that had become a valid reason to pressure him into anything. "You could even take a few art classes at Norwalk Community College, not that you need them." She was dying to mention her contact at SCAD but remembered Bren's advice.

"We'll see," Shannon said, grabbing a piece of toast and taking it with his coffee to his bedroom. Half an hour later, he returned to the kitchen, his long, damp hair pulled back in a ponytail, wearing a clean Grateful Dead T-shirt and black sweatpants, and twirling his keychain around a finger.

"Where are you going?" she asked.

"To Ines's house," he said. "We'll figure out what to do from there."

She hugged him. "It's wonderful to have you back, Shannon," she said.

"It's nice to be back, Mom," he said with a smile. Then he went outside, hopped in his Jeep, and drove away.

Hours later, Bren came downstairs. He was showered, and dressed in a golf shirt and Bermuda shorts. His face was clean-shaven, and he left a refreshing soap scent behind when he kissed her on the cheek.

"When do you have to let Bigstar know if you're taking the job?" he asked.

"He didn't give me a specific deadline, but knowing him, the answer is 'yesterday.'"

"Which way are you leaning?" he asked.

Wow, so many questions about me, Laura thought. She loved the attention. "I've been online, learning as much as possible about Bigstar and his charitable organization. It seems solid, but there are some clear gaps that I can fill to improve it."

"How will you tell Randy you won't be his anymore?"

Laura suddenly averted her eyes. The way Bren asked the question made her wonder if he somehow knew about Randy's advances.

"I'll just tell him," she said. "It's business. Right?"

"If you say so," he said. "I know he'll miss having you."

She studied his facial expression and eyes. Was he probing for something more? "Are you suggesting that I turn down Bigelow's offer?"

"Not at all," he said, patting her shoulder and gazing into her eyes. "You're a talented person committed to a cause. Any boss would be elated to have you, and any boss would be devastated to see you leave."

"I plan to accept the position today," she said, "and I'll call Randy immediately afterward to resign."

"Smart," Brendan said. "In Randy's case, bad news doesn't get better with age."

"Enough of all this attention on me," she said, patting the seat beside her. "Sit and tell me what's in your future."

Bren sat and put his arm around her. "I have no clue," he said. "Could you consider hiring me as the CFO of Future Big Stars? We could work together."

"Don't try to be funny," she remarked. "Seriously, do you have any thoughts about the future?"

"I mulled over some ideas during the trip. Maybe I'll open a high-end bicycle shop in Westport that caters to elite cyclists. I might even combine it with a fitness and nutrition store."

"Retail is always challenging," she said. "Dealing with manufacturers and distributors, hiring employees, managing payroll and taxes, and discerning customer preferences. Does that sound appealing?"

"Ha-ha." He laughed. "Not at all. But the idea of teaching and coaching sounds appealing. I've had a place in my heart for coaching football since our college days. Maybe I'll get my teaching certificate and try to find a job at a school in Bridgeport. You know, working with inner-city kids, trying to give back."

"That's a significant shift from Wall Street," she remarked. "I wouldn't discourage it, but maybe think about volunteering at a school or substitute teaching to see if it's something you want to pursue."

He nodded in appreciation of her suggestion.

"You've saved your money wisely," she said. "Bigelow will pay me three-fifty a year, so we won't have to rely on a teacher's salary. It's disgraceful how little they earn while tackling the difficult task of educating our children.

"I can make some calls for you," she went on. "I've met a lot of school principals through FirstStep. They might be interested in a fifty-year-old washed-up Wall Street guy teaching at their schools."

"Thanks a lot," he quipped.

"I'm getting back at you for suggesting that I hire you at Future Big Stars," she said with a smile. "But seriously, I'll make the calls."

Bren kissed her on the top of her head and went inside. She liked their new life paradigm: family therapy, the trip out West, Bren quitting his job, and her finding purpose and a meaningful career—the recipe was working. She let out a sigh and dialed her phone. "Hello, Bigelow. It's Laura O'Shay."

Brendan

Fall 2009

Shannon stepped onto the back patio, holding a skateboard and a water bottle. Sweat dripped down his face. His blue jeans were damp with perspiration, and the outer edges of his skate shoes were torn from dragging his feet along the grip tape. "What are you reading, Dad?"

"I volunteered to coach JV football at Westport Academy," Brendan said. "Here's the playbook. The plays and techniques haven't changed much since my college days. The key to success at this level is to keep it simple. I trust myself that I can do it."

"That's great, Dad. Um, do you have a minute? I want to tell you what I'm thinking about doing."

Brendan had waited for this moment since Shannon left Painter College eight months earlier. He hoped Shannon wanted to return, but he was ready for anything. Maybe Laura could revive her connections at SCAD. He closed the football playbook and listened.

"I spoke with Jim Merriman today."

"The artist we met at Bryce Canyon. I remember him. An unforgettable character."

"He called today during my skateboarding sesh. He said he would mentor me . . . teach me everything he knows about the craft—sketching, watercolors, portraiture. It's everything I'm interested in."

"And in return?" Brendan said.

"His wife died recently. He needs someone to keep him company, help with chores, chop wood, and help him out at home."

"I don't know, Shannon. What do you really know about this guy?" Brendan asked.

"Okay, Dad," Shannon said. "I see where this conversation is headed." He stood up and went inside.

Brendan could've kicked himself for being so doubtful. He didn't want to drive Shannon away—not again.

Shannon returned a few moments later with his laptop. "Here's Jim's Wikipedia page, Dad. There's a lot here."

Brendan took the laptop and read Jim's page. It listed numerous art awards, teaching fellowships at offbeat workshops, museums exhibiting his work, a few DUIs, and a minor drug possession charge in California. "That was before he stopped drinking. He told me all about it," Shannon said. "And the drug charge was for a bag of weed when Nixon was president. 'Fucking War on Drugs,' he said. The guy's legit, Dad, and he's willing to help. I want to do this. I'm going to do this."

Brendan felt Cassie's uncontainable spirit in Shannon's voice. "I'll talk to your mother."

"No, Dad. I've got this. You focus on your playbook."

A few minutes later, Laura stepped out onto the patio. "I don't want him going to Alaska," she said.

Brendan reached out and clasped her hands. "I don't want him to go either. But it's his life. The worst thing we can do is try to hold him back. We all deserve to strive, to seek, to find, and not to yield."

"Okay, Ulysses," she teased, "you're right. He's not sailing across the Aegean Sea from Troy to Ithaca, though it feels that way." She smiled and wrapped her arms around his waist. "Let's tell him he has our permission."

"He's seeking our acceptance, not our permission," Brendan said. The words felt right, but that didn't ease his discomfort. He didn't want Shannon to leave.

Brendan

November 2009

Brendan opened the large cardboard box in his living room and laid the T-shirts on the floor before breakfast on a Saturday morning in early November. The word "TRUST" was printed across the chest, and the players' names and numbers were printed on the back. "Laura," he hollered, "come in here and take a look."

Laura entered and picked one up, examining the front and back while feeling the soft texture.

"Here," Brendan said, "I made this one for you." It had the name "Laura" and the number "1" printed on it.

"I know the word is cheesy," he said, "but Coach John told us to trust ourselves and each other when I played football in high school."

"Some messages are timeless and universal," Laura said, rubbing her hand on his back. "I don't think it's cheesy at all." She set her coffee cup down, slipped off her bathrobe, and shimmied into the T-shirt. "Too tight?" she asked.

"It looks fantastic on you," Brendan said. She seemed to grow younger with each passing year. "I'm giving them to the guys before our game today," he continued. "We're oh and five, and this is our last game of the season. I hope it boosts their confidence."

"You haven't won a game all year?" she asked. "I would never have known it by your attitude. You've never seemed happier. Do you mind if I come to the game? I'd love to see you in action."

"I'd love for you to come," he said, taking her hand. "The game starts at ten on the lower field and should end by noon. We can go for a hike afterward."

"I'll wear this T-shirt underneath as a gesture of solidarity," Laura said with a smile, "but I'll be dressed for the hike."

An hour before the game, Brendan entered the locker room and opened the box, tossing T-shirts to the players to wear under their uniforms. Just before kickoff, he gathered them in a circle. "Each week this season, we've improved a little. Today is going to be our day. I trust in you, and we trust in each other. Go out there and trust yourself." With that, all twenty-five fourteen-year-old players began jumping up and down, shouting "trust" in unison, getting louder with each repetition. The back of Brendan's neck tingled.

Just before kickoff, Laura stood in the stands behind the team bench. Brendan knew it was silly, but he felt nervous to have her there. He hoped she would be proud of him. When the game started, Brendan shouted encouragement to the players on the field: "Great block, Owen! Nice tackle, Nate! That's how to run, Ricky!" At the end of the game, he shook hands with every player, calling out their names and acknowledging them as individuals to make sure they felt seen. It was his way of affirming their importance. "Can't wait to see you next year, Matty, Jackson, Marcus, Danny, Blair!" The players smiled reflexively, even Oscar, the heavyset kid who struggled with running, and Dante, the tiny ninety-five-pounder who did his best to keep up with the others. Although Brendan loved practices, the games revealed the resilience and confidence many kids didn't realize they had. They were young and awkward in their growing bodies, but they had the potential to become good high school football players in a few years. He wanted to keep them in the game.

After the game, Brendan and Laura drove north to hike the Appalachian Trail in Kent County. They enjoyed the aroma of ripe apples and the colorful foliage. The fallen leaves made the trail slick, and Laura held Brendan's arm tightly. He was excited about how well the boys played.

"When Dante intercepted the pass, I thought he was going to faint," Brendan said. "Then, when he realized he'd done it, his eyes lit up as he weaved around four players to reach the end zone. It's the highlight of my season."

"You mean Dante's season," Laura said.

"No, *my* season. Watching these kids improve is incredibly rewarding."

A hiker approached from behind and congratulated Brendan on his victory.

"How did you know?" Brendan asked.

"I've been trailing you for the past twenty minutes," the hiker said with a smile. "Keep up the good work."

Brendan chuckled. In his years on Wall Street, no one had ever told him to "keep up the good work."

At the top of the trail, Laura and Brendan marveled at the Impressionistic blues, greens, browns, reds, and yellows splashed across the landscape. "I've talked enough," Brendan said. "Share some stories with me."

Laura squeezed Brendan's biceps with her warm hand. She rambled about working with a narcissist like Bigelow Bigstar. Still, she also acknowledged that he wouldn't be spending millions of dollars funding a charity doing so much good if he weren't so narcissistic. Brendan listened quietly, resisting the urge to offer his opinion or solutions. As the sun dipped in the sky, the wind picked up and cooled the sweat on his back. Laura began to shiver as she finished her story. Brendan took off his sweatshirt and handed it to her. She slipped it on and tightened the hood around her head with her amber bangs across her forehead.

"This sweatshirt takes me back to our snowshoeing trip to Abenaki Falls," Laura said. "We should go back someday."

"I'd love to," he said, "but the memory of what happened to Shannon at Painter overshadows our good times there."

"Do your best to forgive yourself," she said. "Shannon seemed happy when he left for Alaska."

"I miss him so much," Brendan said.

"Me too," she said, cradling his cheeks in her hands. "But maybe he's where he's meant to be for now. As for you, Bren, you're exactly where you're meant to be: working with kids and helping them find themselves."

"I regret it has taken me so long."

"Most people, due to ignorance, laziness, lack of curiosity, or lack of opportunity, go through their lives without ever questioning who they are, where they are, what they are, or why they exist. They simply resign themselves to their fate," she said. "Maybe it has taken you longer than you would have liked, but you're on your way."

A gust of wind swept Laura's amber bangs over her eyes. She pushed her bangs aside. "Now let's get back to the trailhead before the sun sets."

●

Back home that night, Brendan picked up a large box leaning against the front door. "It's from Shannon," he said, carrying it inside and opening it with sharp scissors. He unwrapped it, carefully slid out a leather portfolio, and placed it on the kitchen table. Thin sheets of protective plastic separated the sketches.

"There's a notecard," Laura said, nervously reading it aloud: "*Mom and Dad, I hope you like my work, including the* cover. *I shot and tanned the deer myself, like Cassie would've done. I miss you. Love, Shannon.*"

The first drawing was of a solitary fur trapper standing beside a sturdy tent. Equipment was stacked at the entrance: animal traps, coils of rope, blankets, and piles of firewood. The trapper had a long beard and mustache, and was dressed in roughly sewn furs on his head and shoulders, with snowshoes strapped to his boots. A wooden dogsled was near the tent, bound with deer gut lashing at the joints. Four huskies were curled up in the snow. A Piper Super Cub single-prop airplane—its propeller spinning, wings listing in the wind, ski blades landing gear hanging down—circled away with Denali rising up from the tundra, dominating the horizon. The trapper held a rifle in one hand and was waving to the departing plane with the other. A nearby frozen lake mirrored the scene.

As Brendan studied the sketch, he felt a mix of adventure, dread, solitude, and admiration. How could Shannon's artwork evoke such strong emotions in him when he'd never been to Alaska, trapped fur, shot a gun, or spent a winter in a tent?

He flipped through the rest: a moose entangled in a dogsled, the sun rising over the junction of two rivers with a railroad bridge in the background, an otter slapping its tail against the water's surface to warn a lone boy of danger on the riverbank, a moose walking down the town's main street, a bear reaching for leaping salmon in a mountain stream, and more.

"Shannon made the right decision," Brendan said to Laura, who had stood beside him the whole time, awed by the quality and scope of Shannon's work.

"And we almost buried him by sending him to Painter," Laura said.

"I almost buried him," Brendan said. "Never again." This time, his words felt true.

Brendan

December 2009

The air left Brendan's body. He hung up the phone and collapsed to his knees, burying his face in his hands.

"What's wrong?" Laura shrieked. "Not Shannon?"

"No. God, no," he said, looking up at her. "That was Mark O'Donohue. He's invited us to their place in Boston tomorrow. They had twins."

"Twins," Laura said. "It's a miracle. I'm hesitant to ask, Bren, but did he say why they've contacted you after all that talk about wanting their privacy?"

"I didn't ask, and he didn't say. I'm just grateful I can meet Cassie's—"

"Don't think like that, Bren," she cautioned.

"I bet they've changed their minds. Seeing those two beautiful babies made them realize it's okay for me to be part of their lives. What else could it mean?"

"Slow down, Bren," Laura implored. "I don't want you going down a black hole if that's not what they intend."

Brendan nodded, knowing Laura was right, but still . . .

The next day, Brendan searched for a parking space on the narrow, chaotic streets of Boston's South End, but the spots were either covered in snow, occupied by last-minute shoppers, or blocked by lawn chairs. He felt physically and mentally exhausted when they reached Tom and Mark's apartment, a three-story renovated brownstone with a clothing boutique on the ground floor. They rang the doorbell, were buzzed into the building, and took the claustrophobic elevator to the second floor.

"Happy holidays! Come on in," Mark said, kissing Laura on both cheeks and taking their overcoats to a nearby room. He returned with flutes of champagne and led them into the living room. Brendan noticed four stockings hanging from the white mantel above the black marble fireplace, each embroidered with a name: Tom, Mark, James, and Christina. Cassie's kids had names and Christmas stockings. They were real.

"Please take a seat," Mark said, gesturing toward the purple kidney-shaped couch across from a tree adorned with hand-tied gold satin bows and red and white ornaments on every branch. White bulbs hung carefully, illuminating the tree from within and casting an ethereal glow upward and outward. This glow brought life to the silver angel on top, its wings gently brushing against the twelve-foot-high ceiling.

Tom rushed into the room, shook Brendan's hand, and kissed Laura's cheek.

Mark raised his glass, and the others followed suit. "To Cassie. Desire good for all, and the universe will work with you."

Brendan was too emotional to speak and silently thanked God the guys had changed their minds. Laura asked the question he was thinking: "When can we see the babies?"

"Any second now, Laura," Mark said. "They just woke from their naps and the nurse is changing their diapers and dressing them for you." Mark glanced lovingly at Tom and nodded. "We're so new to this—and we're loving it! They're so precious. We'll be right back with them."

Tom and Mark stepped out of the room. Brendan stared at Laura, unable to speak as he sorted through his emotions. It was as if he had played the pick-six lottery and the first five numbers had come up in his favor. Now he was holding his breath, waiting for the sixth ball to drop. A few minutes later, the guys returned with the newborns. Tom handed James to Brendan, and Mark handed Christina to Laura. "We'll leave you four alone to get acquainted," Mark said.

Brendan's and Laura's eyes filled with tears as they gazed and smiled at the cooing infants. "Baby Christina smells like love," Laura said. They sat on the purple couch, gently rocking instinctively, soothing the tiny babies no larger than Brendan's arm. James began to fuss, and Laura took him in her arms before passing Christina to Brendan.

The baby girl opened her eyes and stared up at Brendan. Her emerald-green eyes and tiny nose resembled Cassie's. "I know you're in there, Cassie," he whispered.

He stayed focused on the baby, not wanting to turn to Laura to see her reaction to his words, afraid of her skepticism. Then she whispered, "Christina does look like Cassie. It's uncanny." They passed the babies back and forth as the time—about half an hour—moved too fast, then Tom and Mark returned with two nannies, who took the babies to the nursery. An elderly woman in uniform brought plated lunches for them to balance on their laps.

"Brendan and Laura," Mark said, "you're probably wondering why we invited you here to meet the babies. After consulting with experts, we had a change of heart."

It's true, Brendan thought. They've changed their minds! He was giddy inside.

"We were encouraged to let you meet the babies so that you can find closure."

"'Closure'?" Brendan asked. "Closure suggests the end of something. I was hoping this was the beginning."

"We still wish to raise our children without interference," Tom said.

Brendan slumped in his chair.

"We understand this is difficult to hear, but along with offering you closure, we want to reiterate our desire for privacy. We've accepted jobs in another city, which is quite far away. The internet makes it easy to find us, but please resist that temptation."

"You're confusing me," Brendan said. "You told me I could never be part of these children's lives, which caused me immense pain and suffering that I've never fully recovered from. Then, based on the advice of some so-called expert who's never met me, you lift my spirits by inviting me here and letting me hold these babies. And after I've experienced this ineffable joy, you slam the door shut—again. Do you realize how cruel you are being to me?"

"It may seem cruel to you right now," Mark said, "but the pain will fade, and you'll feel better than you would have if we hadn't given you this chance to meet James and Christina."

"You're a psychologist, but you're not my psychologist," Brendan said. "I can't imagine my present pain giving way to future acceptance. I hope you're right, but this moment feels very wrong."

"We're sorry you feel that way," Tom said. "Nevertheless, we stand by our convictions."

Brendan took a step toward Tom before Laura grasped his arm firmly. "Let it go, Bren," she urged. "You have to let it go."

Brendan gazed into his wife's pleading eyes, searching for the right words to say and the right way to feel. He didn't regret giving the eggs to Tom and Mark, and he knew he had to live with the consequences. The truth was he was going to raise his fist. Instead, he extended his hand to Tom and Mark. "We trust you'll provide a wonderful life for—" he almost said 'Cassie's children' "—your children."

Tom and Mark shook Brendan's hand. The relief on their faces was palpable.

The elderly woman who had served them lunch brought their overcoats. As Laura buttoned up, she nodded to the men. "Wishing you much happiness with your beautiful babies. Farewell . . . and goodbye."

On the drive back to Connecticut, Laura broke the silence. "What just happened back there?" she asked.

"I've been thinking about it for the past hour," Brendan said. "I believe they truly thought they were doing the right thing. Even though I feel so distraught right now, I'll always cherish the memory of holding those babies, smelling their tiny bodies, and looking into their beautiful eyes. Those were Cassie's eyes. I'll always have that moment to cherish. And that's not nothing."

"If it's any consolation—" Laura laughed "—the guys have not one but *two* Cassies to deal with in their future. Those babies will test the limits of their parenting skills and patience."

Brendan erupted into laughter.

"You've come a long way, Bren. Cassie would have been grateful. I know that Shannon and I are."

"That's not nothing, either," he said. "Not at all."

Brendan

December 2009

Brendan drove through snow flurries to New Hampshire a few days after Christmas to visit Cassie's grave and tell her the news about the babies, hoping his words would somehow reach her in the great beyond, if such a place existed. For the moment, he wanted to believe it did. On his way to the cemetery, he decided to see Emily, who had bought Cassie's old house. Emily met him at the door with Nomad.

"What a surprise!" Emily exclaimed as she welcomed him inside, hugging him tightly and kissing his cheek.

"You kept Nomad," Brendan said, reaching down to pat Cassie's dog on the head.

"Of course I did," she said. "What brings you to New Ash?"

"The babies were born," he said. "I met them." His voice broke. "I came to tell Cassie and thought you should know too, if you didn't already."

"When did you become so spiritual?" she asked.

"I'm changing," Brendan said. "I hope it's not too late."

"It's never too late to be better," Emily said. "Come into the sunroom—it's much more comfortable there."

As they walked through the living room and into the sunroom, he noticed the house was spotless, with every piece of furniture in its rightful place and not a speck of dirt or dust. A large framed photo of Cassie hung on the wall opposite the fireplace: She knelt behind a four-point buck she had hunted, holding its head by the antlers. He held Emily's hand as they gazed at the beaver dam and snow-covered hills in the distance. He remembered standing there with Cassie two years earlier.

"What are the babies' names?" Emily asked.

"James and Christina," Brendan said. "I see Cassie in their eyes. It's painful to know I'll never have a relationship with them."

"Don't lose hope, Brendan. The parents can issue restraining orders that would prevent you from pursuing a relationship with the children if it comes to that, and I hope it never does. But they can't stop the children from seeking you out when they are older. Most people have an inherent desire to learn about their origins. Be patient. You don't know how this situation will play out."

He held her tightly and kissed her forehead. "Do you ever wonder what could have been between us?" Brendan asked.

"I'd be a liar to say it never crossed my mind, but you were an ambitious young man," she said with a smile. "I was a free spirit, soaring on the wind. That's all behind us now. How are Laura and Shannon?"

"Laura has stayed by my side, and she's finding herself in her work. Shannon's on his own journey, diverging from the path I carved for him against his will."

"And what about you?"

"I coach junior varsity football at a local prep school. The pay isn't quite the same as Wall Street," he joked, "but the intrinsic reward makes up for it. Luckily, I saved money along the way."

"You're always looking to the future," she said.

He heard the kitchen door open and shut. "That's my daughter from Boston," Emily said. "What a coincidence that you're here. It's finally time for you to meet each other."

Brendan's thoughts lingered on the word "finally."

They returned to the kitchen to find a woman who looked like a twentysomething Cassie.

"This is Sunshine," Emily said as she held her daughter's hand. "And Sunshine, this is Brendan O'Shay." But before they could shake hands, Emily leaned closer to Sunshine and asked, "How are you feeling?"

"The twins were lively in the womb, each eager to be the first to enter the world. And the parents turned out to be quite a handful."

"Sorry," Brendan said. "I'm struggling to keep up with this conversation."

"I'm a gestational surrogate," Sunshine said. "The men I worked with worried about the most absurd things. But they provided me with a lovely apartment and took care of all my needs. They also paid much more than I asked for. Yet, in the end, I'd probably do it for free. It's an act of love."

Brendan turned to Emily. "I'm afraid I know the answer to the question I'm about to ask: Why does Sunshine look so much like Cassie?"

"I've been thinking about how this day would unfold for thirty-five years. Sunshine is why I left Nehoiden High so abruptly," Emily said. "Daddy and Mommy were very Catholic. We were seventeen. Having the baby was the only choice I was given." She hugged Sunshine.

Brendan's head began to spin. He stumbled over to the counter and leaned against it. "Did you get pregnant the night of Cassie's accident?" he asked. "Am I Sunshine's father?"

"That was a terrible night. Cassie's accident was tragic, and I was distraught that you came inside me, even though you denied it. But it turned out that it didn't matter, because a few days after the accident, I found out I was pregnant from all the sex we'd had earlier that summer. And yes, Sunshine is your daughter."

Brendan gazed at Sunshine. What a trip it had been. He'd lost a sister, then he lost a niece and nephew, and now the daughter he never knew existed was standing a few feet away, smiling at him. He didn't know whether to embrace Sunshine or run out the door.

"How could you keep that secret from me?" he asked.

"Football was your ticket to a better life. The last thing you needed was to become a teenage father."

Brendan began to hyperventilate, and Sunshine quickly poured a glass of water for him. After taking a few sips, he settled down. "Were you Tom and Mark's surrogate?" he asked Sunshine.

"I'm not at liberty to say," she replied, nodding her head yes.

He felt lightheaded again. "Are you saying that you, my biological daughter and Cassie's biological niece, gave birth to your biological cousins? That sounds, I don't know, kind of incestuous."

"It's not incestuous at all," Emily interjected indignantly. "A biological connection is preferred," she added. "There's no medical harm in it."

"Do Tom and Mark know about your connection?"

"Of course they do. Tom knows everything. He's the most diligent person I've ever worked with, and Mark is thrilled."

"I need to take a seat," Brendan said. "Are these connections the reason they permitted me to meet the twins?"

"I advised them to do so," Emily said.

"You're the expert they were referring to?"

"Yes. The guys agreed that if you ever found out about Sunshine, you'd pursue James and Christina like Captain Ahab chasing the white whale. Ultimately, meeting the babies should give you closure."

Brendan's vision blurred. What further madness could happen in Cassie's house?

Emily sat beside him and touched his hand. "Desire good for all, and the universe will work with you," she said. "All is good for Sunshine and me, the guys and their babies, and you, Laura, and Shannon. The universe is working with Cassie, too. You'll realize it soon enough."

Sunshine sat on the other side of Brendan and touched his other hand. He clutched their hands to his heart. "I'll need some time to sort this out," he said. "But I won't forget you. For now, though, I have to go."

●

Brendan drove toward Mount Krystal where the forest opened up to a field with a small cemetery in it. Weathered gravestones stood arranged in three rows of five. He trudged through the snow toward Cassie's resting spot, pausing at his mother's grave and praying. As a kid, his mother had told him that a prayer for the dead could push them from purgatory into Heaven. He thought his mom could use the help.

He continued onward to the last gravestone in the last row and stood about where Cassie's coffin was lowered into the ground, losing track of time as he told her the story of James and Christina, wondering if Cassie had known about Sunshine. He began to shiver. It was time to go home. He turned and gazed out over the flat white meadow up to the peak of Mount Krystal. A solitary cloud suddenly obscured the sun, releasing delicate snowflakes onto the stony eyes of the Alaskan Malamute engraved on the front of Cassie's gravestone. A biting wind whipped down off the mountain and across the meadow, nearly immobilizing Brendan. Suddenly the wind shifted, and sunlight broke through a narrow gap in the clouds.

"You orchestrated this, Cassie. Didn't you?"

A ray of light hit Cassie's gravestone just right, and the Malamute appeared to wink.

Brendan brushed the snow off the gravestone as the clouds obscured the sun once more. His ankles felt numb from standing in the snow, yet his heart felt warm. He retraced his footsteps to his car and drove away.

●

When Brendan arrived home in Connecticut, Laura was beaming. She nodded toward the living room. Brendan turned the corner and saw Shannon standing by the Christmas tree. His beard was scruffy, and his thick brown hair was pulled back into a ponytail and secured with a single elastic band. The front of his green T-shirt featured a sketch of a moose strolling down Main Street in Talkeetna.

"I know that sketch," Brendan said, pointing at Shannon's T-shirt.

"I sold a thousand of these T-shirts to tourists passing through town on their buses," Shannon said. "Now my work will be seen in all fifty states . . . and some foreign countries, too." Brendan gave Shannon a big hug. Laura joined in. Brendan never wanted to let them go.

He would tell them about Emily and Sunshine someday . . . just not today.

Acknowledgments

Writing a novel is a solitary experience, but it is not done without the encouragement of others. This novel began as a short story submission for a fiction workshop at the Fine Arts Work Center in Provincetown, Massachusetts, in 2014 and was developed into a novel at the Westport Writers' Workshop in Westport, Connecticut. Throughout my writing journey, many former classmates at Middlebury College in Vermont; neighbors in Weston, Connecticut; and teaching colleagues and students at Brunswick School in Greenwich, Connecticut, and Fairfield County Day School in Fairfield, Connecticut, provided help along the way. In particular, I thank Frank Albanese, a career publishing professional and friend; Allison Dickens, a writing instructor and developmental editor at Westport Writers' Workshop; Adele Annesi, a writing instructor and author in Ridgefield, Connecticut; and David Altfeld, of Manhattan and Los Angeles, for listening to my expressions of self-doubt and providing invaluable support and encouragement. Finally, I thank my wife, Susan. No words can express my gratitude for her love and support—in writing and in life.

www.ingramcontent.com/pod-product-compliance
Lightning Source LLC
Chambersburg PA
CBHW020659110726
47901CB00001B/252